Restoring Order

A Detachment 3 Novel.

B. René Shekmer

ISBN: 979-8-9855-7261-2

Cover design by: B. René Shekmer

Shekmer Publishing
Printed in the United States of America

For my father,

Michael E. Shekmer
1933-2015

ACKNOWLEDGMENTS

A special thanks to my brother, David Shekmer, and my encouraging early readers John Bruha, Mark Rossi, and Roxanne Speck.

CHAPTER ONE

April 1961

With the sun high in the cloudless Guatemalan sky, it was time to try to get some sleep. There would be little time for sleep over the coming days. Mike left the mess tent and started walking back to his own tent. The relentless sun beat down on him as he walked but Mike had become accustomed to it. He stopped walking momentarily as he thought he should see Roberto now, not later. A quick turn and he was walking in the opposite direction.

Roberto Lagomasino was a 27-year-old Cuban exile that Mike had been training in preparation for the invasion of Cuba. Mike was part of the communications link between the invasion force and the Central Intelligence Agency in Langley, Virginia. For weeks he had been training the men who would be the radiomen for their units. They were a great group of guys who were eager and attentive, buoyed by the thought that they were about to make history by taking back what was rightfully theirs, their island, their country.

Mike had developed a special bond with Roberto, an earnest young man, the same age as Mike, who Mike grew to respect. Roberto was a Cuban patriot who had fled to the United States in late 1958, when Fidel Castro's revolution was taking over Cuba. He had lost family members fighting against the communists. He knew the fighting to retake Cuba would be hard, but he believed that they were assured success because the United States was helping them. Roberto was prepared to give anything, including his own life, if necessary, to take his homeland back from Castro. But he was not a reckless man and Mike admired that.

Mike went in search of Roberto. He found him in his tent, fully dressed in the camouflage fatigues and boots they all wore. Roberto was too tense to get any sleep.

"Mike, how good to see you, my friend," Roberto said, as Mike slipped into Roberto's tent.

Roberto's English was very good but, as a native Spanish speaker, sometimes he phrased things a little differently than an American would. Mike did not care. He had no trouble communicating with Roberto and Roberto had helped with translation, when necessary, during Mike's training of the Cubans. It was much needed assistance as Mike's Spanish was not great to begin with and was a more formal Castilian dialect, while most of the trainees spoke in the Cuban vernacular. Some words just did not translate from English to Spanish. Mike would explain what he meant to Roberto and Roberto would explain to the men.

"Are you ready?" Mike asked. "Is there anything I can help you with?"

"No, I'm ready," Roberto said. "I can't sleep in the middle of the day. Not today. Please. Sit down. Sit with me."

Mike sat down on a flimsy, green canvas cot. Roberto sat on an equally flimsy, green canvas cot across from him. For the next several hours, they talked and laughed as only friends can do. They talked about everything: their families, their close friends, growing up in Cuba versus growing up in Pennsylvania, and the things they each loved to do. Mike's wife was almost eight months pregnant when he had left Virginia and headed down to Guatemala. He shared with Roberto his wonder and excitement about having a child.

They were as relaxed as they could be under the circumstances. They never once talked about the mission but, as always, Roberto radiated a sense of confidence and responsibility. All too soon it was time for Roberto to gather his gear and head for his unit's rally point.

"Thank you for everything you have done for me, Mike," Roberto said. "I will catch you on the radio."

"Give them hell, Roberto," Mike said, as he grabbed Roberto by the hand and shook it. "But keep your head down."

Roberto laughed. "Will do," he replied, with a big smile, repeating the phrase he had heard Mike use many times during their time together.

They parted and Roberto went to join his unit for transfer down to Nicaragua, where they would board ships and boats for the invasion of Cuba. Mike went to the commo tent, realizing that the time for sleep had passed.

* * *

American B-26 planes, flown by Cuban exiles and disguised as Cuban military planes, bombed the Cuban airfields a couple of nights before the invasion. The idea was to deny Castro air support and any chance of air superiority.

The invasion force left for Cuba while it was still daylight, planning to arrive under the cover of darkness. Mike and his colleagues were busy pre-invasion testing and re-testing the radio equipment and passing status reports to Langley. The invasion began before midnight on April 17, at Playa Girón, in Bahía de los Cochinos, the Bay of Pigs, on the southern coast of Cuba. It did not go well right from the beginning.

There was heavy radio traffic as some units landed and others came under fire. Mike worked the radios non-stop, without much sleep. The invasion force had some early success when it was able to defeat the local militia. As expected, the request for air support came from the invasion force. Mike passed the message on to Langley and was told to hold.

The invasion force was able to capture the local airfield at Playa Girón. Then, when the Cuban regular military units joined the fight, more requests for American air support came in and Mike relayed the requests to Langley. Again, he was repeatedly told to hold.

As time passed, Langley remained silent on providing air support and there were no American planes in the skies above Cuba. The requests for air support became more desperate and Mike continued the pass the urgent pleas to Langley. He knew the answer was to hold but he felt obligated to push every request through. Something was wrong. Everyone in the commo tent could feel it. Finally, Mike got an answer. Request denied. There would be no air support.

Mike fought back the rising feelings of contempt. President Kennedy had promised there would be air support if the invasion force needed and requested it. The B-26 pre-invasion bombing had been intended to give the invasion force the edge by denying air support to Castro and clearing the way for American air superiority over Cuba. Without their own air support, the invasion force was being overrun. No air support was a death sentence and Mike knew it.

He pushed down his emotions because he had a job to do conveying the message back to the units. No air support would be coming. It was the last message Mike had been expecting to have to send.

As the hours passed, one by one the invasion force units began to fail to respond to Mike's calls. One by one, they dropped off the air. When Roberto came on the air for the last time on April 19th, his message was brief.

"Mike, *voy con Dios ahora*. Out." Then he also went silent.

Mike tried to raise him repeatedly but got no response. Roberto had broken protocol by calling Mike by name. He would not have done that unless he knew he was about to die and wanted his last radio transmission to be personal, to someone who cared. Mike knew Roberto was dead. He felt it profoundly and undeniably and a part of Mike also died.

On April 20th, the remaining invasion forces surrendered. The invasion was over. A failure of American resolve, with a cost of more than a thousand Cuban exile lives, either dead or imprisoned.

* * *

Roberto had died and Mike was sick about it. He felt guilt for being involved in a massive betrayal. Stunned and semi-dazed, Mike set about cleaning up and packing to leave. The next day, he received the news that his wife had given birth to a son. A son born on the same day that Roberto had died. Mike was conflicted, grieving the loss of Roberto and the failure of the mission and, yet, excited about the birth of a son.

Hoping his wife would get the message before formally naming their son, Mike sent an encrypted reply and requested the message be delivered to his wife as soon as possible. "Name our boy Michael Roberto Turek. Roberto, not Robert. You'll understand why when I get home. Miss you. See you soon, Mike."

CHAPTER TWO

Present Day

Sofia opened the old, massive wooden door at the entrance to St. Cyril's Byzantine Catholic Church in the old city section of Athens. Inhaling deeply, she stepped out of the blazing Grecian sun and entered the cool, dark foyer. Out of respect, she placed a long black lace scarf over her blonde hair as she ventured deeper into the solemn building. The smell of incense hung thick in the air as she walked slowly into the ornate nave. She closed her eyes as a familiar presence washed over her. Sofia stood still for a moment and savored the feeling of calm and well-being that came with the presence of her mother.

After a moment, she opened her eyes and peered into the dark depths of the church. Her eyes were adjusting from the bright sunlight she had left outside to the darkness of the inside of the church. She could see the iconostasis at the far end of the church. It was filled with icons, large, richly colored paintings of saints with large golden halos. Off to the left was an alcove with racks of candles. She headed there first.

After lighting a long white tapered candle in the rack, she bowed her head, oblivious to everyone and everything as she spoke softly to her mother through prayer. Only in the Byzantine Catholic church did she feel the closeness with her mother that she had missed daily for six years. The deep pain of the loss receded as she filled her mother in on the lives of her father, her two brothers, and herself. They were all together in Greece for the summer and Sofia was certain that her mother would be pleased.

When she had no more to say, Sofia said goodbye to her mother and reached into her purse for a ten euro note, which she placed into the small offering box next to the candles. She turned and looked again at the iconostasis. Her mother would have loved it. Sofia began to walk to the center of the church and down the main aisle to the front of the church for a closer look.

She was slightly startled when a man came close to her and placed a hand on her arm. She turned in his direction as he leaned into her to speak.

"Come with me quietly or your brothers will be killed." He whispered, in French.

"No!" Sofia thought, as she looked into the man's serious brown eyes. She was immediately torn. Resist or go with this man. Her instinct was to resist, to scream at the top of her lungs and make a scene. But she could never put herself above the well-being of her brothers Peter and Matthew. The man spoke to her in French, not English or Greek. He knew that she spoke French. In that instant, her momentary indecision resolved into resignation. This was not some random crime. She had not been singled out because she looked like a tourist. He clearly knew who she was.

Sofia saw that a second man had joined them in the center aisle of the church. It was not just her against one man, it was two men. At least two men that she could see.

"Walk to the door," the first man said quietly to Sofia, in French.

They all walked to the massive wooden front door of the church. Near the end of the pews, Sofia looked into the eyes of a woman who was standing still and looking directly at her.

"*Help me!*" Sofia silently screamed in her head. But she said nothing aloud. At the door, the man speaking French told her to remove her headscarf. She pushed the black lace scarf back off of her blonde hair, letting it hang from her neck, and silently beseeched her mother to watch over Peter and Matthew. Then the heavy door was opened, and they walked out into the bright sunlight of the Mediterranean midday

CHAPTER THREE

The low hanging morning fog had yet to begin to burn off as Mick ran around the high school track, in Warrenton, Virginia. It was very early on a Thursday morning in the spring. The day would get warm but for now there was a chill in the air.

His mind was on duty and responsibility. He couldn't help it. Whenever he ran, his mind drifted to the things buried in his subconscious. Things that were bothering him, that were normally crowded out by the demands of his daily life, bubbled up into his consciousness when he ran. Today it was duty and responsibility owed to the legacy of two good men. It all revolved around his name, Michael Roberto Turek, Jr.

Mick's great-grandfather had been named Michael Turek. But everyone called him Mick, not Michael, not Mike. He was born in a small village in eastern Slovakia and immigrated with his family to the United States in the early 1900's, before he was old enough for school.

Mick's grandfather had been named Michael Edward Turek. But everyone called him Mike, not Michael, not Mick. He was not technically a junior because he had a middle name and his father did not but, sometimes, his aunts and uncles called him Junior. He was the first generation born and raised in America.

Mick's father was named Michael Roberto Turek. But everyone called him Michael, not Mike, not Mick. He had died when Mick was young, before Mick was old enough for school. Mick had no actual memory of him of his own but felt that he knew his father because his grandfather had spoken of him so often.

Finally, Mick had been named Michael Roberto Turek, Jr. In the family naming tradition, they were back around to Mick again. So, everyone called him Mick, not Michael, not Mike. He was a real junior. But no one ever called him Junior. It was as if calling him Junior would remind him every time that his father was dead; so, the family had reached some unspoken agreement to never call him Junior.

What weighed on Mick as he ran was his middle name, Roberto. Because his father had died when Mick was very young, his grandfather, Pops to Mick, was the only real father figure that he had truly known.

Pops was the only person who ever called him Roberto. And then, only when they were alone, never in front of anyone else. It was like a secret they shared together. As Mick grew older it dawned on him that Pops only called him Roberto when he was proud of something that Mick had achieved, like graduating from high school, graduating from college, or joining the military. Pops would pull him aside and say something innocuous like, "Hey, Roberto, let's go fishing tomorrow." And Mick knew that what Pops was really saying was that he was proud of him and, to celebrate Mick's accomplishment, they should go fishing together, just the two of them. Mick loved spending time with Pops and time alone with Pops was Mick's favorite time.

Roberto is not a normal middle name for a kid of Slovakian heritage. When Mick asked about it, Pops told him that he carried that name for an extraordinary man who could no longer do so and who had not had a son to leave it to as his legacy. Pops never really went further, except to say that Roberto had been his friend.

A few weeks before Pops died, Mick heard the whole story for the first and only time. Pops had gotten sick in January. They knew almost immediately that the doctors gave him only a couple of months to live. Cancer. An aggressive and relentless cancer. Mick was with him as much as he could be, weeks on end. They talked about everything. Pops had led an interesting and extraordinary life and Mick wanted to hear everything before it was too late.

One evening, when the two of them were alone, Mick was in search of a topic for their evening conversation. They had covered so much already. Mick had asked Pops, "If you had the opportunity to do just one thing in your life differently, what would that be?" He had no idea what Pops' answer would be, but he was curious.

Pops went very still and closed his eyes for a long moment. When he opened his eyes, silent tears rolled down his face. It was the only time Mick had ever seen his grandfather cry.

Mick's grandfather laid it all out in excruciating detail, like it had happened yesterday. About the weeks in Guatemala training the young Cuban exiles. About Roberto Lagomasino and how much Pops liked and respected him. About how Roberto died and how much guilt Pops felt about it. About Roberto's last radio transmission, "Mike, *voy con Dios ahora*. Out." He regretted that he had encouraged Roberto because he had trusted the government. Had he known better then, he would have made sure that Roberto had a Plan B, if the government betrayed him, as it did. A Plan B may not have saved Roberto's life, Mike was realistic about that. But knowing that the United States may not provide needed support for the fight, at least he could have prepared Roberto for what could happen if he ended up on his own out there.

In Mick's mind, Pops was his father in every way that counted and he was a puzzle—with obvious missing pieces. A patriot who spent the majority of his life in service to his country, he loved America and her people. That didn't prevent him from having a deep mistrust of the government he served. Because of his sense of duty, he concealed his distrust from everyone but those closest to him. Instead, others around him saw an extreme insistence on self-reliance. To always be thinking of what could go wrong in any plan and how he would deal with it himself.

Mick, of course, grew up knowing all about Plan B. Pops would tell him that Plan B is yourself. No matter what you think is going to happen or what you are told is going to happen, always have a Plan B for how you are going to get yourself out of whatever mess you find yourself in. When Mick came back from missions, Pops would listen attentively to descriptions of what he had done, the problems he had encountered, and how he solved those problems. They would talk it all through as a way for Mick to review the mission before compartmentalizing and filing it away in his brain. Done, reviewed, and stored in memory. But when Mick was done with his review, the conversation was never done. The conversation always entered the next phase, with Pops asking the same question.

"What was your Plan B?"

Pops would point to a particular part of the mission where Mick had relied on the government, usually for extraction. Mick had created and reviewed his Plan B for numerous scenarios. So far, he had never really had to use it. Nevertheless, it was important to Pops that Mick always had a Plan B and that he was always ready to put it into action.

The legacy of Roberto Lagomasino's death in Cuba in 1961, as passed on to Mick by his grandfather, was extreme self-reliance. Hope for the best but plan for the worst. And the worst was that your government would not be there for you when you needed it. Mick had always understood that Pops had a core distrust of the government. Only when Pops lay dying did he learn why.

March came and went, and the doctors were surprised that Pops was still hanging on. He made it to April. In April, the doctors said any day, every day. Pops was clearly losing steam and was hardly speaking at all, but he kept hanging on. He was both tough and stubborn like that. He would go in his own time. The last real two-party conversation that Mick had with him had been about Roberto Lagomasino. Pops made it to April 19th.

On the day he died, surrounded by family, Pops looked out at each of the familiar faces around him before settling on Mick. Mick was holding his right hand. With clear eyes, Pops had looked directly into Mick's eyes and said, softly, "Roberto, *voy con Dios ahora.*" Then Pops closed his eyes. Mick knew it was the end and he squeezed Pops' hand. Pops squeezed back, weakly, but Mick felt it.

He held on to his composure solely for Pops. It was emotionally the hardest thing that he had ever faced. In less than an hour, Pops was dead. He had never opened his eyes again and had never said another word. He died 59 years to the day after Roberto Lagomasino. He died on his own schedule, in one last tribute to the man whose name Mick carried on.

Now, Mick was running around a track and thinking about Pops and Roberto and the duty he owed to them to make sure that their legacies lived on and did not die with him. Mick needed a son. A tall order for a man who was not married and was not even dating someone at the moment. But he was not getting any younger and he could not ignore this particular duty forever.

Mick ended his run with no idea how many laps he had run. When he was in the zone, his mind took over and he just ran until he ran out of things to think about or until he was physically exhausted. He reached for a towel in his duffel bag and wiped the sweat from his face.

He looked down at his hands and arms, a very dark golden brown. He had the same skin as Pops. There was a very slight natural olive tint to his complexion. But just a short time in the sun and he tanned without effort. He never burned, he just got darker. Various parts of his body were different shades of brown. His face and hands were the darkest, his arms were a little lighter, his torso and legs were just a little lighter still, and below his waist and above his thighs was the natural very pale olive. With his skin coloring, and his thick black hair and brown eyes, just like Pops had, Mick could pass for multiple different ethnicities easily; and he often did, when working. Pops had been better at it. At five foot, eleven inches tall, Mick was about average for an American man. But in much of the rest of the world, he was on the taller side. Pops had been five inches shorter. Short for an American man. But Pops had been able to blend seamlessly in much of the rest of the world.

In the distance, Mick saw flashing blue lights, haloed by the fog, on Waterloo Road. That was never a good sign. He grabbed his duffel bag and walked briskly toward the parking area while guzzling water from a plastic bottle.

A black sport utility vehicle with dark tinted windows came to a stop near him. The blue lights stopped flashing as a tall, thin, prematurely greying man stepped out of the SUV. The man walked to the front of the hood and met up with Mick, who kept moving toward his Jeep Cherokee, while asking, "What's happening, Roger?"

"A probable kidnapping in Greece," Roger replied.

Mick pulled his wet T-shirt off over his head and asked, "Do I have time for a shower?"

"Only if you find time in transit," Roger responded, with a shrug of his shoulders.

Mick yelled over his shoulder, still headed for his Jeep, "Flying or driving?"

16

"Flying out of Brandy," Roger replied, as he returned to the SUV.

Mick threw his wet shirt and duffel bag into the Jeep, grabbed his go-bag, locked the Jeep, and got into the front passenger seat of the black SUV. Had they been driving to northern Virginia; he might have dropped the Jeep at his house on the way. But his place was not on the way to Brandy. Brandy was a reference to the Culpeper Regional Airport, which was located closer to Brandy Station than to Culpeper, both in Culpeper County, in central Virginia. But Mick was not worried. He was friends with the Assistant Principal of the high school. His Jeep would still be in the parking lot when he returned.

Roger wasted no time moving the SUV back onto Waterloo, then turning right and heading South on Route 29 toward Culpeper. Mick dug deep into his go-bag, withdrew a clean shirt, and put it on. Next, he found a pair of pants. He removed his shoes and pulled the khaki pants on over his running shorts then put his shoes back on. He just needed clothes decent enough to navigate the small regional airport without attracting a lot of attention.

They arrived at the airport and fast-walked to a nondescript, white, private aviation hangar. Outside, on the tarmac, there was a helicopter with rotors already spinning. Roger asked if there was anything that Mick needed for him to do and, when the answer was no, he slapped Mick on the back and pushed him toward the helicopter, while yelling, "I will see that you have a change of clothes."

Mick gave Roger a thumbs-up as he bent down slightly to brace against the wind being thrown off by the rotor blades, ran to the helicopter, and jumped in. A crewman slammed the door shut and the helicopter began to simultaneously rise and move forward.

Mick watched the countryside go by through the fading fog during the ride. There were cows grazing and horses running in the rich, green fields on rolling hills below. A small herd of five deer that were munching the dew-covered grass in a field near a tree line ran for the trees at the sound of the helicopter. Mick's sense of home in the hunt country of central Virginia waned as the countryside fast gave way to the congestion of northern Virginia. First came the housing tracts, then the business districts. The farther north the helicopter flew, the taller the buildings and the more congested the roads below became. It became impossible to tell from the air where one town ended and another town began. Rush hour in the northern Virginia/metro D.C. area lasted far longer than an hour and, even with many people choosing staggered work schedules, it was hard to beat the hours long morning rush to work. Mick was glad to be flying above it and glad that during his down time he did not live in it.

The helicopter landed on the top of an eight-story building, not at Langley. Mick was met by a man who took him to the stairwell, then down to the elevator, and to the fourth floor, without saying more than "follow me." The man escorted Mick into a conference room occupied by a half dozen people, each with eyes glued to the screen of a laptop computer or cell phone. As Mick walked into the room, they all looked up at him. An auburn-haired woman announced to the group that Mick had arrived, but they were still waiting for Taylor to show up. Five faces nodded at Mick and went back to watching their screens.

Bronwyn Richards rose from her seat and walked around the conference table to Mick. Without hesitation, she wrapped him in a bear hug. Mick returned the hug as if Bronwyn were a familiar relative not seen in years. Mick was not a touchy-feely kind of person, but Bronwyn was a welcome sight, and, for her, he would always make an exception. Bronwyn, the consummate professional woman, had never married. She sometimes joked that she was married to her job. She had unofficially adopted Mick after a mission some years prior. The knowledge that Bronwyn was involved stateside knocked down a bit of the stress that had been building in Mick and he felt the muscles in his shoulders loosen slightly.

As Mick and Bronwyn disengaged, Taylor Cole walked into the conference room weighed down by two oversized gear bags and one disposable plastic suit bag on which "Turek" had been written on a piece of masking tape stuck to the bag. From the look of it, Taylor had gotten notice after his morning shower. He was clean-shaven and dressed in a hunter green polo shirt, black tactical pants, and black hiking boots. He looked put together and mission ready. Mick glanced down at his own wrinkled khakis, faded blue T-shirt, and running shoes. He rubbed his unshaven jaw and decided once again that a shower was not worth the madness of living in northern Virginia.

Mick and Taylor silently shook hands as Bronwyn announced to the room that Taylor had arrived and the meeting was to begin. One of the analysts rose from his seat and walked to the front of the room where a large screen monitor was mounted on the wall. Mick and Taylor took seats at the conference table.

"We have a probable kidnapping in Athens," the analyst began.

"Sofia Sopko, college student and daughter of Ambassador Peter Sopko, was visiting her father in Athens during summer break," he continued, as a photograph of a pretty, young, blonde-haired woman with green eyes flashed on the large monitor. Mick felt a twinge of recognition as he stared at the photograph. The woman looked vaguely familiar, but Mick could not place her. Maybe she just looked like someone else he knew or had once known.

The analyst addressed the politics first. "Ambassador Sopko was a late term political appointment as U.S. Ambassador to Greece." Ambassador Sopko's photograph flashed on the large monitor. "His predecessor died suddenly. Brain aneurism, this time last year. Ambassador Sopko was a safe and easy confirmation pick. He is a Republican but not overtly political. He is, however, well connected. The new administration asked him to hold over and does not seem to be in too much of a hurry to replace him. So far, not even a rumor of a nomination to replace him."

The analyst then turned to Sofia's details. "Sofia Sopko, a twenty-year old, Junior at the University of Richmond. Actually, she just finished her junior year. She was spending the summer in Greece, with her widowed father. As a dependent of the Ambassador, Sofia travelled on a diplomatic passport. By all accounts, Sofia is a model daughter of a United States diplomat. She is a serious student with good grades. She has no known suspect relationships."

"Sofia is the oldest of the Ambassador's three children. The other two children are also in Greece; eighteen-year-old Peter, Jr., on summer break from George Washington University and sixteen-year-old Matthew who lives with his father in Athens." Photographs of each displayed as the analyst spoke. "Their mother died of cancer when Sofia was fourteen years old." No photograph of the mother. "The Ambassador and his sons worship Sofia. According to the Ambassador, Sofia is the glue that kept him and the boys from falling apart after the death of his wife."

"In short, Sofia is smart, devoted to her family, and not reckless in the least," the analyst concluded.

A second analyst replaced the first at the front of the room to detail what was known about the day Sofia was taken.

"Sofia was taken today at just after noon from a church in the Plaka, the old shopping district in downtown Athens, in the shadow of the Acropolis," he stated, as an aerial photograph of the area flashed onto the large monitor. "That is, Sofia was taken today, at five o'clock this morning, our time."

Mick reflexively glanced at his watch. Eight-twenty in the morning.

"According to her father, Sofia and her brothers were driven to the Plaka by an Embassy driver to do some shopping. According to the driver, a Greek national working for the Embassy, the morning was uneventful as the kids visited various shops and purchased multiple tourist items. At some point, the kids split up. The boys went to look at some old ruins and Sofia went to a Byzantine Catholic church." A photograph of the exterior of the old church filled the large monitor. "Sofia told the driver to take the parcels to the car while she was in the church and that she would wait there for him to return. They all planned to meet up for lunch at a restaurant just a few blocks from the church."

"As Sofia entered the church, the driver went to the car. The driver claims it only took him between twenty-five and thirty minutes to get to the car, put the parcels inside, and return to the church. Motor vehicles in the Plaka are limited to motorbikes and delivery vehicles. The area is largely pedestrian with narrow streets, so the driver had parked some distance away in a public parking lot.

"When he returned to the church, he waited outside for Sofia for about twenty minutes. As the time approached one o'clock, when the kids had arranged to meet at the restaurant for lunch, the driver entered the church to remind Sofia of the time. The driver searched everywhere but could not find Sofia. He located a priest and asked about Sofia. The priest had not seen her. Others in the church were asked if they had seen Sofia and only one woman claimed to have seen her. The woman claimed that she had seen Sofia leave the church with two darker olive-skinned, black-haired men, roughly an hour earlier. The woman claimed that Sofia did not look happy, as if she had been given bad news. The woman remembered Sofia and she thought it odd that the blonde woman was being escorted by two 'Turks'."

The analyst inserted the fact that the hatred and mistrust between the Greeks and the Turks is millennia old, before continuing with the facts as they were known. "The driver then immediately called the Embassy, explained that Sofia had been taken, and was ordered to call the police. The Embassy sent a team out to the Plaka to secure the boys, secure the driver, and follow up on any additional leads."

"While this is a full-blown international incident, at the Ambassador's request, the Greek government and police are cooperating fully and keeping it quiet," the analyst said. "So far, no media."

Taylor whispered under his breath, so only Mick could hear, "But for how long?"

Mick nodded knowingly to Taylor and then asked the analyst, "What do we have on the identities of the two men or where they took her?"

A third analyst answered Mick's questions. He said that there was no positive identification of the two men yet. He showed video surveillance from various building security cameras and automated teller machine cameras on the large monitor. None of the images of the men were particularly clear although they did appear to be vaguely middle eastern, possibly Turkish, with olive skin and dark hair. Both men were thin, clean-shaven, and dressed in business casual clothing. Instead of suit coats they wore black, light-weight jackets with their matching dress pants and shoes. White button-down dress shirts were the only part of their attire that stood out from their otherwise dark and mysterious look. One of the men appeared to have a gun in his pocket pointed at Sofia's side as she walked.

The woman in the church was right, it did look odd for Sofia to be walking out of the church with the two men, especially given the concerned look on her face. One of them was walking very close to her on her right side and just a half step behind, she appeared uncomfortable with him in her personal space. As he led her from the church, his right hand was in the pocket of his light jacket and he was holding it against his stomach. Mick and Taylor looked at each other and nodded, seeming to agree with the assessment that the man had a gun pointed at Sofia. Sofia kept glancing down at the non-existent space between them. The other man walked along on her left side, giving her a little more space but clearly giving her directions as he occasionally leaned in to speak to her. He wasn't using any hand gestures so Sofia must have understood what he was saying to her. As the three exited the church, they all turned to the right and appeared to walk calmly off into the crowd.

"Does Sofia speak Greek or any other language besides English?" Mick asked.

"She does not speak Greek," one of the analysts responded. "She does speak French in addition to English."

"So, the man on the left is speaking either English or French while talking to Sofia," Mick said.

"French, we think he is speaking French," the analyst replied. "At one point, it appears he's telling her which way to go because she turns to the right. Our linguists believe from the movement of his lips that he is speaking French, not English."

"So possibly Lebanese or North African," Taylor surmised.

Mick nodded. French is widely spoken in Lebanon and parts of northern Africa, in addition to Arabic, as Lebanon and parts of northern Africa were once under French rule. Speaking French in Greece would greatly cut down on the possibility of being overheard and understood by the people they passed, even more so than speaking English.

"Where did they go?" Taylor asked.

The analyst said that they had fairly good coverage of them walking about two blocks to what appeared to be a white delivery-type van and getting in the van. Sofia and the man on the right got into the back through the passenger-side rear door. Then the man on the left got into the driver's seat. According to the local police, the license plate was stolen from a delivery van sometime in the prior few days.

Once the van was moving, the coverage became intermittent as the van moved into and out of coverage of various surveillance cameras. It drove through Athens and headed north toward Thessaloniki. Coverage was non-existent once the van left the Athens suburbs and it has not been seen in Thessaloniki. Thessaloniki is the second largest city in Greece and is a busy port on the Aegean Sea. Either the van went to one of the smaller towns or seaports on the way to Thessaloniki or they switched cars somewhere. There have been no sightings of the van since it left the Athens area.

"What else do you have?" Mick asked.

"Nothing, really," the analyst said. "We are still working on identifying the two men. Greek police and security officials are on the lookout for Sofia, the two men, and the van. There has been no ransom demand or other contact yet."

"Okay." Bronwyn said. "That's it. Mick and Taylor, you will be flying out of Dulles International Airport within the hour for Athens. Additional information received while you are airborne will be transmitted to you in route."

Both Mick and Taylor nodded.

"You are going in almost completely blind," Bronwyn acknowledged. "A full kit will be waiting for each of you on the plane with two sets of identity papers. You will be flying into Athens under your own names with diplomatic passports. Should you need to leave Greece, you can travel under your alias identities, blue tourist passports, at your discretion. Appropriate credit cards for each identity have been included. As always, there is also cash. Euros and dollars."

Again, both Mick and Taylor nodded. They rose in unison and walked to the gear bags Taylor had left near the door. Bags in hand, they followed Bronwyn down to the basement garage to a waiting black SUV with a driver. They stowed the bags in the SUV. Then they walked back to Bronwyn.

"Why are we involved in this?" Mick asked.

"As you heard in the briefing, the Ambassador is well connected," Bronwyn replied. "A request for your team came in through a back channel."

"Well connected is a serious understatement," Mick said, surprised that any Ambassador would have knowledge of his team or the wherewithal to request the assistance of his team so quickly, if at all. "That's a hell of a back channel he has."

"The Ambassador is not only wealthy," Bronwyn said, "he is powerful and he has seriously powerful friends. You might try to remember that when you deal with him."

"You are not kidding," Mick said.

"Are we going to have problems with State?" Taylor asked. "Are they trying to handle this themselves?"

"No," Bronwyn replied. "After we agreed to send your team, a formal request for assistance came over from the State Department. We are officially lead on this."

Mick handed Bronwyn his cell phone. Then, he reached up to his neck and snagged a long gold chain with a small but heavy gold cross on it with his thumb and forefinger. He pulled it off over his head. He reached into his back pocket, pulled out his wallet, and removed his driver's license. Then he placed the cross and chain inside his wallet and handed the wallet to Bronwyn. Finally, he reached into his pants pocket and removed his car keys, which he also handed to Bronwyn.

Taylor did the same thing, only he removed his gold wedding band and put it in his wallet before handing the wallet to Bronwyn. He checked his pants pockets to make sure there were no other personal items. There were none.

As they turned to go to the SUV, Bronwyn called out to Mick. He turned back toward her and she wrapped him in a hug, which she held for a long moment.

"Be careful," she whispered in his ear. "And play nice with the Ambassador. Just imagine the stress he is under."

Mick nodded to let Bronwyn know that he understood. The team did not deal with families. They were sent after Agency employees and, oftentimes, the employee's family did not even know their family member was in trouble. They certainly did not know that the team was involved. Dealing with the Ambassador was going to be a new experience adding a new dimension to their usual work.

Then Mick and Taylor both got into the SUV. Bronwyn stood and watched as they drove away.

CHAPTER FOUR

The driver dropped Mick and Taylor off at a nondescript private aviation hangar at Dulles International Airport. Once they stepped inside the office portion of the hangar, they were shown to a small lounge area and advised that wheels up would be in about thirty minutes. Taylor sat down to wait. Mick grabbed his go-bag and the plastic suit bag and headed for the restroom which he knew from prior experience had a shower.

"See if you can find some coffee while I shower." Mick called out to Taylor as he walked into the bathroom. Fifteen minutes later, Mick emerged from the bathroom, shaved, showered, and changed. He wore the same black tactical pants and black hiking boots as Taylor. His shirt was a dark blue polo and he also wore a light-weight black jacket.

As Mick approached Taylor and set down his bag, Taylor handed him a tall cup of coffee. Mick was just putting the cup to his lips when a man entered the lounge and said, "Load up, gentlemen." Mick glanced at the full, steaming cup of coffee regretfully for just a moment before putting it down on a table.

Loaded down with their gear bags, and sans coffee, Mick and Taylor walked out of the hangar, across the tarmac, up the stairs, and into the waiting jet. It was a government-owned plane, so it did not have the luxury interior that many private jets had. Even so, it was spacious inside, with wide comfortable seats and plenty of leg room. It could seat thirteen passengers.

They stowed their gear in the rear of the cabin, next to their kit bags which were already aboard, picked their seats, and buckled in. They were the only passengers on the plane. A steward came by, glanced at their seatbelts, then sat down and buckled in as well. Within minutes, the jet was taxiing to the runway. Mick watched as they rolled past numerous planes lined up for their turn at take-off. The jet moved to the head of the line and took off.

Once at cruising altitude, the steward came back to Mick and Taylor. The steward handed each of them a large manila envelope then turned and went to the galley. Minutes later, the steward was back with two steaming cups of coffee and two cold bottles of orange juice.

"Gentlemen, it's a long flight to Athens," the steward said. "You will probably want to get some sleep on the way so you can hit the ground running. If you like, I can get you meals now. We have both breakfast and lunch options."

Mick ordered breakfast. Taylor ordered "second breakfast" and cracked a joke about being on the Hobbit diet. Mick laughed. He liked Taylor and thought he was a very capable operator, but he was definitely obsessed with all things Lord of the Rings. Lucky for Taylor, the steward appeared to be in on the joke and enthusiastically went about putting Taylor's "second breakfast" together.

Mick opened his envelope and began to sort through the contents. There was a black diplomatic passport in his name with two credit cards also in his name, a blue tourist passport in one of his fictious identities with two additional matching credit cards, a significant number of euros and dollars, and a bunch of photographs. The photographs contained nothing new. They were just color copies of the photographs they had seen earlier in the morning and black and white stills from some of the surveillance recordings. Mick studied each photograph, committing the faces to memory. He looked at Sofia Sopko's photograph the longest.

"Hey, Taylor, have you ever seen the girl, Sofia, before?"

"Don't think so," Taylor responded. "There is something about her, though. I think I would remember her if I had seen her before."

There was something about her and Mick could not escape the feeling that he had seen her somewhere before. Mick had an excellent memory. He could place faces with names years after the fact which was a valuable skill in his work. But he was drawing a blank and could not imagine where they would have come in contact. She was about a decade younger than he was. It was not likely they had any social connection.

Mick put the photographs away when breakfast arrived. They ate and talked about the odds and ends of everyday life. Taylor's oldest boy was learning to play ice hockey and, to hear Taylor tell it, it was a good thing that Taylor's wife was a doctor. Mick was planning to plant grapes on the property he had inherited from his grandfather with the thought of trying to make wine.

Mick and Taylor worked well together. They both had similar backgrounds. Both were prior military with service in Afghanistan and Iraq. Mick had served in the Army and Taylor had served in the Marines. Both had gone into federal law enforcement after the military; Mick as a Special Agent with the Drug Enforcement Administration and Taylor as a Special Agent with Homeland Security Investigations. Each had been recruited by the Central Intelligence Agency. They met during Agency training and had quickly become good friends.

They were not spies. They were part of a paramilitary counter-terrorism team with a broad field of play. When the shit hits the fan and spies find themselves in real trouble, rapid response guys, like Mick and Taylor, are the ones the CIA sends in to save their butts. The members of the team had various backgrounds and areas of expertise. Mick and Taylor were the closest thing to detectives, so they were the investigators.

Mick thought of himself as a fixer. In the simplest of terms, his job was to put things right when they had gotten out of whack. Mick did not really think about it much beyond that because he never really talked with anyone, except Pops, about his job. People inside the Agency did not ask questions. When he had to talk to someone outside the Agency about his job, he lied.

Mick was glad that Taylor was on his team. Both Mick and Taylor could turn it on and turn it off. Guys that got into mission mode and could not turn it off wore Mick down over time by causing him to live in a state of hyper-stress.

After the steward cleared the remnants of breakfast away, both Mick and Taylor checked the contents of the kit bags and their gear bags. Kit was the equipment that the Agency thought they would need; gear was their own personal equipment and clothing. Mick also had his go-bag, an abbreviated version of a gear bag which Mick kept in his car. He was able to consolidate the three bags into two. They rearranged the contents the way they each preferred them to be, semi-automatic Glock 19 handguns on top. Mick removed a half-dollar sized waterproof bronze compass from his go bag and clipped it to a belt loop. It had been a gift from his grandfather and Mick took it on every mission. Their gear bags always included an empty wallet for each identity they would use on the mission. Mick and Taylor carefully loaded each wallet with the matching ID cards and credit cards, one always held their real identity, before distributing the euros and dollars between each of their two wallets. When they were finished, they headed back to their seats to review their alias documents and make sure they were very familiar with each other's alternate identities.

Mick's alias for this mission, if he needed to use it, was Roberto Lagomasino. He had done a double take when he had first seen it after removing the documents from the envelope the steward had handed him. Mick had kept the Roberto Lagomasino alias active, along with multiple others, but he had never actually used it on a mission before. It felt a little strange that he had been given this particular alias to use on the same day that he had started his morning with thoughts of the very real, but long deceased, Roberto Lagomasino. Taylor's alias was Daniel Redman.

They were 25,000 feet in the air, there was nothing more they could do until new information arrived, so it was time to relax while they still could. And sleep. Mick knew he needed to get a good eight hours of sleep, if possible, because this might be his last chance at a full sleep cycle for a while. They reclined their seats and settled into sleep. It was an eleven-hour flight. Mick hoped he would sleep through the rest of the flight.

Mick was startled into full wakefulness. Looking around, he recognized the plane interior and saw Taylor still sleeping. Mick took a deep breath, commanded his body to relax, and checked his watch. They were about two hours out. He got up from his seat, grabbed his ditty bag, and headed to the bathroom. Returning to his seat, he went over the photographs again.

The steward came to Mick with a cup of coffee and asked if he wanted anything to eat. Mick thanked the steward and said that he would wait for Taylor. The smell of coffee would wake Taylor in short order. Sure enough, Taylor began to rouse from sleep within minutes. Taylor, not a morning person, headed to the bathroom to take care of business without saying a word.

When Taylor returned to his seat, the steward was waiting with a cup of coffee for him and a continuation of Taylor's joke. The steward asked Taylor, with a straight face, "Are you ready for luncheon or were you thinking of breaking the rules and going for third breakfast? We could just call it elevenses."

Taylor laughed loudly and ordered third breakfast.

"What about you? Second breakfast or luncheon?"

Mick replied, with a smile, "Second breakfast. Thanks."

Taylor laughed at Mick being sucked into playing along. Mick laughed too as the steward walked to the galley. Mick wasn't going to ruin their fun. Taylor and the steward were enjoying the Hobbit references. An hour after they had eaten, the steward advised them that they would be landing soon.

The approach to the Athens International Airport and the landing were uneventful. The plane taxied away from the regular terminal to the area which housed private aviation hangars. Knowing the drill, Mick and Taylor stayed seated even after the plane engines were shut down and the stairs were lowered to the tarmac.

A Greek immigration official boarded the plane and, in perfect English, asked for passports. They each handed him two passports. He stamped the two diplomatic passports and the two tourist passports, without a glance at the names or photographs. The official then went to the door, waved two men into the plane, and deplaned himself. The two men introduced themselves, said they had a car to take them to the U.S. Embassy, and asked what bags needed to be put in the car. Once Mick and Taylor had both retrieved their handguns from the bags, grabbed their kit bags and handed their gear bags to each of the two men, they deplaned into the warm humid darkness of pre-dawn night in Athens.

As Mick walked into the empty lobby of the American Embassy before dawn that Friday, he saw the Marine guard move into action. Clearly, they were expected as the guard quickly buzzed open the secure door through which they all went. They were escorted to the Ambassador's conference room where it was equally clear they were the last to arrive. It was half past five o'clock in the morning and yet the conference room was full.

Ambassador Sopko stood up from his seat at the head of the large conference table and came around to shake hands with Mick and Taylor. There was a glassiness to the Ambassador's eyes and an urgency in his voice that telegraphed the stress he was under. But there was a firmness in his handshake that conveyed formidable strength. Mick's first impression was that Ambassador Sopko would move mountains to give them whatever assistance they might need, or at least try to.

There was no small talk or pleasantries; just names and handshakes. Then the Ambassador introduced Mick and Taylor to each of the others present. On the American side, there was the Central Intelligence Agency station chief, the Department of Justice legal attaché, the U.S. military liaison, and a couple of lesser functionaries. On the Greek side, there were the heads of the Greek equivalents, internal security, justice, military, and the Athens Chief of Police. The last to be introduced was the Greek detective working the case, Kostas Panopoulos.

Mick looked Kostas straight in the eyes and, once he had his full attention, gave him a subtle nod in recognition of the fact that he might be the most helpful person in the room when it came to actual movement on the ground. Mick was relieved to see Kostas' equally subtle response to that recognition from Mick.

Mick and Taylor moved to the only two vacant chairs at the conference table and sat down. More than half of the people in the room did not need to be there but Mick and Taylor needed information and they had to sit through whatever was planned to get it. There had been no updates on the plane. Either there was no new information, or it was being held here in Athens awaiting their arrival. Now was the time to find out which. All eyes turned to the Ambassador.

"As you know, a little after noon yesterday, my daughter Sofia was taken from the Byzantine Catholic church in the Plaka by two men," Ambassador Sopko said, with equal parts sadness and frustration in his voice. "There has been no ransom demand or contact of any kind from the kidnappers. Sofia was last seen on video surveillance getting into a delivery van with the two men. The men are still unidentified. The van was last captured on surveillance camera on the highway to Thessaloniki. That is it. That is all we know."

"The Greek police and security forces have assured me that they are combing every city and town looking for Sofia and the van," Ambassador Sopko continued, clasping his hands together tightly on top of the table. "So far, nothing. It is as if they vanished on the road to Thessaloniki."

With a brief pause that emphasized the stress the Ambassador was under, he turned to Mick and Taylor. "I don't want you to waste a minute in this room unnecessarily." The Ambassador lowered his head before looking back to them with anxiety radiating in his every word and continued, "I have been waiting for you to arrive. I am told that you are the best men to handle this kind of situation. You are here now. And, frankly, right now, you are my only hope. Tell me what you need me or anyone else in this room to do to help you find my Sofia and it will be done."

Both Mick and Taylor were somewhat taken aback. There was no new information. No contact from the kidnappers. There was to be no dog and pony show for them to sit through. At that moment, Mick knew that the chances of retrieving Sofia quickly were not good. The kidnappers had made a clean escape with Sofia. But he hoped for Ambassador Sopko's sake that luck would be on their side. Mick could tell that the Ambassador was placing all his faith in them and Mick felt that weight settle on his shoulders.

"We need to speak to the following people in the following order," Mick began. "Your two sons, separately. Sofia's driver. The woman at the church who saw the men. We also need to visit the church with the woman who saw the men, possibly with the driver. Then we need to follow the path that the men and Sofia took to the van and that the van took until it disappeared. We also might want to talk to the owner of the stolen license plate. We will be re-covering the ground that I am sure the local police have already covered but with different eyes."

"Finally, we will need Kostas Panopoulos available to us twenty-four hours a day," Mick demanded, looking straight at Kostas. Then looking back to Ambassador Sopko, Mick said, "But first, do you know why Sofia went to that church?"

Ambassador Sopko sighed loudly. Mick could hear the pain of loss in the voice of the Ambassador as he explained.

"Sofia went to the church because of her mother. My wife died six years ago. Sofia was only fourteen and very close to her mother. We are a Roman Catholic family but my wife, Victoria, was raised Byzantine Catholic. Victoria and Sofia loved going to Byzantine churches wherever we went. Victoria liked to point out each of the icons in the iconostasis and identify the saints. Now Sofia goes to visit these ornate churches to talk to her mother."

As Ambassador Sopko stopped talking, a single tear rolled silently down his face. He made no attempt to wipe it away.

"That seems like a personal and private thing that Sofia does," Taylor said. "Not something she would necessarily share with people. Who would know about Sofia going into Byzantine Catholic churches? Your sons did not go with her?"

"Other than immediate family, I don't know," Ambassador Sopko said. "I know, her brothers know. The boys don't go with her because that is Sofia's private time with their mother. Looking at the icons was something that Sofia and her mother loved and shared together. I am not aware of her ever taking anyone with her."

"In the United States, there are not too many Byzantine Catholic churches compared to, say, Roman Catholic churches," Ambassador Sopko explained. "So, it is not like this is a daily or weekly thing for Sofia. Quite frankly, I didn't think about it until I was told where Sofia had been taken from. Even in Greece, Greek Orthodox churches greatly outnumber Byzantine Catholic churches."

Taylor turned to the Department of Justice legal attaché. "Get a list of all foreign students attending the University of Richmond," Taylor directed. "And get their photographs. Then go to the Byzantine Catholic church closest to the school and find out if they know Sofia or anyone else on that list. Keep checking Byzantine Catholic churches in an expanding radius from the school until you find someone who knows Sofia."

The legal attaché wrote notes and nodded in response. Then, without a word, she got up from her seat and left the room.

"Okay," Mick said, turning to the Ambassador. "When and where can we speak with your sons?"

"They are at the residence," the Ambassador said. "Follow me."

As they all began to rise from their seats, the station chief handed Mick and Taylor cellular telephones.

"The names and personal telephone numbers of everyone at this table are already programmed into these phones," the station chief said. "There are also other numbers that may be helpful to you programmed in as well. The phones are not secure."

Mick and Taylor took the cell phones and they each handed him an envelope for safekeeping. The envelopes contained their alias identity documents, the blue tourist passports and the wallets with the matching credit cards and money.

"Kostas, we will need you, too," Mick said as they began to leave the room, following the Ambassador. Kostas fell in line behind Taylor.

CHAPTER FIVE

At the Ambassador's residence, Ambassador Sopko introduced Mick, Taylor, and Kostas to his sons, Peter and Matthew. Despite the early hour, both boys were fully dressed. The boys were clearly having a rough time but trying not to show it. However, there was no hiding their red and puffy eyes.

Ambassador Sopko showed Mick, Taylor, and Kostas into the formal dining room with Peter. Everyone took seats at one end of the large table, with Peter at the head of the table. Then the Ambassador and Matthew went into the living room to wait.

"Peter, tell me about the day Sofia went missing," Mick said. "Start from the beginning and we will interrupt with questions, if necessary, as you go."

It was now Friday morning and Peter began with the night before Sofia was taken, which was Wednesday night. He said that, during dinner, Sofia said she wanted to go shopping at the Plaka to get gifts for some of her friends back at school and she wanted to do it now so that she would not wait until the last minute and not be able to get the best gifts or best deals. Sofia and Peter had only arrived in Greece the week before and they had not seen or done much yet. Matthew was still in school when they arrived. His last day of school had been Wednesday. And their father had planned to take the coming week off to take them to the islands.

Peter immediately wanted to go along to the Plaka because he wanted to see the ruins of Hadrian's Library which are in the area of the Plaka. Matthew wanted to go along too. He wanted to spend time with Sofia and Peter. Their father thought it was a good idea and made arrangements for his car and driver from the Embassy to take them.

The next morning, at eight o'clock, the driver picked them up at the residence, dropped their father at the Embassy, then drove the kids to the Plaka. They spent much of the morning walking in and out of the various stores looking at the souvenirs for sale. They saw the same things at multiple stores with slightly different prices. Sofia was determined to get the best price, so they made a game of keeping track of which store had the lowest price for each item she wanted. When they came to a store that sold sandals made to order, they each had their feet traced and ordered a pair of sandals to be ready in a weeks' time. When they got tired of walking through the Plaka, they began to retrace their steps, stopping to buy the items at the stores with the cheapest price along the way.

As they neared the end, Sofia told the boys that she had seen a Byzantine Catholic church that she was going to stop in and visit. Sofia told the boys to go on to the ruins and to meet her at one o'clock and they would decide where to eat lunch. The driver was with them the whole time and he suggested a particular restaurant close by, which was between the ruins and the church, so they all agreed to meet there at one o'clock. The driver wrote the name of the restaurant and a crude map on the back of a receipt and gave it to Peter. The boys then split off from Sofia and the driver and went to the ruins. That was the last time they saw Sofia.

Just before one o'clock, they went to the restaurant and waited. Neither Sofia nor the driver showed up. They were picked up by men from the Embassy who said that Sofia was missing.

Mick and Taylor questioned Peter about whether he saw anyone following them, particularly when they turned back to reverse their path. Peter could not remember anyone following them. Peter said it was Thursday and the narrow streets of the Plaka were crowded. They were not paying attention to other people because they were having so much fun just talking and joking around with each other. Since Peter had started college last year, Matthew was all alone. Matthew and their father moved to Greece just after getting Peter settled into George Washington University. Sofia wanted to know everything that had happened in both Matthew and Peter's lives while they had been apart. She was especially interested in Matthew's life and how he was getting on in Greece. Whenever Matthew and Peter ran out of things to say, Sofia would remind them of a funny thing they had seen or done together and would have them all laughing in no time. They just were not interested in the people around them.

Mick asked Peter to look at photographs of the two men who took Sofia to see if he recognized either of them. Peter stared at the photographs.

"I want to recognize them, but I don't," Peter finally said.

"Why didn't you go to the church with Sofia?"

"Because that is her special time with mom," Peter said, tears forming in his eyes, threatening to spill over.

"Now, I wish we had gone with her, but we didn't, we never did," Peter trailed off at the end, barely a whisper.

Taylor got up from his seat and came around to Peter.

"It is not your fault, Peter," he said, as he ushered Peter from the dining room to the living room. Taylor returned with Matthew while Peter waited with his father. Matthew hesitated at the entrance to the dining room.

"Don't be afraid," Taylor said. "Come on in and take a seat, Matthew."

Taylor handled the questioning of Matthew while Mick and Kostas looked on. Matthew gave the same account of the morning that Peter had given. He also did not pay attention to whether anyone was following them. When shown the photographs of the two men with Sofia, silent tears began to fall from Matthew's eyes. Like his father, he refused to wipe them away or even acknowledge them.

"I don't know if they were following us or not," Matthew said. "There are many Muslim men in Greece."

"Why do you think they are Muslim?" Mick asked.

"I don't really know," Matthew responded. "They don't look Greek. They look like the Muslim men I see in downtown Athens all the time."

Taylor thanked Matthew for helping them and went into the living room to let Ambassador Sopko know that they were done. They left the boys at the residence and drove back to the Embassy to speak with the driver. During the ride back to the Embassy, the Ambassador spoke of his children and how they had attended a security briefing before he and Matthew had left for Greece. Ambassador Sopko said the security briefing kept replaying in his mind.

Ambassador Sopko was clearly deeply devoted to his children and put on no airs. He explained that, since the loss of his wife, he was torn between seeing that the children had every opportunity to grow, to learn, and to strike out on their own, and selfishly keeping them close to him. He would not have accepted the opportunity to be the Ambassador to Greece except that the children, especially Sofia, had encouraged him to do so. While he enjoyed the posting, he hated being so far from Sofia and Peter. And Matthew missed them daily. This summer with all the children in Greece together was something he and Matthew had talked about and looked forward to for months.

"This is my fault," Ambassador Sopko said. "I should have sent security with them. I didn't think. All three kids were together. And they had Nikolas with them. I never even considered that they would separate."

No one responded. There was no response that could be made.

Once at the Embassy again, they were taken to the Ambassador's conference room where the Ambassador left them. The driver was standing outside in the reception area. He followed them into the conference room. The driver introduced himself as Nikolas Pappas. He was a fit man with a light complexion, dark brown hair, and brown eyes, wearing a subdued black business suit, white shirt, and black tie. He took the seat indicated at the table and, in perfect English, proclaimed that he was prepared to answer their questions.

Nikolas Pappas related how he came to be a Greek employee of the American Embassy. Nikolas said that his father was Greek, and his mother was American of Greek heritage. He grew up in Greece and learned both Greek and English. Although he considered himself Greek, he has dual Greek and American citizenship as his mother never gave up her American citizenship and registered his birth with the Embassy shortly after he was born in Athens. He had vacationed multiple times in the United States as his mother used vacations as a chance to see her American relatives. He had attended the American Academy in Athens where the American children, like Matthew, and other European nationals in Greece go to school. Instruction at the American Academy is in English. His mother was insistent that Nikolas speak fluent English. She claimed that English was the international language of business and, therefore, Nikolas had to speak English.

After compulsory service in the Greek Army, Nikolas applied for a position at the American Embassy. He was hired and most of his work consists of driving and translating. For the past nine months, he has been Ambassador Sopko's personal driver. He has worked for the Embassy for almost three years and is saving his money to attend college in the United States.

When the questions turned to the day of the kidnapping, it was clear that Nikolas felt a heavy sense of responsibility. His description of the morning was just as Peter and Matthew described. He enjoyed being with the children although he did not participate in their conversations unless spoken to directly. He understood everything they said, and he was amazed at how easily Sofia drew Matthew into conversation. Since he had known Matthew, he had never seen Matthew so obviously happy as that day walking in the Plaka with Sofia and Peter.

When Sofia suggested that they split up, with the boys going to the ruins and her going to the church, Nikolas was at first concerned. While not a bodyguard, he was responsible for getting the children safely back to the residence. However, he could tell from the body language and expressions of the children when Sofia spoke of going to the church alone that there was something he did not know. He felt like that was the plan all along and he was the only one that did not know ahead of time. So, he went with it.

The ruins were not far away, and he suggested a taverna where the children could meet for lunch. Nikolas took all the bags from the boys and he and Sofia walked to the church. At the church, Sofia said that she would be a while and asked Nikolas to take the bags to the car and return for her. She said that she would meet him in front of the church when she was done and that she would stay at the church until he returned. Again, Nikolas hesitated but thought it was a church, there are few places safer than a church. And Sofia clearly wanted to be alone in the church. So, again, he agreed. Nikolas watched Sofia go into the church before he began walking to the car.

Nikolas was gone for less than thirty minutes before he returned to the church. As Sofia was not outside waiting when he returned, he opened the door and looked into the entryway for her in case she was waiting just inside to stay out of the sun. Not seeing her in the dark foyer, he stepped back outside the church and waited for her to come out. About ten minutes before one o'clock, Nikolas went inside the church to remind Sofia of the time and tell her they needed to head to the taverna. Sofia was not in the church. He asked the people in the church if they had seen Sofia. He found only one woman who had seen Sofia and she said that Sofia left with two Turks.

Nikolas explained the woman's use of the word Turks, "The Greeks and the Turks have been enemies forever. During the Byzantine Empire, much of modern-day Turkey belonged to Greece. The historically famous city of Troy was a Greek city in what is now Turkey. Istanbul was once Constantinople and before that Byzantium. Constantinople was the center of the Byzantine Catholic church. However, later, during the Ottoman Empire, much of Greece was occupied by the Ottomans."

"More recently," Nikolas continued, "in the 1970's, Turkey invaded Cyprus, an island with residents of both Greek heritage and Turkish heritage. The two countries almost went to full out war over Cyprus and today the island is cut in two with a Greek side and Turkish side and a border in between. The Greek hatred of the Turks runs deep."

"The woman thinks the men are Turks because the Turks are the historic enemies of the Greeks?" Taylor asked.

"No," Nikolas replied, looking to Kostas for assistance. "She is using the word Turks to mean more, to mean someone Muslim."

"Just as with other European countries," Kostas explained, "there has been a relatively recent influx of immigrants from the middle east, north Africa, and other Muslim countries into Greece. To some Greeks, anyone Muslim is a Turk. The use of the word Turk expresses all some Greeks need to know about a person, he is not to be trusted, he is the enemy."

"Yes, exactly," Nikolas agreed. "When the woman in the church used the word Turks to describe the two men, I knew she did not mean Turks literally but was using the word to mean Muslims. That is why I knew immediately that Sofia was likely taken and I called the Embassy."

Just as Nikolas finished speaking, Kostas' cell phone began vibrating on the table. Kostas waved them on as he looked at his phone. Mick placed photographs of the two men with Sofia on the table before Nikolas, but he waved them away.

"I have stared at those photographs for hours," Nikolas said. "The police showed them to me first. And Ambassador Sopko has copies of them. I have never seen them before. I did not see them on the day Sofia was taken."

Kostas slid his cell phone over to Nikolas and said, "Scroll through, there are four photographs."

Nikolas did as requested. On the final photograph, Nikolas exclaimed, "Him, I saw him near the car when I dropped the bags off."

Kostas took the cell phone and slid it over to Mick and Taylor.

"Those photographs have just come in from a bank across from the parking lot where Nikolas parked the car," Kostas said. "The automated teller machine was out of order on that day. The technician came to fix it today and pulled those photographs from the machine's camera which apparently was still working while the automated teller was not."

The photograph Nikolas had reacted to showed a fit man, early to mid-twenties, black hair, clean shaven, with a light olive complexion, dressed in jeans, a T-shirt with some sort of graphic on it, and running shoes. He was standing next to a building, leaning back on it, facing the automated teller machine camera head on and talking into a cell phone.

"Based on his appearance, I would say that man is not Greek," Kostas said.

"He could be of Arab descent," Taylor suggested.

"He could be Israeli, too," Mick said.

"His facial expression looks tense, but his body language looks like he is trying to look casual," Mick added. "And his dress is very casual, like a tourist."

"In my opinion, he looks Arab, but he is dressed like an American tourist," Kostas said.

"We need to see what is on his shirt," Mick said, as he zoomed in on the picture as far as the cell phone would allow. He still could not make out what was depicted on the shirt, which was partially blocked by the man's arm.

"Kostas, get us copies of every photograph taken by the ATM camera from nine o'clock in the morning until three o'clock in the afternoon," Taylor said.

Kostas took the cell phone back and began making the call. As Kostas was speaking in Greek on the phone, Taylor went in search of the CIA station chief and the DOJ legal attaché.

Everyone assembled back in the conference room, including Ambassador Sopko, who had realized that something more than an interview of his driver was happening. To his credit, Ambassador Sopko came into the room quietly, chose a seat at the far end of the conference table, and did not speak.

Mick asked for and received Kostas' cell phone. He showed the station chief and legal attaché the four photographs and explained where they had come from. Then he pointed out the photograph of the man Nikolas had identified. Mick explained that more photographs would be coming in from the bank, through Kostas, and that he wanted them scrutinized by Langley for identities. He also wanted to know what was on the man's T-shirt. He needed multiple copies of these four photographs immediately. Throughout, Ambassador Sopko remained silent. As the legal attaché and station chief left the room with Kostas and his cell phone, Taylor moved down to the Ambassador's end of the table.

"Sorry, but we don't want to waste a minute transmitting the photographs back home," Taylor said. "As soon as we have copies printed, you will see them. Remember, we don't even know if they will lead to anything or not, yet."

"I understand," the Ambassador replied. "Thank you."

As the Ambassador began to leave the room, he turned and said, "Just find my daughter, please." With that, he left.

While waiting for Kostas to return, Mick went to the bubble to transmit a secure update to Bronwyn. The bubble, or vault, is a secure communications room in the belly of the Embassy. It is the safest place in the Embassy. With high security, very limited access, and bomb proof walls, floor, ceiling, and door, it can withstand almost anything. From the bubble, Mick sent his secure message. It was just a hunch but the young man by the parking area did not look like a professional. Mick really wanted to know what was on his T-shirt. Mick wanted to know who he was, and, with luck, his T-shirt may be a clue to finding out.

CHAPTER SIX

Mick, Taylor, and Kostas left the Embassy in a black Embassy SUV with diplomatic license plates. Their gear was in the back. Against U.S. government regulations, Kostas drove since he was the most familiar with the streets and traffic of Athens. They headed to the home of the woman that had seen Sofia in the church. She lived just a few blocks from the church in the Plaka. Kostas had some difficulty finding somewhere to park the large SUV on the narrow streets, many of which were pedestrian only. With diplomatic plates and a policeman driving, Kostas was not worried about getting a parking ticket. There was just nowhere to park. He ended up backtracking toward the church and parking near where the white van had been parked as it was the only place he could find.

As they got out of the SUV, Kostas told Mick and Taylor that the white van had been parked just a few car lengths up the street. They walked to the space Kostas directed them to and looked around. It was a no parking area reserved for commercial deliveries. The street was full of small shops. The white van had looked like a delivery van. It would have aroused no suspicion.

"This all has the look of planning," Mick remarked, as he looked at the scene.

They walked down the narrow street to the woman's home. She lived above a corner ice cream shop. The neat two-story building of beige stucco with bright royal blue trim had blooming purple bougainvillea growing up along the whole of one side, casting part of the narrow side street below in shadow. Small wooden tables and chairs, painted the same bright royal blue color as the trim on the building, filled the area of the street directly in front of the shop. The entrance to the home was around the corner from the entrance to the shop.

Kostas knocked at a blue painted, wooden door, in the shadow of the bougainvillea. The door was opened by a handsome dark-haired woman in her late forties or early fifties. She was dressed in a black skirt and white blouse with a colorful blue and gold scarf draped over her shoulders. The woman welcomed Kostas warmly and invited them all inside. They went up a flight of wooden stairs and into a small but nicely furnished living room. The woman and Kostas spoke in Greek the entire way up the stairs. Once in the living room, the woman gestured for Mick and Taylor to be seated. They each took a seat on the couch, leaving the two chairs for the others.

Kostas introduced the woman as Athena Vassaly. He explained to her that Mick and Taylor were American law enforcement and that they were there to talk about Sofia. Athena spoke little English, only pleasantries and what was necessary for a shopkeeper to serve English-speaking tourists. Mick and Taylor spoke no Greek so they were thankful Kostas was able to translate as they tried to get more information from Athena.

Athena Vassaly explained that she owned the ice cream shop below them. She goes to the Byzantine Catholic church almost every weekday sometime after noon to light a candle for her late husband. On Thursday, she was at the church for just a short time, maybe only five minutes, when a young blonde woman came up beside her and lit a candle. The young woman was unusual, so

Athena noticed her. Sofia was dressed in jeans like a tourist, but she was wearing a head scarf inside the church and seemed to be deep in prayer after lighting the candle. Athena thought that she must be Byzantine Catholic because the tourists that come into the church almost never covered their heads and rarely prayed, preferring to wander the church looking at the ornate architecture, statues, and icons. After a few minutes, Sofia concluded her prayer by crossing herself in the Byzantine Catholic manner, right to left, not left to right like the Roman Catholics. Then Sofia placed a ten euro note in the offering box by the candles. Again, not usual for a tourist. Tourists gave coins as offerings, if anything at all. Athena confessed that the young woman intrigued her. She wondered who she was and where she was from. She wanted to try to talk to the woman, but she hesitated too long.

Sofia left the candles and walked toward the iconostasis at the front of the church. The moment to talk with her had passed and Athena needed to get something to eat for lunch and get back to her shop. Athena headed toward the door. On the way, she turned back once to look again at the young woman. That is when she saw Sofia flanked by two men. The men were both foreigners. "Turks," Athena said, looking directly at Kostas, who nodded. Sofia appeared to have received bad news and the three of them walked quickly toward the door. They walked right by Athena who had stopped at the sight. Sofia looked directly at Athena for just a moment and Athena saw sadness and uncertainty in her eyes. At the doorway, one of the men spoke to Sofia and she pulled the scarf from her head. Then they left.

Athena stood in place. She was overwhelmed with concern for the young woman. She went to the nearest pew, sat, and began praying for the young woman. Athena was struck by the certainty with which she just knew that she needed to stay at the church and to pray for the young woman. The minutes ticked by and Athena stayed in the pew. Finally, after what seemed much longer but was less than an hour, a very agitated, young Greek man began asking people in the church if they had seen the blonde-haired woman.

Athena went up to the man and told him what she had seen. The man asked many questions about the men and became even more agitated. Athena, while still concerned for the young woman, felt a sense of relief. She felt that this was why she had been compelled to stay at the church, to tell this man what she had seen. She spent the rest of the afternoon at the church, talking to various policemen, each of whom asked her the same questions.

"Now you are here asking the same questions again," Athena concluded, as translated by Kostas from Greek to English.

Mick nodded affirmatively then handed a number of photographs of the men with Sofia to Athena and asked that she look at them. Athena looked at the photographs and said that they showed the two men she had seen in the church with Sofia. She added that she had already seen these photographs and had already told Kostas that these were the two men.

Kostas explained to Athena that the Americans were just trying to be thorough. Athena nodded and told him that she wanted to help in any way that she could. Mick asked Kostas to show her the photographs on his cell phone, but she didn't recognize anyone in the pictures.

Mick turned to Kostas, "Ask her what her impression was of the two men. Like what she thought of Sofia when she first saw her. What did the way they were dressed or how they carried themselves make her think of them?"

"When I saw the men, I thought Turks," Athena replied to Kostas. "Honestly, I was alarmed and thought, why are Turks in this church?"

Athena went on to explain that the presence of the two men didn't make sense. They appeared to be Muslim, but

Muslims don't come into the church. They were dressed like Greek waiters with their black pants and white shirts with the short light jackets. When they approached Sofia, they seemed far too familiar with her. They got very close and one of them appeared to be giving her orders. She explained that perhaps they worked for a wealthy Muslim man, like they could be drivers or guards of some type.

Athena hesitated then said that, while she was praying, she prayed that the young woman was not a girlfriend of a wealthy Muslim man. She told them that the only thing that made the scene make some sort of sense was that the two men were chaperones for the young woman. Athena explained that based on the look on Sofia's face, it was not likely that these men were her chaperones. Nothing about Sofia's appearance suggested she was the type of young lady who often went out with chaperones, so Athena was very concerned about what she saw. She told the men, "In my heart, I knew something was wrong, that's why I had to stay to see if someone came looking for her."

"Could you hear what language they were speaking?" Taylor asked and Kostas translated.

"No, I could not hear them," Athena replied.

Mick asked, "Would you go with us to the church and show us exactly where this happened?"

Athena agreed and they all walked two blocks down the pedestrian street, deeper into the Plaka. They passed several shops and restaurants with tables and chairs out front. After a brief stroll, they reached the church.

As Mick and Taylor opened the large and heavy front door of the church, they commented on the artwork and sculptures. There were only a few people inside the dark, quiet church. The solemnness and the rich history of the Byzantine faith were apparent as the smell of incense hung in the air.

A priest came from the front of the church to the back and spoke to both Kostas and Athena in Greek. After a minute or two, the priest looked to Mick and Taylor and gestured for them to enter further into the church. Then he went to the doorway and stood there. Kostas said that, after he explained why they were at the church, the priest insisted on keeping tourists out of the church while Mick and Taylor looked around.

Athena took them to the set of candles which she and Sofia had stood before on Thursday. She stood in her place and had Kostas stand where Sofia had stood. At Athena's direction, Athena and Kostas re-enacted Sofia's movements. When Kostas went toward the iconostasis, Athena gestured for Mick and Taylor to go with Kostas. They were to play the parts of the two men who took Sofia. Kostas was not even halfway to the iconostasis when Athena told him to stop. Then Kostas said that Athena wanted Mick and Taylor to go on either side of Kostas. Then Athena took her place closer to the door behind the last row of pews. Athena motioned for the men to walk toward the door and they did. They stopped at the door and Athena, still behind the pews, patted her own head. Kostas reached up as if removing a scarf from his head. Then Athena went and took her place in the pew and lowered her head in prayer.

From the re-enactment it was clear to everyone that the two men intercepted Sofia on her way to the iconostasis and turned her to the door. They were either in the church before Sofia or they entered shortly after her and walked down the main aisle and waited for her. Neither Athena nor Sofia would have seen them enter the church while facing the candles in the small alcove by the wall. Athena explained that the only other door out of the church was behind the iconostasis where only the priests were allowed to go. It was also equally clear that Athena saw Sofia and the two men clearly. While it was dark in the church, they walked right by her, less than ten feet away.

They spent a few more minutes looking around the inside of the church then headed for the door. At the door, Mick and Taylor thanked the priest, with the assistance of Kostas, before leaving. Outside the church, Mick and Taylor thanked Athena for her assistance. Then they followed Kostas as he walked the route taken by the two men and Sofia back to their vehicle.

After following the route the white delivery van had taken out of Athens on the way toward Thessaloniki, they returned to Athens and Kostas took Mick and Taylor to a hotel. It had been a long day. They were hungry and tired.

The hotel was a small boutique hotel on the edge of the Plaka. Kostas knew the owner. With one phone call, Kostas had secured two rooms for Mick and Taylor. The hotel was similar in appearance to the outside of Athena's ice cream shop. The two-story building was covered in a pinkish stucco with a bright royal blue trim. There were several brightly painted wooden tables and chairs on the street outside the main entrance, where guests could sit, order drinks from the hotel, and people watch.

The hotel, both inside and out, had a relaxed island feel. When they entered, Kostas was immediately swarmed by two pretty girls in their mid-teens. His God-daughters, he explained to Mick and Taylor. The girls were followed by a middle-aged man, who Kostas introduced as his good friend and a distant cousin, Mateo. Mateo welcomed Mick and Taylor and checked them in without more than a swipe of their credit cards. Mateo spoke English and assured them he would assist them in any way possible while they were his guests. He explained that they could go out for food or he would see that food was brought in. He owned the bakery next door and the taverna just two doors down the street.

After Mick and Taylor were shown to their rooms on the second floor, Kostas said that he would be returning to his home to get a change of clothes and would return to the hotel a little later. He explained that dinner was served late in Greece and he would be back in time to take them out for a feast. He suggested that, while he was gone, they get settled in and perhaps check out the neighborhood.

Though they were tired, Mick and Taylor decided to get quick showers and head outside. They each took a seat at a small table out in front of the hotel. One of Mateo's daughters was quick to show up with a tray of drink options. Mick took a cup of espresso while Taylor opted for a refreshing bottle of Orangina. They hadn't eaten since the plane, so Mick suggested they go for afternoon tea. Afterall, it was far too late for elevenses or luncheon and Kostas would be back for dinner soon enough. Taylor appreciated the Hobbit humor and agreed they should look for somewhere to get something light to eat. However, before they finished their drinks, Mateo's other daughter appeared with a tray of fresh bread, two types of cheese, a bowl of olives, and a bottle of olive oil. The men decided this would do nicely until dinner and dug in.

After satisfying their immediate hunger, Mick and Taylor began making calls to check in and see if anything new had been learned about Sofia's kidnappers. Both the Agency station chief and the legal attaché wanted to come see them later in the evening at their hotel. They arranged to meet after dinner that night.

Kostas returned to the hotel around seven o'clock with a small suitcase. Kostas put the suitcase inside the hotel and took a seat at the table outside with Mick and Taylor. Mick asked about paying the bill for the food and drinks and one of the owner's daughters waved her hands and shook her head to indicate that there was no charge. Kostas confirmed that she was saying there was no charge. Mick placed two ten-euro bills on the table under an empty bowl as a tip for the two girls.

Then, they all walked two doors down the street to the taverna. They were seated at a quiet table for four inside, in the rear of the restaurant. All three men headed for the two seats which placed their backs to the wall. Mick recognized what was occurring and made the snap decision to be the one with his back to the door. Taylor would keep his eyes open. And Kostas, being a local, would probably have a better innate sense of whether something was not right than either Taylor or Mick. A small thing, but Kostas went up a notch in Mick's eyes. So far, Kostas was performing better than he had expected.

After dinner was ordered, Kostas said, "I hope I did right by introducing you as American law enforcement today."

Taylor chuckled. "That is what you are here for, Kostas," Taylor said. "You know your own people and we do not. You tell whoever whatever they need to hear to get us what we need. You are doing just fine."

Mick nodded in agreement. Kostas then asked if they would discuss the case at dinner.

"No," Mick said. "We are not barbarians. We will enjoy dinner then return to the hotel where we will brainstorm together."

Kostas broke into a smile and his posture became more relaxed. In reality, Mick and Taylor would not talk about the case in such a public place for security reasons. Kostas was feeling them out, just as they were feeling him out.

Mick, Taylor, and Kostas enjoyed their meals while engaged in pleasant non-work-related conversation. Mick learned that Kostas' family had a small vineyard and made their own wine. The dinner conversation involved grape growing and wine making. By the conclusion of dinner, Mick, Taylor, and Kostas were relaxed and comfortable with each other.

As they walked into the hotel, the station chief and legal attaché were waiting for them in the lobby. Kostas directed everyone to a small lounge room off the lobby and closed the door after everyone had entered. The station chief deferred to the legal attaché.

"We have determined what is on the shirt of the guy in the photograph," she said. "It is the University of Richmond mascot, a spider."

"We have also located a Byzantine Catholic priest in Williamsburg, Virginia, who knows Sofia," the legal attaché continued. "The Ascension of Our Lord church in Williamsburg is the closest Byzantine Catholic church to Richmond. Still, it is an hour away by car. The next closest Byzantine church is in Virginia Beach. No one there knows Sofia."

"How often has Sofia been to the Williamsburg church?" Mick asked.

"The priest said that she comes in about once a month, lights a candle for her mother, prays for a time, and often talks with the priest before leaving," the legal attaché replied. "You should know that the priest considers Sofia one of his flock. He knows her name; that she goes to college in Richmond; that her father is the U.S. Ambassador to Greece; that her mother was Byzantine Catholic; and much more."

With more urgency, Mick asked, "Has the priest seen anyone with Sofia?"

"Yes, a young man," the legal attaché replied. "The last few times that Sofia went to the church; she was driven by a young man. The priest could not recall his name but did recall that Sofia mentioned once that he was Maronite. The priest remembered that because he doesn't know many Maronites. It was something unique about the young man. The man waited for Sofia and wandered around the church or sat in the back until Sofia was ready to leave."

"Maronite," Taylor repeated. "That points to Lebanon. The Maronite Church is an Eastern-rite church in communion with the Western-rite Roman Catholic Church. The Maronite church is largely unique to Lebanon and the Levant. The lay language of the Maronite people is Arabic. Due to the heavy influence of

France on Lebanon, many Lebanese, particularly Christians, speak French in addition to Arabic."

"Was the priest shown the photograph of Spiderman?" Mick asked with mild sarcasm. Mick liked to give nicknames to his 'persons of interest' in a case. He decided this was an appropriate name for the guy holding up the wall across the street from the automated teller machine.

"Yes, he was," the legal attaché said. "He said that it looked similar to the young man, but he could not be sure as the photograph was from too great a distance."

"What about the foreign students at the university?" Taylor asked. "Was he shown those photographs?"

"Not yet," the legal attaché answered. "The Federal Bureau of Investigation received a list of over two hundred names but are still waiting on the photographs."

"While at school, Sofia goes to a Byzantine church with a Maronite," Mick thought aloud. "Maronites are most concentrated in Lebanon. Lebanese Christians are likely to speak French. Spiderman appears Arabic and could be Lebanese. One of the men who took Sofia spoke to her in French."

"Get the photographs of all foreign students from Lebanon expedited," Mick ordered. "And run the list of names through the Department of State for student visas, pull any matches from Lebanon."

Taylor asked the station chief to have someone with regional expertise review a list of the names of all students at the university. The list of names needed to be reviewed for names that could be of Lebanese origin.

"We can't over-look the fact that Spiderman might be American of Lebanese descent," Taylor said. "If he is American, he will not be on the list of foreign students or on a student visa. During the civil war in Lebanon in the 1970's and 1980's, many Christian Lebanese families immigrated to the United States. The grandchildren of those immigrants could be the age of Spiderman now."

After the station chief and the legal attaché left the hotel, Mick, Taylor, and Kostas reviewed what they knew. The kidnapping was clearly well thought out. The kidnappers knew that Sofia would be in Greece for the summer; that she visited Byzantine Catholic churches regularly and alone; and that she spoke French in addition to English. Lebanon was the odds-on favorite for the country of origin for the kidnappers. The fact that Sofia's male friend was Maronite cut both ways. It was a sign pointing to Lebanon which explained the use of the French language, but no one could think of a logical reason why a Maronite would be involved in the kidnapping of the daughter of a United States Ambassador.

CHAPTER SEVEN

Mick rose very early in the morning on Saturday. The window in his room looked out onto the street below. Early deliveries were occurring at shops along the narrow street. There were few pedestrians. Those people that were out and about were dressed neatly for work and were walking determinedly, not with the casualness of tourists.

Mick went downstairs to the lobby. He was met by the bright smile of one of Mateo's daughters. She quickly darted into a room at the back of the hotel and soon returned with a cup of espresso, which she handed to Mick. She directed him to a table outside and ran off to the bakery next door. Mick sat and sipped at the espresso while watching the early morning routine of the neighborhood. Mateo's daughter returned with a tray piled high with various breads and pastries, which she sat in front of Mick before going back into the hotel. Mick drank, ate, people watched, and checked his cell phone for non-existent messages.

Taylor and Kostas joined Mick at the outside table with cups of espresso of their own.

"Good morning," Mick said. "Anyone have anything new?"

Both Taylor and Kostas shook their heads negatively as they took seats at the table. It was not long before Mick saw the station chief and the legal attaché walking down the street towards him. He alerted Taylor and Kostas and all three stood up, took their cups of espresso and the bakery goods, and entered the hotel. When the station chief and the legal attaché entered the hotel, they again all went into the lounge off of the lobby and Kostas closed the door. Mick noticed that the lounge door now had a sign on it saying "Reserved" in both English and Greek.

"We have a positive identification of the man who accompanied Sofia to the church in Williamsburg," said the legal attaché, as she provided them with copies of a student identification card and a student visa application.

"Sami Musa, twenty-two years old, from Beirut, Lebanon," the legal attaché announced. "He has been attending the University of Richmond for two years and returns to Lebanon each Christmas break and summer break. The priest in Williamsburg has positively identified him from his student identification card photograph as the man who drove Sofia to the church several times."

"We have nothing on him," said the station chief. "But we are doing a deep dig on his family now."

"It looks like Spiderman is Sami Musa but let's not jump to conclusions until we verify that Sami Musa is in Greece," Mick said. "Kostas, can you find out if, how, and when Sami Musa entered Greece?"

Kostas nodded, stepped away with a copy of the visa application, and made a phone call.

"Any contact from the kidnappers?" Mick asked.

"No, no contact," the station chief said. "And no claim of responsibility. It appears the kidnappers are maintaining a media blackout for now. That works better for us but we can't count on that lasting. They can go public whenever it suits them so we need to be ready."

"They will not go public until they are feeling secure, unless we force their hand," Taylor said. "Two days seems like a long time to have a captive, but it is not a long time if they have to get the captive to a secure location when they are in a foreign country. It could be that they are not feeling secure yet."

"We will know soon if Sami Musa is in Greece," Kostas said, as he returned to the group. "Two days is not a very long time, especially when you are operating in a foreign country where you do not speak the language. I would think that they would want to get out of Greece and into a friendlier country as soon as possible."

"Or they have a place in Greece with the necessary support," Mick injected. "Crossing a border with a captive is dangerous for the kidnappers."

"But Greece is mostly surrounded by water," Kostas said. "There are a great many boats and ships coming and going all of the time. They could get her out easiest by sea."

"For that matter, they could keep her on a boat or ship at sea and not have to deal with random people seeing her," Taylor suggested.

"Right," Mick agreed. "Kostas, can you get a list of all foreign flagged vessels that were in Greek ports between Athens and Thessaloniki since last Thursday?"

"That will take some time," Kostas said, as he again stepped away from the group to make a phone call.

Before Kostas could make the call, his cell phone rang. The group waited impatiently as Kostas spoke into his cell phone in Greek. When the call was completed, Kostas turned back to the group.

"Sami Musa flew into Athens from Cyprus on Monday of this week, three days before the kidnapping," Kostas said. "There is no record of him leaving Greece. If he left by private boat, it is possible that we would not know."

"Cyprus is a member of the European Union," Mick said. "Once he cleared through immigration into the EU in Cyprus, he could travel easily and without much scrutiny. Smart planning on someone's part. Less scrutiny when arriving in Greece from another EU country."

Mick asked Kostas if he could find out where Sami Musa had stayed in Greece. Kostas agreed to have police officers begin contacting hotels in search of Sami Musa. The search would begin in the Plaka and radiate out from there. The police would tell the hoteliers that the man was a possible witness to a crime and was wanted for questioning. Everyone agreed that finding Sami Musa at a hotel was a long shot; but one that they could not ignore. If he was part of the kidnapping plot, he was most likely not staying at a hotel. But then again, he did not look like a professional and maybe Sami Musa was a weak link in the plan.

After Kostas made his calls, the group tried to make sense of what they knew. The station chief expressed his opinion that Sami Musa was not going to turn out to be Maronite. The Maronite thing was a red herring, he believed. He had been stationed in Beirut for several years and believed that Musa was going to be Shia. He explained his complicated but detailed reasoning to the group.

"There are three primary religious groups in Lebanon and more than a dozen lesser represented religious groups," he began. "The Maronites are the largest of the Christian groups. The two largest Islamic groups are the Sunni and the Shia."

"Lebanese Christians, including the Maronites, look to France and other western powers, like the United States, for support when times are tense in Lebanon. It makes no sense for a Maronite to be involved in the kidnapping of the daughter of an American diplomat.

"The Sunni Lebanese look to Saudi Arabia for assistance when tensions roil in Lebanon. Sunni Islam is the religion of the Kingdom of Saudi Arabia. Former Prime Minister Rafic Hariri was killed by a truck bomb on February 14, 2005, in Beirut. The United Nations Special Tribunal for Lebanon charged four Hezbollah members with the assassination of Rafic Hariri.

"The Shia Lebanese look to Iran for assistance. Shia Islam is the religion of the Islamic Republic of Iran. Hezbollah is the leading power among the Shia in Lebanon. At the end of the Lebanese civil war, Hezbollah fighters were the only ones that did not disarm. Hezbollah argued that it was a protection force against outsiders, along with the Lebanese Army, and would never turn their arms against fellow Lebanese. In truth, Hezbollah operates as an armed terrorist group in Lebanon with impunity.

"For example, in July of 2006, Hezbollah fired rockets from Lebanon into Israel as a diversion, and then kidnapped two Israeli Defense Force soldiers from inside the border of Israel, while leaving three others dead. Hezbollah demanded the release of Lebanese prisoners in Israel in exchange for the two Israeli Defense Force soldiers. Israel refused and began a bombing campaign which became a 34-day war between Israel and Hezbollah; known in Lebanon as the July War and in Israel as the Second Lebanon War. The Lebanese Army stood by helplessly while Israel bombed the southern part of Lebanon where the Shia Lebanese live next to the border with Israel. Only in Lebanon could another country go to war with just one segment of the country's population and the nation's army just stand by and watch. Hostilities were ended by a United Nations agreement between Lebanon and Israel which included both the disarming of Hezbollah and United Nations peacekeepers positioned in Lebanon on the border with Israel. The bodies of the two kidnapped Israeli Defense Force soldiers were returned to Israel as part of a prisoner exchange. To the surprise of no one familiar with the region, in spite of the UN agreement ending the war, Hezbollah has never been disarmed.

"Coming forward to present day, since the beginning of the Syrian civil war in 2011, Hezbollah has been fighting on the side of Syrian President Bashar al-Assad at the direction of Iran. Bashar al-Assad's religion is Alawite. Alawis represent less than twenty percent of the Syrian population, which is predominantly Sunni. The Syrian civil war pits the Sunni Muslim population against the Alawite Syrian ruling family.

"The current Syrian President's father, Hafez al-Assad, assumed power by coup in 1970 and declared himself President. Since the Syrian Constitution required that the President be Sunni Muslim, Hafez al-Assad changed the Constitution to require only that the President be Muslim. Then to solidify that al-Assad met the new Constitutional requirement, Musa al-Sadr, a leader of the Shia in Lebanon and founder of the Lebanese Amal Movement, issued a fatwa that Alawis were a community of Twelver Shia Muslims.

"Theologically, it makes no sense. Alawis have beliefs that are heretical to both Sunni and Shia Muslims, drinking wine and belief in reincarnation just to name two. Therefore, Alawis have been considered ghulat, meaning exaggerators, by mainstream Shia Islam, and infidels by Sunni Islam. But Hafez al-Assad's need for the Alawis to be recognized as Muslims in a predominantly Sunni Muslim country and Musa al-Sadr's desire for political influence and patronage combined to create the political expediency of the Alawis as a branch of Shia Islam.

"As a matter of geo-political convenience, Iran accepts the Alawite al-Assad family as the rulers of Syria, a majority Sunni country. The Syrian civil war is a battle between the Sunni Arab world and the Shia Persian world for control of territory in the heart of the Arab world. Just as the world accepted that Hezbollah and Israel were at war in 2006, but that Lebanon was not at war and was merely a helpless victim, the world now accepts that Hezbollah is fighting in the Syrian civil war, but that Lebanon is not. Such is the enigma that is Lebanon, a country with an armed, Iranian proxy fighting force within its borders that shrouds itself in Lebanese patriotism while loyal, first and foremost, to Iran. Christian and Sunni Lebanon are held hostage by Hezbollah which really means that Lebanon is held hostage by Iran.

"Hezbollah's strength continues to grow in Lebanon. Currently, Hezbollah holds most of the significant cabinet positions in Lebanon.

"I would bet money on the fact that Sami Musa will turn out to be Shia," the station chief concluded.

Mick sought clarification. "So, if Sami Musa is involved, you think that it is a Hezbollah operation?"

"Let's just say that I wouldn't be surprised," the station chief said. "Hezbollah has a history of kidnapping Americans. Remember, in 1984, Hezbollah kidnapped, tortured, and murdered William Buckley, the station chief in Beirut, and later sent videos of Buckley being tortured to the United States Embassies in Athens and Rome. Also, in 1988, Hezbollah kidnapped, tortured, and murdered Marine Colonel William Higgins, while he was assigned to the United Nations peacekeeping mission. And there are plenty of journalists and others who were kidnapped as well."

"But those kidnappings occurred inside of Lebanon," Taylor said. "Wouldn't it be a stretch to think that Hezbollah is acting outside of Lebanon or Syria?"

Mick answered for the station chief. "No, Taylor, Hezbollah operates outside of Lebanon. Argentine intelligence believes that Hezbollah, at the direction of Iran, conducted the 1992 bombing of the Israeli Embassy in Buenos Aires that killed 29 people and wounded over 200 others; and the 1994 truck bombing of the Asociacion Mutual Israelita Argentina in Buenos Aires where 85 people were killed and over 300 were injured."

"Recently, Argentina froze the assets of the Lebanese ex-pat Barakat clan in Argentina due to their belief that the Barakat clan launders money which is then funneled to Hezbollah and Hezbollah is designated as a terrorist organization due to those bombings," the legal attaché added. "I remember reading a notice sent out because the United States has joined with Argentina and is also freezing the assets traceable to the Barakat clan."

Kostas spoke up for the first time. "Why in Greece? Why this girl?"

"It would sure help if we knew why," Mick said. "My thinking right now is that it was a target of opportunity."

Mick explained his reasoning. "Sofia Sopko has been at the University of Richmond for three years; Sami Musa for two years. Somehow, they came in contact and Sami Musa either intentionally or unintentionally mentioned her while at home in Lebanon. Sofia's father did not become Ambassador to Greece until this past Fall. Sami Musa did not begin accompanying Sofia to the Williamsburg church until this Spring. Sami Musa was in a position to get close to Sofia while at the university when Sofia was not on guard. He was also in a position to find out if, and when, she was leaving for Greece."

"Greece is a major tourist area during the summer which makes it easier for foreigners to move about freely without a lot of notice," the station chief added. "In addition, there has been an influx of Muslims into Greece in recent years making it even easier for Muslim men to move about in Greece without attracting much attention."

"Meanwhile, the United States and Iran have been enemies since the Iranians took 52 American diplomats and civilians' hostage in 1979," Mick said. "Iran and the United States are currently on opposite sides in the Syrian civil war where Hezbollah is fighting. And the United States has designated Hezbollah as a terrorist organization."

"Maybe that is it," Taylor said. "Sofia was a Hezbollah target of opportunity, which they intend to use to try to influence American policy in Syria."

"Well, we won't know unless we find Sami Musa," Mick concluded. "And we are not going to do that sitting here." They all headed out of the hotel and to their cars.

Mick, Taylor, and Kostas were allowed immediate access to the Embassy and into the Ambassador's conference room. Ambassador Sopko hastily concluded the meeting he was having in his office and joined them. Mick and Taylor brought him up to date on the investigation. They left out their suspicions of Hezbollah involvement.

Mick asked the Ambassador, "Did Sofia ever mention a young man named Sami Musa, maybe just Sami, or Sam?"

"Yes," the Ambassador replied. "Sam. In one of her e-mails, she mentioned a student named Sam in a conversational French group she attended."

"Can you get us a copy of the e-mail?"

"Yes, but I have to go through all of the e-mails," the Ambassador said, as he got up and walked toward the door to his office. "I only recall her mentioning the group a couple of times and one time she mentioned Sam."

"While you look, we have other things to do in the Embassy," Mick said, as they headed for the legal attaché's office.

The legal attaché was acting as the repository for all recordings, photographs, and documents. She was simultaneously tracking all evidence for any potential criminal prosecution of the kidnappers and keeping multiple copies of everything available to Mick and Taylor for their investigation. As a federal prosecutor prior to becoming a legal attaché, she was thorough and organized. In her office, they obtained a stack of enhanced photographs of the two men who took Sofia, the white van, Sami Musa in Athens, and Sami Musa's school identification, as well as copies of Sami Musa's visa application.

Mick directed the legal attaché to obtain Sofia Sopko and Sami Musa's full university transcripts. She was to look for classes they had been in together. She was also to find out about a conversational French group that Sofia Sopko and Sami Musa attended. Mick asked that each of the group members be tracked down and questioned as to when Sofia and Sami started attending the group and, specifically, how Sami Musa represented himself to the group. Where was he from? How good was his French? What was his religion?

The legal attaché said she would get the FBI on it immediately.

Mick also asked the legal attaché to request to review all of the e-mail messages between the Ambassador and his daughter. She was to read all the e-mails and pull out for their review only those e-mails that might have significance to the investigation. Mick wanted a source other than the Ambassador with knowledge of the contents of the e-mails to avoid potentially sending the Ambassador down emotional rabbit holes. The legal attaché agreed to approach the Ambassador after they left the Embassy.

They next went to the station chief's office. The station chief had a grim look on his face.

"I just received information from Beirut," the station chief said, as they walked into his office. "Sami Musa's family is Shia, living in a mixed area of Beirut since 2006, but originally from the outskirts of Dahiyah, before the July War. Dahiyah is a Shia area and a Hezbollah stronghold. It was heavily bombed by Israel during the war."

"What else do you have on the family?" Taylor asked.

"Sami's father has been married twice," the station chief said. "By his first wife, he had two sons and a daughter. His first wife died when the children were young. His oldest son was killed while fighting Israel during the July War. His second oldest son is believed to be fighting with Hezbollah in the Syrian civil war. The daughter is married and lives near Dahiyah. The father had two more children with his second wife, Sami and the youngest boy, five years younger than Sami, 16 years old now. They no longer live in or near Dahiyah."

"What is the father's involvement with Hezbollah?" Mick asked.

"None that we know of," said the station chief. "The father appears to be apolitical. He neither supports Hezbollah nor speaks ill of Hezbollah, which is the only safe position for a Shia in Lebanon to take if they are not a supporter of Hezbollah."

"But two of his sons have fought with Hezbollah," Taylor said.

"All I can do is try to explain what I learned while living in Lebanon," said the station chief. "The Shia were historically treated as second class citizens in Lebanon. Hezbollah filled a gap left by the government by providing services to the Shia in areas that they controlled. As a Shia in Dahiyah, you don't bad-mouth Hezbollah, even if you don't agree with them."

"Hezbollah has tremendous influence on the youth in their areas of control," the station chief continued. "Hezbollah propaganda is everywhere you look, everywhere you go in Dahiyah. Even if the father did not approve of Hezbollah, he would have to be careful about what he said, even to his own children.

"As I said before, Dahiyah is a Hezbollah stronghold and was heavily bombed by Israel. But it has now been largely rebuilt. So, it may be significant that the father never moved back to Dahiyah or anywhere near it. It may also be significant that he is financing Sami's education in the United States. There are universities in Lebanon that Sami could attend for less money. Sami's father is not a wealthy man.

"All of which is to say that Sami's father may not be a Hezbollah supporter and, yet, two of his sons could end up as Hezbollah fighters. Maybe Sami works for Hezbollah or maybe his father sent him to the United States to get him away from Hezbollah."

"Or maybe Sami's father sent him to the United States to remove him from Hezbollah's influence and it did not work," Taylor suggested.

"That is a viable scenario as well," the station chief acknowledged.

"Now I really want to know what the conversational French group members knew about Sami Musa's religion," Mick said.

"Absolutely," Taylor replied. "If he was representing himself as Maronite, not Shia, that is evidence of his complicity in the kidnapping. Otherwise, there would be no need for the ruse."

The station chief's desk phone rang. He answered, listened for half a minute, then said, "Right away." Hanging up the phone, the station chief announced that the Ambassador had the e-mail mentioning Sam and was waiting for them in his office.

Mick, Taylor, and Kostas walked into the Ambassador's office without knocking. It was their first time in the Ambassador's office and Mick stopped short when he saw the photograph on the credenza. The Ambassador saw that Mick was looking at the photograph.

"My wife, Victoria," he said.

"I believe I met her once," Mick said, struck by the certainty of it. "Years ago, at Great Meadow. I was there to watch my sister compete. She introduced herself as Vicky. I never knew her last name."

The Ambassador smiled. "After her children, her greatest passion was horses."

"Sofia looks so much like her," Mick said, as the pieces fell together. He had never seen Sofia before; he had briefly met her mother.

"Yes, she does," the Ambassador said, wistfully.

After a moment, Ambassador Sopko turned back to the matter at hand and handed each of them two pieces of paper, two different e-mails from Sofia. The first e-mail was from late January and mentioned that a student named Sam had joined the conversational French group Sofia attended.

"Good news on the French practice front," Sofia had written. "A new guy joined the conversational group. We are now 7. We need the new blood. I hope Sam continues with the group so we can have someone new to talk with."

It was a largely innocuous passage in the e-mail, but it did give the impression that Sam's joining the group was the first time Sofia had met him. The second e-mail was from March.

"Sam, from French group, has a car," Sofia had written. "He offered to drive me when I need to go anywhere that requires a car. We went grocery shopping and it was great to be able to stock up at one time for a change. I think that next year I would like to have a car on campus. It would be so much easier for getting to job interviews as I near graduation. If I get the car in the fall, I could drive to DC and see Peter when we have breaks from school."

"So, first he joins the French group and then he offers to drive Sofia wherever she wants to go," Mick mused. "Good work by Sami. Meet Sofia through a mutual interest and ingratiate yourself to her by becoming her driver."

"How did Sofia get to the church in Williamsburg before Sami began driving her?" Taylor asked the Ambassador.

"Rental car, I imagine," the Ambassador said. "Both Sofia and Peter have credit cards on my account. There are occasionally rental car charges on Sofia's portion of the bill. The children can charge anything they need, and I have never questioned any of their charges."

Kostas' cell phone began to ring. He answered the phone and spoke in Greek. As the conversation progressed, Kostas became more animated and it was obvious from his tone that he began barking orders into the phone. At the conclusion of the call, Kostas turned to the others.

"We have Sami Musa in custody," Kostas announced. "He was at a hotel in downtown Athens. I have directed that he be taken to the closest police station for questioning. We should go now."

"I want to go, too," Ambassador Sopko said immediately.

"Sir, you do not want to be there," Mick responded. "You cannot be there while we question him." Mick was short and firm with the Ambassador.

"It will not help us do our job," Taylor interceded, to soften the blow. "We don't know how this is going to go down and it is better for you to not be there."

"But I will just watch, he doesn't even have to know I am there," the Ambassador argued.

"Enough," Mick said, more sharply than he intended. "Ambassador, this is not an American criminal investigation where you can watch us work from behind a two-way mirror. This is first and foremost Sofia's recovery operation. We are going to do whatever we need to do. As a diplomat, you must maintain plausible deniability. So, you cannot go."

"Of course, you are right, I understand," the Ambassador said, accepting the rebuke, as Mick, Taylor, and Kostas headed for the door.

CHAPTER EIGHT

Mick instructed Kostas to park either underground or on the street at least a block from the police station due to the diplomatic license plates on the SUV. It was better not to publicly announce their identity or presence.

Upon arrival at the police station, Kostas pulled the SUV into an underground parking area with a secure sally port where prisoners are booked and taken to the holding cells. Kostas affixed his police badge to his belt and led the way through the maze of offices to a small interview room.

Sami Musa was sitting alone at a small plastic table in the interview room. There were only two vacant plastic chairs in the room so, before entering, Kostas went into another room and obtained another chair. Kostas opened the door, slid the chair into the room, and walked in. He was followed by Mick and Taylor. They all sat on the opposite side of the small table from Sami.

Kostas began to speak to Sami Musa in Greek. Sami just sat there listening for a minute or so. When Kostas paused for a second, Sami held up a hand and said, in Arabic, "I do not speak Greek."

Mick wanted to see how Sami would respond to French before they moved on to English.

"*Parlez-vous français?*"

"*Oui*," Sami replied and began to speak in rapid-fire French, which none of them could follow.

Kostas held up both of his hands to get Sami's attention. "Do you speak English?"

"Yes," Sami replied hesitantly, while switching to English.

"Good, we will all speak in English," Kostas said.

"You are Sami Musa?"

"Yes," Sami responded.

"You are Lebanese?"

"Yes," Sami responded again.

"Why are you in Greece?"

Sami did not respond. First, he looked to Mick and, then, to Taylor. Then, he lowered his head and looked at his hands in his lap. Kostas moved on.

"When did you arrive in Greece?"

"Monday," Sami replied, still not looking up from his hands.

"Where have you been staying?"

"At the hotel where the police arrested me."

"The whole time from Monday until now?"

"Yes."

Kostas tried again, "Why are you in Greece?"

Again, Sami did not respond but, instead, looked up at Mick and then Taylor. Again, Kostas moved on.

"What is your religion?"

"Islam."

"What sect?"

"Shia."

"Why are you in Greece?"

Again, no response from Sami. However, when he looked to Mick and Taylor this time, there were tears brimming in his eyes.

Mick stood up. Kostas and Taylor immediately followed suit. Kostas hit a button on the wall which notified someone in a control room to open the door. A moment later, the solenoid switch in the door could be heard engaging. Mick led them out of the interview room. When the door was closed, he led them a short way down the hallway, far enough to rule out any possibility of Sami overhearing their conversation.

"This may be the break we have been looking for," Mick said, in hushed tones. "He is telling the truth in answer to your questions. He is refusing to answer the question of why he is in Greece rather than lie to us."

"He knows we are American," Taylor interjected. "He keeps looking to you and me even though Kostas is asking the question he is refusing to answer."

"Yes, he is not stupid," Mick said. "He is clearly scared. But I don't think it is us that he is afraid of. What do you two think? Kostas, you first."

"First, I agree that he is scared," Kosta said. "Second, I agree that he does not fear us, meaning you, the American authorities, and me, the Greek authorities. Third, I think he knows exactly why he is sitting in that room at this police station. And finally, I think he wants to tell us, but he does not know if he can trust us. To that end, he sees you, the Americans, as the power players, not me, representing Greece."

"I agree with Kostas," Taylor said. "I vote to see where going easy gets us before we go down a road we can't come back from."

"Okay, we are all reading it the same," Mick said. "Kostas, can you get us something to drink, four of anything, and a box of tissue or a roll of toilet paper, something for him to wipe his face with?"

Kostas went further down the hall and turned the corner. Mick and Taylor waited for him to return. When Kostas returned, they all went into the small interview room and took their seats. Sami watched them silently.

"Okay, Sami, we are back," Mick said, as he slid a Fanta and a box of tissues in front of Sami. "As you have probably guessed, this man on my right and I are Americans."

Sami audibly exhaled and his shoulders slumped.

"Now, you are going to tell us everything that you know about the kidnapping of Sofia Sopko," Mick continued.

"They took her?" Sami's voice was soft, almost inaudible, as he reached for a tissue.

"I can't talk to you," Sami said louder. "They will kill my brother."

"Okay, that is a start," Mick said. "You have decided to trade Sofia Sopko's life for your brother's life. I assume you mean your little brother."

"It's not like that," Sami responded, with a small voice. "You don't understand. There is no choice. I have no choice."

"Well, Sami, I disagree," Mick responded. "Everyone has a choice. It may be a choice between two evils but, still, it is a choice. And maybe we do understand. Maybe we do understand that your family lives in Lebanon and the choice you have made involves your whole family, and not just your little brother."

Sami looked up into Mick's eyes. He seemed to be searching for something, but he remained silent.

"Sami, I am giving you a choice right now," Mick said. "You can try to help me find Sofia and I will try to help you. Or you can remain silent and maybe Sofia dies, and maybe your family dies, too, either now, or in the future, the next time, or the time after that, when you are again threatened and finally decide the cost is too high to bear."

"You don't know who you are dealing with," Sami said quietly. "How can you help me?"

"Let me guess," said Mick. "The party of God. Hezbollah. Is that who we are dealing with, Sami?"

Sami's eyes again filled with unspilled tears and he quietly whispered, "Yes."

"I promise you, if you help us, we will help you," Mick said. "We can get your father, mother, and little brother out of Lebanon."

Sami asked, hopefully, "And my sister and her family?"

"Possibly, but that will be harder," Mick said. "All I can promise is that we will try."

"Will you take them to America?"

"One thing at a time, Sami," Mick said. "I am promising you safety for them; final destination is not something I can promise you right now. But you need to tell us everything now."

Sami physically deflated as the fight or flight adrenaline rush began to ease its effects on his body. Mick and Taylor both noticed and immediately knew the deal was done.

"One of us needs to start the wheels moving on our end," Mick said, while looking at Taylor.

"I'll go," Taylor said. As he rose to stand, he reached into his pocket, removed a micro recording device and set it on the table in front of Mick. "Kostas, will I have any problem getting out of here?"

"No," Kostas said. "The door to the interview room opens from the outside. Once inside, to get out, you must be released by the control room which you call by pushing the black button on the wall. Don't push the red button. That's a panic button. It sets off an alarm and brings an armed response. But, wait, let me make a call and you will have a police driver to your destination."

Kostas made the call. Within minutes, a police officer appeared at the door to the interview room, opened the door from the outside, and Taylor and the officer left.

The police officer dropped Taylor in front of the United States Embassy. While in route, Taylor had texted the station chief, "Meeting. Your office. 15 min."

When Taylor entered the Embassy, the station chief was waiting for him at the main entrance. The station chief led Taylor to the Ambassador's conference room. As they had passed the turn to the station chief's office, the station chief had said, "Too many people are involved in this to fit comfortably in my office."

When Taylor entered the conference room, he recognized the legal attaché and two men with whom he was very familiar. The rest of the team had arrived. Thankfully, the Ambassador was not present, so Taylor did not have the uncomfortable task of removing him from the meeting.

Taylor walked directly to David and Jason and gave them each a handshake, while saying, "Glad you are here, we need you both."

Taylor was too keyed up to sit at the table, so he stood at the head of the room and addressed the group. He began by telling everyone that the situation was still very fluid. Even so, promises had been made and they needed to get into action to fulfill the commitment made.

Taylor cautioned that they did not yet have a full debriefing from Sami Musa as Mick was still handling that part. However, the working scenario is that Sami Musa is being threatened with harm to his family in Lebanon unless he helped in the kidnapping of Sofia. Therefore, preparation for the removal of Sami Musa's family from the field of play was a priority right now.

The family includes father, mother, and teenage little brother in Beirut that are part of the deal. Exfiltration of Sami's sister's family, including the wife, husband, and kids is highly desired but not expressly part of the deal.

"The sister has two small children," the station chief advised the group.

Taylor answered the questions posed by those in the room as best he could. The questions were many and Taylor's ability to answer them was limited.

"David and Jason, you two are in charge of everything relating to the removal of Sami Musa's family from Lebanon from this moment forward," Taylor said. "That means approvals, personnel, arrangements, money, everything. Just don't make any overt move in Lebanon without speaking to me or Mick first."

"I have to get back to Mick and the main mission, Sofia," Taylor concluded, and then departed.

Sami Musa told his story and answered every question put to him by Mick and Kostas. He appeared honest, both in tone and body language, and relieved to be telling someone.

Sami Musa had been contacted while in Lebanon over Christmas Break from school. One day, Sami went to see his sister and his nephews near Dahiyah. Before going back home to Beirut, he stopped by the cemetery to pay respect to his oldest brother. While at the cemetery, two men approached him and took him to a house he did not know. There, they told him about Sofia Sopko, that she went to his school in Virginia, and they told him that he was to get close to her and to find out as much as he could about her. They would not say why they were interested in her or why they wanted the information. When Sami refused, first, they derided his loyalty to Hezbollah. They reminded him that his oldest brother died fighting with Hezbollah and his other older brother was fighting with Hezbollah in Syria. When he still did not relent, they threatened his family and they also said that they would pay his tuition next year in exchange for help. Sami did not want the money. He was not even sure that they would pay even if he did want it. But he did not want his family to be harmed or killed. He did believe that they would take revenge if he did not help them.

Before they took him back to his car at the cemetery, they gave him a piece of paper with an e-mail address and password on it. They told him to go into the e-mail account, draft an e-mail message with the information he needed to transmit but not to send the e-mail, just to leave the e-mail there as a draft.

Sami went home to his family in Beirut and did not tell anyone about the two men or the threat to his family. Sami said his father hates Hezbollah and blames them for throwing away the lives of his two oldest sons in the service of Iran. His father wants his children to get an education so they can live good, prosperous, and peaceful lives, preferably somewhere other than Lebanon. Sami believed that if he told his father, his father would make a big problem and Hezbollah would hurt or even kill him.

Sami returned to Richmond and located Sofia Sopko. He followed her periodically for a few weeks to see where she went when not in class. He saw that she attended a conversational French group on Tuesday and Thursday evenings. Since he speaks French, he joined the group to meet her. They became acquaintances at first. One day, when it rained, she started a conversation in the French group about the weather which then veered into all the things you cannot do when it rains, like going grocery shopping.

Sami reported Sofia's activities in the e-mail drafts as instructed. He wrote about how Sofia did not have a car and could not get groceries when it rained. He was just writing anything so they would not hurt his family.

A week later, he came home to his room after class one day and found an envelope taped to his door. Inside the envelope was a set of car keys and a note which said, "Your car. 2014 blue Ford Taurus. Parked out front." Sami went outside and located the blue Ford Taurus by using the key fob and watching which car the lights flashed on. Then he tried the key in the car and it fit. Inside the glove compartment, he found a vehicle registration and insurance card, both in his name.

Sami mentioned in the French group that he had gotten a car. Afterwards, he told Sofia that he could drive her anywhere she needed to go. Sofia asked him to take her to the grocery store every couple of weeks. They became friends. One day, Sofia asked him if he wanted to take a drive to Williamsburg on Saturday or Sunday. He agreed and they drove to a church in Williamsburg on Saturday. When they got to the church, Sofia casually asked him what religion he was. He panicked and said Maronite. It was the only thing he could think of because he did not want to say Muslim. Sami is not a practicing Muslim and has never attended a mosque while in the United States. They spent the morning at the church then went to Colonial Williamsburg in the afternoon. He took her to the Williamsburg church three times total. It was a long drive, an hour each way. They had a long time to talk. Sofia was very open. Sofia always insisted on paying to fill his gas tank up before and after every trip.

Sami continued to report on Sofia through draft e-mails in the e-mail account, including about the visits to the Byzantine Catholic church in Williamsburg and why Sofia went there. Each time he went to write a new draft e-mail, the old one was gone from the draft folder. Sami never received instructions of any kind through that e-mail account.

At the end of the school year, Sami returned to Beirut. He was only home for two days when he received a telephone call telling him to visit his brother's grave the next day. He went to see his sister and nephews then went to the cemetery. He was approached by one male who told him that he was going to spend some time in Greece, and he should prepare his family for that fact. He tried to talk his way out of going to Greece but, again, threats against his family were made.

Sami returned home and the next day he told his father about a girl he knew from school who lived in Greece and who had invited him to visit with her family in Greece. He did not use Sofia's name. He made up the name of Helen. It was the name of one of the other girls in the French group. He hated lying to his father, especially because his father was so pleased that he had a friend from a prosperous family that had invited him to visit with them in Greece. His father's only question of concern was, "Her father approves of your visit?" Sami's father even offered to pay for his airfare. One lie led to the next. Sami could not bear the thought of betraying his father by taking his father's money to fly to Greece for Hezbollah. Sami had to lie even more about having gotten money in a refund from the school as a result of a small scholarship so as not to have to take any money from his father.

A few days later, Sami received another phone call. This time he was told when he was flying to Greece and to be prepared. The following day, he was called again and told to go to his brother's grave again. He went the next day and was met by a man who gave him an envelope containing an airplane ticket, one thousand Euros, and instructions to wait at baggage claim in Athens for someone to meet him.

On Monday of last week, he went to the Beirut airport and used the ticket to fly first to Cyprus then to Athens. In Athens, he waited at baggage claim. Two men approached him and introduced themselves as Ahmed and Ali, no last names. They all took a taxi to the hotel in Athens where Sami was ultimately arrested. Sami had his own room. Ahmed and Ali had a separate room on a higher floor. They gave Sami a cell phone to use in Greece. He was not to call outside of Greece. He was told to answer the phone whenever it rang.

Sami described Ahmed as a Lebanese man, about 35 years old, about five foot eight inches tall, short black hair, brown eyes, and clean shaven. Sami described Ali as a Lebanese man, about 30 years old, about five foot nine inches tall, short black hair, brown eyes, and clean shaven. Sami was shown the photographs of the two men who had taken Sofia from the church. Sami positively identified the two men as Ahmed and Ali. The man on Sofia's left was Ahmed. The man on Sofia's right was Ali.

Sami said that Ahmed and Ali went out of the hotel every day, leaving in the early morning and returning very late in the afternoon. Sami stayed in his room and went out alone only to get lunch. Sami had no trouble getting around and ordering food in English. Twice in the evening, they all went out to dinner together. Sami never heard Ali speak anything but Arabic. However, Ahmed speaks French as well as Arabic. Ahmed would ask for a French speaking waiter whenever they entered a restaurant. Once, when there was a French speaking waiter, Ahmed ordered food for himself and Ali in French. Sami also ordered in French. When no waiter in the restaurant spoke French, Sami ordered food for everyone in English. Ahmed always paid the bill for everyone with euros.

On Thursday morning, Ahmed and Ali went out in the morning as usual. Sometime around nine o'clock in the morning, Ahmed called Sami and told him to be ready to move. A while later, Ahmed called and instructed him to meet them at a location in the Plaka. Sami took a taxi as far as he could before the taxi driver told him that no cars were allowed past a certain intersection so he would have to walk the last block. Sami walked the block and met Ali near a parking lot. Ali told him to wait there and call if he saw Sofia or anyone getting into a black SUV which he pointed out to Sami. Sami waited and watched for about two hours. No one came. Then finally, a man came and put parcels in the black SUV then left the way he had come. Sami called Ahmed and told him. Ahmed was whispering and short with Sami. He told Sami to stay there and not to leave until told to. It was more than two hours later before Sami was told by Ahmed in a phone call to go back to the hotel and wait. Sami went to the hotel and had been waiting ever since, going out only to eat.

Ahmed calls once a day, almost always around nine o'clock in the morning, to check in with Sami. Ahmed called this morning, the day of Sami's arrest, to check on him. Ahmed will call again tomorrow morning.

Kostas asked where Sami's cell phone was, and Sami said that the police took it when they arrested him. Kostas made a call and shortly after a policeman came to the interview room with a cell phone in a plastic evidence bag and small, soft-side suitcase. Kostas removed the cell phone from the plastic bag and turned it on. It was standard practice to turn cell phones off to preserve the battery and to avoid inadvertent changes being made to the phone. After the phone powered up, Kostas found that the phone was not security-lock enabled. He checked for missed phone calls.

"There are no missed phone calls," Kostas said to Mick.

"Go to the call history and take photographs of the entire call history," Mick said to Kostas.

Kostas laid the cell phone flat on the table, brought up the call history, stood up to get a direct view of the face of the phone, and took several photographs with his own cell phone.

"Check for text messages, contacts, and photographs," Mick directed Kostas.

Kostas did as directed.

"No texts," Kostas said. "Only contacts are A1 and A2. There are a few photographs."

"Photograph the contacts; send the photographs to yourself," Mick said.

When Kostas was done with the cell phone, he handed it to Mick. Mick took the phone and opened the contacts first which he showed to Sami.

"A1 is Ahmed; A2 is Ali," said Sami, without needing to be asked.

Mick then opened the photographs. There were only six. He opened each photograph and looked at them. Then, he started at the beginning and placed the phone in front of Sami.

"I was trying to get photographs of Ahmed and Ali without them knowing that I was taking their photographs," Sami said. "But you already have photographs of them."

Mick asked, "Why did you risk trying to take their photographs?"

"Look, I didn't know what was going on, but I knew I didn't like it," Sami said. "I only knew that they are threatening my family. I thought it might be insurance. If I had proof of who they were, maybe they would leave me and my family alone. Or, if something did happen to my family, I could take the photographs to the police."

Mick and Kostas reviewed the call history together. The calls lined up precisely as Sami had described, including the call from Ahmed at nine o'clock that morning. Mick checked the phone power level and saw that it was at eighty percent full. Mick turned the cell phone off and slipped into his pocket. Just then Taylor knocked on the door to the interview room.

"Sit tight, Sami," Mick said. "We need to talk. We'll be back in a bit."

Mick turned off the micro recording device and slipped it in his pocket. Then, Mick and Kostas joined Taylor in the hallway and again walked away from the interview room. Taylor told Mick about David and Jason being in Athens and that he had teed them up and set them loose with the Lebanon portion of the mission. Mick was relieved to hear that they had support on the ground so they could focus on finding Sofia. David and Jason were perfect as both spoke Arabic and French.

David was a shooter, a strong tactical member of the team. However, there were an abundance of shooters around to choose from. David was chosen for the team because of his language skills, Arabic and French, his encyclopedic knowledge of geography, his navigation skills, and the fact that he could fly, both rotary and fixed wing.

No one could say that Jason was not a shooter. However, he was also chosen for the team based largely on his other skills. For language skills, he spoke Arabic and French, like David. More importantly, he was a trained medic with combat field experience.

"What are we going to do with Sami?" Taylor asked.

"We can keep him in custody," Kostas offered.

"No, we don't want to treat him like a criminal," Mick said.

"But he is a criminal," Kostas insisted.

"Yes, he is a criminal, but we need him to answer his cell phone if it rings," Mick said. "The phone stays with us, so Sami stays with us. At least for now, we need him."

"We can't take him to the Embassy, Mick," Taylor said.

"But we can take him to our hotel and have someone sit on him," Mick said. "Kostas, can we get a plain clothes officer to assist us in watching Sami?"

"I'll make the call," Kostas responded. "Someone will meet us at the hotel."

CHAPTER NINE

The ride to the hotel from the police station was not a problem. The problem came when they had to park half a block from the hotel and walk back to it. Kostas wanted to cuff Sami for the walk. Mick vetoed the idea.

"If the three of us cannot keep a hold of him, he dies when the three of us shoot him," Mick said to Kostas, with a straight face.

Then Mick looked Sami directly in the eye and said, "You understand, Sami?"

Sami nodded his head affirmatively, with eyes as wide as saucers. Kostas smiled slightly, while Taylor cleared his throat. There was no escape attempted during the short walk to the hotel.

As they entered the hotel, Mateo met them and said he had a room ready for their guest next to Mick's room. Mick handed Mateo a credit card and told him to use it for the room and any other charges that come from that room, like food. Mateo took the credit card, swiped it, then showed them to Sami's room. Once Mateo left the room, Taylor set down Sami's suitcase that had been taken by the police when he was arrested. Then he opened the bag and searched it. It contained Sami's passport, money, clothes, and toiletries. Sami watched as Taylor took the paper money, placed it inside the passport, and handed the passport to Mick, who slipped the passport into his pocket.

"I'm hungry," Mick announced. "You hungry, Sami?"

"Yes," replied Sami.

Mick asked Kostas to order food for everyone, including the officer on his way to the hotel, from Mateo's taverna and to have it all delivered to the lounge downstairs. Kostas made the call.

As Mick and Kostas went down to the lounge, the plain clothes police officer arrived. Kostas introduced Spiros to Mick. Then he took Spiros upstairs to show him the room, let him stow his overnight bag, and introduce him to Taylor and Sami. In the room, Spiros handed Kostas copies of the information the hotel had for Ahmed and Ali. Kostas scanned the information then handed the hotel information to Taylor and they all went to the lounge downstairs to eat. Registered guest, Ahmed Karim, plus one. The credit card was in the name of a business in Beirut.

Mick left the lounge to make a phone call. Sami had to eat, and they did not want to treat him too harshly while they still needed him, but he did not need to hear Mick's phone calls. Mick called the station chief, brought him up to speed, and asked him to drop by the hotel and to bring a thumb drive to be able to copy photographs from Kostas' cell phone.

The food arrived first and Mick followed the food into the lounge. Salads, souvlaki, tzatziki, pita bread, and bottles of Fanta and Coke, enough for a small army. Rice pudding and baklava for dessert. No one made a move for the food even after the waiter had left. So, Taylor grabbed plates and started passing them out which broke the hesitation. Everyone began to dig in.

Kostas' phone rang and he answered it quietly in Greek. When he hung up, he signaled for Mick to follow him out of the lounge. Kostas told Mick that Ahmed Karim, with a Syrian passport, had arrived in Greece on a direct flight from Cyprus the same day Sami had arrived. There had been someone named Ali Hakeem, also with a Syrian passport, on the same plane.

The station chief arrived while plates were still being filled in the lounge and Kostas and Mick were still in the lobby. Mick told the station chief about the names Ahmed Karim and Ali Hakeem. The station chief confirmed the spellings with Kostas. All agreed they were most likely aliases and the passports were most likely fake, but they needed to be checked out. Mick handed the station chief Sami's passport and money for safekeeping.

Mick asked for and received Kostas' cell phone. He handed it to the station chief and showed him the photographs. Mick explained that the photographs were screen shots of and photographs from Sami's phone. The station chief copied the photographs over to the thumb drive then onto his own cell phone before handing the cell phone back to Kostas.

"Get on those phone numbers," Mick said. "Find out who they are calling besides Sami. We also need a team to trace and triangulate on them. The one called Ahmed calls Sami's cell phone every morning about nine o'clock. We must be ready when the next call comes."

Then Mick handed the station chief the micro recording device.

"I need you to make several copies of this recording, it's Sami's statement," Mick said. "Have a transcript made immediately, then have the transcript translated into Arabic. We may need it when dealing with Sami's father."

The station chief asked, "Can I let the Ambassador hear this?"

"Yes," Mick responded, after hesitating for a moment. "He is going through hell. But you better stay with him while he hears it and do not let him have a copy. Once he hears that recording, make sure someone is prepared to be with him for the duration. It is one thing to know Sofia was taken, it is another to know that it was planned and carried out by Hezbollah. There is just no telling how he is going to react to this."

"I'll take care of it," the station chief said.

"Make sure the legal attaché gets copies of everything," Mick concluded, before returning to the lounge while the station chief left the hotel.

Only Mick, Taylor, and Kostas were still in the lounge when David walked in. Sami and Spiros had returned to Sami's hotel room. Mick introduced Kostas to David. Then David explained that Ahmed's first name was Ahmed but that his last name was believed to be Bari. He is a known entity, confirmed by facial recognition, a Hezbollah operative. Ahmed is suspected of two assassinations for Hezbollah in the past four years. He keeps a low profile. He seems to just appear on the scene periodically to do a job then disappears again. There is still no positive identification of Ali. The Beirut business name on the credit card used by Ahmed is a shell company with no physical address. Treasury is attempting to trace the credit card usage and the source of any payments.

David updated them on the plan to exfiltrate Sami's family by boat from Lebanon. The road to the Beirut airport runs right through the Hezbollah controlled area and is considered too dangerous for the exfiltration. A boat is safer and can easily accommodate a varying number of passengers, the immediate family, plus the sister's family, if that pans out as well. Assets were being put in place now.

David explained that the initial contact with Sami's father was being debated. David wanted Sami to write a note to his father for possible use in convincing his father of their bona fides at first contact. For ease of transmitting information over non-secure devices, Mick and David agreed upon code names for Sami, Sami's father, and Sami's sister. They had to assume that

Hezbollah was monitoring all communications within Lebanon.

Mick sent Taylor to Sami's room to get a handwritten note from Sami to his father, rather than have Sami see another team member. The note had to be written in Arabic and David would read it before leaving the hotel to make sure that it was acceptable.

Mick, Taylor, and Kostas were sitting outside at a table in front of the hotel in the late afternoon shade when Kostas received a phone call. After concluding the call, Kostas advised the others that it was believed that the white van had been found in a small fishing village on the coast. The van, with no license plate, had been reported as a suspicious and abandoned vehicle.

After confirming with Kostas that no one had touched the van yet, Mick sent Kostas to tell Spiros that they would be gone for a while and to make arrangements for additional officers to come and assist with watching Sami. Mick contacted the station chief and advised him that they would be headed to the village.

The drive took just over two hours. Mick watched the scenery out the window for most of the way while lost in his own thoughts. Taylor slept almost the entire way. Kostas drove and made arrangements over the phone for a bomb squad and a forensic team to meet them at the van.

The fishing village on the Aegean Sea was quite small and far away from any tourist destination. The white van was parked at the rear of a commercial boat repair building. It had been reported to the police by the manager of the business. Kostas spoke to the manager and learned that the van had been there since sometime in the night on Thursday because it was first noticed on Friday morning. The manager did not give it much thought on Friday but, when it was still in the lot on Saturday, he approached it and saw that there was no license plate. As the van was snugged into the far end of the rear of the building, next to a wall, he had not noticed the missing license plate until he went up to the van for a closer inspection.

Kostas introduced Mick and Taylor to the forensic team. One of the forensic team members gave them each latex gloves to put on before approaching the van. Mick advised the forensic team that they were particularly interested in obtaining DNA evidence from inside the van and asked them to swab the surfaces as the first priority, after photographing the exterior and interior of the van. The second priority was fingerprints. Then Mick and Taylor would search the contents. However, before anyone opened the van, the bomb technicians were to make sure that it was not booby trapped.

Kostas spoke to the bomb squad members as they donned thick white bomb resistant suits to approach the van. The two men moved to the van carrying mirrors attached to long poles and began going around the van while the mirrors were positioned to look at the under carriage of the van. They each made a full pass around the van and neither saw anything out of the ordinary.

Then, one of the bomb techs approached the driver's door of the van and attempted to open it. Locked. The second bomb tech took his place and jimmied the lock. The door opened. No explosion. The bomb tech reached inside and popped the hood then backed away. The first bomb tech raised the hood and, after a minute, gave an all-clear sign to his partner. The second bomb tech then went around the van opening every door and looking inside. Still no explosion. The two bomb techs walked over to Kostas and signaled that he could approach the van.

Just then, a pickup truck with large lights mounted in the bed pulled up near the van. The sun was setting and the light was fading. However, when the truck driver turned on the lights, the van was illuminated at if it was noon on a clear sunny day.

Mick watched as the forensic team went over the van. First taking photographs, then DNA swabs from various surfaces, and finally dusting for fingerprints. It was an exceedingly slow process. Mick and Taylor patiently waited their turn to look inside the van. If DNA and/or fingerprints were found for Sofia, Ahmed, and Ali, it would be evidence in any possible criminal prosecution. Mick did not dwell on the fact that Sofia's death was the most likely way there would ever be a criminal prosecution. He was here to do a job, recover Sofia alive but prepare for any other eventuality.

When the forensic team was done, Mick and Taylor approached the van. The glove box was empty, not even vehicle ownership papers. The floor was clean, no loose litter, no receipts, no nothing. Taylor looked under the front passenger seat and saw something wedged into the bottom of the seat. He reached under the seat, grabbed what looked like a piece of cloth with his latex gloved fingers, and pulled it out. It was a piece of black lacey material. Kostas photographed the piece of material then provided a plastic evidence bag for Taylor to put the material in. Other than the one piece of material, nothing else was found in the van.

Kostas arranged for the van to be towed to the police station. The trio headed there as well and met in the conference room around a large map of that section of the coast. Kostas spoke to the policeman in charge and translated as the officer explained the coastal activity. The area was off the beaten path for tourists. It was largely a commercial fishing area. Most of the boats that came into dock were owned by local companies or people. Occasionally, foreign boats came into dock but usually only for fuel or repairs.

It was decided that, in the very early morning hours, the local police would contact the fishing boats before they set out to sea to determine if anyone had seen a foreign boat within the past week. Then they would contact the local businesses to see if any foreign boats or crew had recently been in any of the other towns nearby.

Mick knew that he and Taylor would be of no assistance to the police because they did not speak Greek. With nothing left to do, they had no option but to return to the hotel. During the two-hour ride back, Mick, Taylor, and Kostas reviewed the case developments to date and speculated on the anticipated telephone call from Ahmed to Sami the next morning. They were all tired but talking helped keep them awake.

CHAPTER TEN

They got to the hotel in the wee hours of Sunday morning and only had time for a short nap before they needed to be ready for Ahmed's phone call to Sami. Too soon, they were up, showered, changed, and ready for a cup of coffee. Kostas went next door to the bakery to get breads and pastries for the group. Mick and Taylor got five cups of coffee and regrouped in Sami's room. Spiros and Sami were up, dressed, and sitting in their room. They were each handed a cup of coffee and then Mick placed Sami's phone on a small table near where Sami was sitting on a bed.

"You need to keep Ahmed on the phone for as long as you possibly can," Mick told Sami. "We need a few minutes to track his location. The longer you can drag out the call, the better it is for us. But don't do anything to arouse his suspicion."

Sami silently nodded his head in acknowledgment of Mick's instructions.

"Do you have any questions?" Mick asked.

"No," Sami replied. "We have been over it. I am ready."

Kostas had just arrived with breakfast when Sami's phone rang. Taylor immediately made a call using speed dial on his phone. He stepped just outside the room and watched Sami through the doorway while listening to his own phone. Kostas went with Taylor, while Mick stayed with Sami.

It was time. Sami cautiously answered the phone once Mick gave him the signal that they were ready. Ahmed and Sami spoke in Arabic. Fortunately, they had arranged for an interpreter to relay the conversation on Taylor's phone. Sami tried to remember the things Mick told him when they prepared for this call. When Ahmed asked how Sami was doing, Sami told him he was bored, and he wanted to get out of the hotel. Sami asked when he could go home or if he could at least go out for a walk and to see the sights. Ahmed told Sami that he would be able to go home soon. Surprisingly, Ahmed told Sami it was fine for him to go out and look around a bit but to be sure to have the phone on him and answer immediately if it rang. Sami tried to thank Ahmed, but he had abruptly hung up.

"Damn that was short," Mick complained. "Good phone security on his part, seems Ahmed may have experience with dodging call traces. I hope it was enough for them to get at least a general location."

Kostas placed a bag of breads and pastries on the table for Spiros and Sami. Then Kostas, Mick, and Taylor went downstairs to the small lounge area to eat. Mateo brought them all fresh coffee and asked if he should take coffee to their friends in the room upstairs. Mick said yes and Mateo left the lounge. After they finished eating, Mick, Taylor, and Kostas headed to the Embassy.

In the Ambassador's conference room on Sunday morning, the Ambassador looked shaken and desperate. Mick could tell just by looking at him that he had listened to the tape of Sami Musa's interview.

The Ambassador rose from his seat and, with desperation in his voice, asked, "Is Sofia alive?"

Mick quickly glanced at Taylor. It was a not-so-subtle request for assistance because Mick knew his own limitations. He was short with people, too short sometimes. Taylor had what Mick thought of as a doctor's sympathetic bedside manner. He could say essentially the same thing as Mick, but people usually took it better from Taylor. Without hesitation, Taylor stepped up.

"We have no reason to believe that she is not alive, sir," Taylor began. "The kidnappers have not made contact and we don't know what they want. It wouldn't make sense for them to hurt her before they have made a demand. In the meantime, she is their insurance. I know this is difficult but try to stay calm until we know more about why she was taken and what they are after. We are working hard to find her and we won't give up."

"You know that Hezbollah is behind this," the Ambassador said. "It is hard to remain calm when my daughter is in the hands of a terrorist organization."

The Ambassador was far too shaken to be buoyed by platitudes. Like the others, he knew that Hezbollah's involvement upped the stakes for his daughter.

"I also know that Hezbollah always has a political agenda," Taylor replied. "They took her for a reason. They want to use her in some way, as a bargaining chip. They have no reason to harm her."

As the truth of Taylor's statement sunk in, the Ambassador took his seat at the table. As he sat down, Mick noticed that there was a new addition to the Embassy personnel in the conference room. Seeing the direction of Mick's gaze, the station chief stood up, motioned toward the new man, and introduced him as a Navy doctor, here to assist the Sopko family in any way necessary. Ambassador Sopko had no reaction to the introduction of his medical minder. He would not rock the boat in any way. His love for his daughter allowed him to endure any humiliation necessary to see this through. Mick understood and, therefore, made the effort to address the Ambassador directly throughout the briefing.

Mick brought the group up to speed with the finding of the van, its location, the forensic processing although no results would be known immediately, and his thought that the search should turn offshore. After Mick finished, Ambassador Sopko asked to see the piece of material that Taylor had found. Taylor reached into his pocket, retrieved the plastic bag containing the piece of material, and slid it over to the Ambassador. The Ambassador picked the bag up and carefully examined the black lace material. He placed the bag back on the table and his fingers traced the outline of the material inside.

"That is a piece of Sofia's scarf," he said, softly.

"Are you sure?" Taylor asked.

"Yes, I am positive," the Ambassador replied. "It belonged to my wife. She gave it to Sofia shortly before she died. It is a family heirloom. It had belonged to my wife's mother. She brought it from Slovakia when she immigrated to the United States as a young woman. Sofia carried it with her always, in her handbag. She even made a cloth pouch to keep it in so that it would not get dirty or torn."

"In that case, given the location where I found it, Sofia must have torn that piece off of the scarf and placed it there intentionally," Taylor said. "There is no way it could have accidently gotten stuck up under that seat."

"Sofia left us a bread crumb," Mick mused aloud. "Now we know for certain that the van was the one used to take Sofia. I am even more convinced that we need to be looking offshore."

The conversation quickly turned to satellite imagery. It made sense for them to take Sofia offshore. That way they could keep her out of sight of prying eyes and it would be almost impossible for Sofia to escape unassisted. And, if Sofia was trying to help them find her, they needed to have people looking at every ship and boat for Sofia's next clue.

Before leaving the Embassy, Mick went to the bubble to communicate directly with Bronwyn. She would see that the satellite imagery was analyzed properly.

The station chief arrived at the hotel just after they had finished eating lunch. He laid out a map of Greece and said that Ahmed's call had been hitting off a cell tower a few villages south of the village the van was found in. It was not satellite or ship to shore. Either Ahmed was in that village or on a boat that was coming close enough into shore to make the call.

Mick asked the station chief to have Bronwyn narrow the focus of the satellite and aerial search in and around that area of the coast. Mick also asked that a boat, equipped with their full kit and with two sets of scuba gear, be placed on standby for them, in case they needed it. The station chief informed them that he had a boat that would work at the port of Piraeus, just south of Athens. After the station chief left, Kostas, Mick, and Taylor agreed to try to relax since there was nothing more to do without more information. Oftentimes, when things broke, they broke fast. And the more rested they were, the longer and harder they could pursue the next leads.

CHAPTER ELEVEN

David stood inside a doorway half a block from Sami
Musa's parents' apartment building in Beirut, Lebanon.
Surveillance had revealed that Mr. Musa had left his
apartment, walked to a small food market, and bought
groceries. He was expected to walk past this doorway on
his way home. David waited patiently and unobtrusively.

Mr. Musa, carrying a shopping bag in one hand, walked
up the sidewalk. Just as he came to the doorway where
David was standing, David stepped into the sidewalk and
right into Mr. Musa. Before Mr. Musa could recover,
David placed a piece of paper in his free hand and
whispered to him in Arabic, "It is a message from Sami;
do not look at it until you are inside your home."

With that done, David apologized loudly and walked
down the sidewalk away from Mr. Musa. Surveillance
observed Mr. Musa gather himself and continue on to his
home without looking around or looking at the paper in
his hand.

Once inside his apartment, Mr. Musa kissed his wife,
handed her the shopping bag, and then went directly to
the bathroom. With the door closed, he sat on the toilet
and stared at the folded paper in his hand. After taking a
minute to steady himself, he opened the paper and saw
Sami's handwriting. He read the note once then he read it

again. Tears filled his eyes as he stared at the words on paper.

"Father," Sami had written. "I am sorry. I lied to you and I have let you down. I am being held by American authorities in Greece. I came here because Hezbollah threatened our family if I did not help them. They have done something terrible and I made it possible. May Allah forgive me. The Americans have promised to try to help us. They will take you, mother, Reza, Layla, and her family away from Lebanon, away from Hezbollah, if you will go. Please talk to them. Give Reza the chance to be the son that you deserve. Your son, Sami."

The name and address of a restaurant was at the bottom of the note, in different handwriting, with a time. Once Mr. Musa made his decision, he walked to the sink and splashed water on his face. After wiping his face dry with a towel, he walked out to the kitchen and announced to his wife that they were going out to eat tonight. She began to protest but Mr. Musa placed his hand over his own mouth and stared at her intently. She knew immediately to keep quiet. Mr. Musa took his wife by the hand and told her to get ready to go out to dinner and to tell Reza to get ready as well. Within twenty minutes, the family was walking out of their front door.

They made their way to downtown Beirut, to the address that had been given at the bottom of the note. It was seven-thirty when they arrived at an obviously expensive French restaurant. They walked inside and Mr. Musa approached the maître d'.

The maître d' greeted him, "Welcome. Your name, sir?"

"Musa, a table for three please."

"Yes, of course," the maître d' said, before showing them to a table in a secluded dining room separate from the main dining room.

There were only four tables in the room and only one was occupied. The family sat down and looked at the menu which was in French, Arabic, and English. After a few minutes, a waiter appeared and placed a basket of bread on the table. He spoke to them in French and Mr. Musa placed their drink orders in French. When the waiter left, Reza asked his father if he thought the waiter was French or only spoke French. Mr. Musa chuckled.

"He speaks French because it is a French restaurant," Mr. Musa said, in French.

"If tomorrow he works in a Lebanese restaurant, he will speak Arabic," Mr. Musa said, in Arabic.

At the next table, both men smiled at Mr. Musa's explanation.

The waiter returned with their drinks and took their dinner orders, again, in French. When the waiter left, Jason arose from the next table and walked to the Musa table where he asked, in French, if he could sit. Mrs. Musa and Reza looked confused as Mr. Musa motioned for Jason to take the empty chair at their table. Jason continued by asking if he could speak freely in front of the family. Mr. Musa nodded affirmatively.

Jason proceeded to explain, in abbreviated form, that Sami had gotten involved with Hezbollah and that the family was in danger. Sami was in American custody but was unharmed. Preparations had been made to take the Musa family away from Lebanon in the next few days. But Jason explained, there was no time to pack or make any arrangements of any kind. If they chose to leave, they would leave on the terms given, or not at all. Then Jason left the family and returned to his own table so they could talk among themselves while Jason and David listened from the next table.

The family had many questions. What kind of trouble was Sami in? Where would they go? What about their daughter? What about their possessions?

After their meals were delivered to their table, Jason returned to the Musa family and again asked for permission to sit, which was granted. Having already heard their questions, Jason began to answer them one by one as the family picked at their meals.

He could not tell them anything about what Sami had been involved in, except that it was very serious. Their final destination was unknown, but it would be somewhere where they would be safe. If they chose to go, a refrigerator box would be delivered to their apartment tomorrow. A total of four suitcases or bags for the family of three would be placed inside the box and carted out to the truck by the deliverymen for their future use. They should pack light, no more than one week of clothing each. The remainder of the space should be used for family remembrances, photographs, and valuables. Anything that did not fit in a suitcase could not go and was to be left behind. There was to be no giving anything away, no matter how valuable or sentimental. They could tell no one of their plans, absolutely no one.

"What about my daughter and her family?" Mr. Musa asked.

"That depends on what you tell me truthfully tonight and on them," Jason replied.

Jason asked about the daughter and her husband and their allegiance to Hezbollah. Mr. Musa assured Jason that given the opportunity to leave, they would leave. Jason explained that once they left, there would be no coming back, ever. Then Jason asked if he was sure that his son-in-law would willingly walk away from his own family forever.

Mr. Musa stated plainly, "Honestly, my wife is a better judge of people and their attachments."

Mrs. Musa, who had been silent while her husband and Jason talked, took a deep breath, and released it. "Yes, I think that he would be willing to leave, even under those circumstances," she said. "It will pain him, but he will do it for his children."

"Do you trust him to never expose your whereabouts?" Jason asked.

"I trust him never to place his wife or his children in danger which means that he will protect us as well," she replied.

The discussion turned to logistics. It was agreed that the refrigerator delivery to the Musa's apartment would occur first thing in the morning. Once the deliverymen were gone, Mrs. Musa would go to her stepdaughter and explain the situation. A refrigerator delivery would be made to the daughter's house in the late afternoon. Again, one suitcase per person and one extra. Because the suitcases would be gone before her husband returned from work and she could speak to him, Jason assured Mr. and Mrs. Musa that if the daughter's family chose not to go, their suitcases would be returned to them through the delivery of another appliance or another method so as not to arouse suspicion. Beginning the day after the suitcase pickup, the families were to be prepared to leave at a moment's notice, taking nothing with them but the clothes that they were wearing. Jason confirmed Mr. Musa's and his daughter's telephone numbers and provided an address near the corniche that they were to go to immediately upon receipt of a call from someone inquiring about the service they received during the refrigerator delivery. Then Jason arose from the table, told Mr. Musa that the bill for dinner had already been taken care of, and departed with David.

The Musa family sat silently for a few moments, each lost in their own thoughts. Then, they too arose from the table. Mr. Musa placed a tip on the table, and they left the restaurant. They had work to do to be ready by morning.

CHAPTER TWELVE

Mick relaxed and napped uninterrupted until the late afternoon. When he awoke, he checked his phone and saw no new messages or missed calls. He showered, dressed, and went downstairs. Taylor and Kostas were sitting at the tables outside, drinking Fanta, and people watching.

Mick went in search of coffee, which he found quickly, before joining Taylor and Kostas at the table outside. When Mick asked if there was anything new, they both said no.

This operation had entered the waiting period. Mick was refreshed and ready to work but there was nothing to do. So, they sat and waited before heading off for dinner. The station chief stopped by after dinner, but he also had nothing new.

Mick lay in bed that night replaying every move they had made, trying to determine if they had missed anything. Mick also thought about Sofia. Maybe it was better if she was at sea. At sea, they might not feel the need to drug her. Mick also wondered why there had yet to be a demand made, or a claim of responsibility. What purpose did it serve to maintain silence once they felt relatively safe? For hours, Mick's mind spun around and around until finally he drifted off to sleep.

Mick was awakened before dawn on Monday morning by Taylor calling him on his cell phone. Taylor explained that satellite and aerial imagery was being delivered soon. Mick got ready and headed downstairs to the lounge. There was coffee, breads, and pastries filling the table. Kostas was speaking in Greek into his phone and Taylor was drinking coffee as Mick walked in. Mick had just finished getting a cup of coffee when the station chief arrived.

They made room on the table and the station chief unrolled large aerial photographs of the Greek coastline and surrounding waters. They each took a moment to orient themselves with the first photograph and identify the village where the van was found and the village where the cell tower was located. The photographs were of the same basic area, in different enlargements and at different times of day. Ships and boats that had been ruled out by the analysts were not numbered. They were military ships from Greece or other friendly nations, commercial cruise ships, and the like. The ships and boats that were considered possible locations for Sofia had been numbered so that the same vessels and their locations could be seen on each photograph. Two ships and four smaller boats had been numbered.

One of the ships had been traversing the Aegean Sea at an unusually slow pace. Kostas spoke up and volunteered that that was not completely unusual. If a container ship was ahead of schedule and a berth was not available for unloading and loading, the captain would reduce speed and creep along until given the word to come in.

The second ship was anchored off the coast. Again, Kostas explained, instead of creeping, sometimes they just anchor and wait. If they knew the names of the ships, they might be able to find out where they were heading and find out why they were acting in the manner they were. Also, because they were in Greek waters, they could send the coast guard out to check on the ships. The station chief provided the names of the two ships to Kostas as those were the two that were positively identified.

The third vessel was a yacht. It was mostly anchored but would occasionally move a short distance away. No one had an explanation other than possibly fishing.

The fourth vessel was also a yacht. It was working its way down the coast at a leisurely rate, occasionally putting into a port then, after a time, going back out to sea and moving further south. Everyone agreed that appeared to be a pleasure cruise stopping into port for fuel, provisions, or to spend the night tied up at a dock.

The fifth and six vessels were both commercial fishing boats. They were staying off the coast and not coming into port. Kostas again gave an opinion. That was unusual because most boats returned to port every night to empty their catch and for the crew to go home for the night. He ventured a guess that one reason to stay offshore was because they were fishing in Greek waters illegally.

After some discussion, it was agreed to have the coast guard contact and board the two ships, numbers 1 and 2, and to go near the two fishing boats, numbers 5 and 6. Kostas believed that if they were fishing illegally, they would leave the area when the coast guard came near. Kostas would also send an undercover detective to scout out the yacht that came into port frequently, number 4, to see who was on the boat. The yacht, number 3, was perplexing. They agreed not to approach number 3 until they had checked all of the other ships and boats out. In the meantime, they would continue aerial surveillance of the yacht and the station chief would direct enhanced surveillance of all six vessels with high-definition photographs of each during daylight hours.

Mick, Taylor, and Kostas looked again at each vessel in each photograph, looking for a clue left by Sofia, but identified nothing.

CHAPTER THIRTEEN

At eight o'clock in the morning, on Monday, in Beirut, a large box delivery truck pulled up in front of the Musa's apartment building. Two men got out and unloaded a large refrigerator box. They wheeled the refrigerator box on a hand cart into the apartment building, into the elevator, and rode up to the Musa's floor. At the Musa's door, one of the men knocked loudly.

Mrs. Musa opened the door and ushered the men and the refrigerator box inside. The two men quietly opened the box. The box was reinforced inside to keep its shape even when empty and weighted to give it the appearance of heft. The box would not tip over or blow away in a strong wind. The men inserted the four suitcases waiting in the foyer into the box. Then they explained to Mrs. Musa that they needed to wait at least thirty minutes before they could leave so as not to arouse suspicion. Mrs. Musa invited them into to the kitchen where she served them tea. They all sat in silence, sipping their tea, and waiting for the minutes to pass.

When enough time had passed, the two men hauled the refrigerator box back into the elevator, then went down to the ground floor and back to the delivery truck. Once the box was loaded, the truck drove off. Mrs. Musa readied herself for the trip to her stepdaughter's house. Within minutes, she left the apartment. As she rode down in the elevator, she practiced once again in her mind what she would say to her stepdaughter.

Later that morning, Mrs. Musa walked up to her stepdaughter's house and knocked on the door. The door opened and her stepdaughter, Layla, came outside to hug and greet her. They went inside, with Layla exclaiming what a surprise it was to see her.

Mrs. Musa carried on as if it was a normal visit while trying to figure out how to broach the subject of leaving. Layla made tea and Mrs. Musa asked to sit outside in the backyard because it was such a beautiful day. Layla looked puzzled but put shoes on both the children, grabbed a couple of toys, and they all went outside. Layla distributed the toys to the children then Layla and Mrs. Musa sat on white plastic chairs. Layla handed her stepmother a cup of tea. They both drank in silence for a minute.

Mrs. Musa worked up the courage to broach the subject at hand. "Layla, I must tell you something and I need for you to say nothing until I am done."

"Okay," Layla said, with a look of concern on her face.

Mrs. Musa told Layla about Sami being in trouble, about the family leaving Lebanon, and offered that she and her family could go too but she had to decide right now, today. Layla became more frightened the more Mrs. Musa spoke. By the time Mrs. Musa was done, Layla had tears in her eyes but a resolved expression on her face.

"We will go," Layla said. "We must think of our children. What do I have to do?"

Mrs. Musa explained how a refrigerator delivery would be made late that afternoon and that she would have to have five suitcases packed before the delivery arrived. Mrs. Musa explained that Layla could talk to her husband when he came home from work and that, if he refused to go, their suitcases would be returned as another appliance delivery in a few days. Layla had many questions and Mrs. Musa had few answers but she answered the best that she could. Mrs. Musa filled Layla in on the detailed instructions they were given by Jason as they finished their tea and watched the children play.

They decided to take the children inside to begin packing. Before going inside, Mrs. Musa cautioned Layla not to speak of the trip inside the house. She was frightened about the possibility of listening devices, although she was embarrassed to say it. Mrs. Musa watched the children play in the house while Layla packed.

When Layla was almost finished packing, Mrs. Musa realized that she had been gone for some time. She rose to leave. Layla followed her out to give her a quick hug goodbye. While the two embraced, Mrs. Musa quietly whispered to Layla, "Everything will be fine, but we won't be able to speak again until we're out of Lebanon. Please be careful. We'll see you soon."

As she walked away from the home, she prayed that Layla's husband would agree to go and that that was not the last time she would ever see Layla.

CHAPTER FOURTEEN

At half past eight o'clock on Monday morning, in Athens, while they were waiting with Sami for Ahmed's daily call, Kostas received a call. The Coast Guard reported in on their assessments of the two commercial ships. Both were awaiting docking facilities, their paperwork was in order, and the captains were completely cooperative.

Nine o'clock came and went with no call from Ahmed. By ten o'clock they all knew there would be no call. Mick was disappointed but not surprised. Keeping in contact with Sami after he had Sofia had been error on Ahmed's part. It had allowed Mick to locate Ahmed's general vicinity by cell tower. Now, the connection they had was severed. There would be no further calls which they could use to help track down Ahmed and, with him, Sofia.

Mick, Taylor, and Kostas left Spiros and Sami in the room and went downstairs to the small lounge room off the lobby. Mick asked no one in particular, "Did he not call because he is out of range of a cell tower? Or, did he not call because he knows he can't possibly need Sami for anything further?"

Kostas received another call from the Coast Guard. The two fishing vessels began to leave the area when the

Coast Guard was within sight and headed their way but then one stopped and waited to be intercepted. The Coast Guard boarded the vessel and seized it for fishing illegally. The vessel was being brought into port. The second fishing vessel left the area. As instructed, the Coast Guard did not attempt to pursue the fleeing fishing vessel.

"If the two fishing boats were together, it could be that the one with the smaller catch sacrificed itself so the one with the larger catch could escape," Kostas speculated.

"Or the one sacrificed itself so that the boat with Sofia on board could get away," Taylor suggested.

Mick called the station chief and requested continuous aerial surveillance of the fishing vessel that got away. Then, the Coast Guard reported in on one of the pleasure craft. It was an Italian family on vacation, sailing around Greece and the Greek islands. They pulled into port almost every night and whenever they needed fuel, food, or entertainment. When not in port overnight, they claimed they stayed near land to keep clear of the shipping channels at night.

"If Ahmed was on the fishing vessel that left when the Coast Guard arrived, he was definitely out of range at nine o'clock," Kostas said.

"I think he would have called Sami if he could have," Taylor said. "If only to tell Sami to go back to Lebanon. If he didn't need Sami anymore, he should have wanted Sami out of Greece as soon as possible and safely back in Lebanon."

"That sounds reasonable," Mick said. "But Sami played no part in actually taking Sofia. He never even saw her in Greece. Ahmed has no reason to think Sami would be a suspect in anything. They stayed in separate rooms, on separate floors, in the hotel. The only thing they did together was go out to dinner a couple of times. Ahmed could be thinking that sending Sami back to Lebanon too soon might draw unwanted attention to Sami. Better to wait a reasonable time and make it look like Sami is just another tourist. I guess I have to agree. Ahmed would have called if he could. He has to know Sami was scared enough to stay at the hotel until his money ran out if Ahmed never actually told him to go back to Lebanon. After a reasonable time, Sami is a loose end that Ahmed needs to tie up, if he can."

Taylor asked, "What more do we know about the other fishing vessel?"

Mick and Taylor both looked at Kostas. Kostas pulled out his phone and started making calls. Within twenty minutes, Kostas ended his phone conversation.

"The crew of the other fishing vessel are Lebanese," Kostas said. "They are being detained. The captain is admitting that they were fishing illegally."

"That's it," Mick said. "They were the blockers. They were only there to run interference so the primary could get away."

"Do you want to go talk to them?" Kostas asked.

"No," Mick said. "They are meant to waste the time of anyone who could cause trouble for the primary fishing vessel. Every minute we spend on them is a minute we are not chasing Ahmed. We need to go after Ahmed."

Mick called the station chief and arranged for him to meet them at the boat on standby in the port of Piraeus. Taylor could see that Kostas did not completely understand Mick's choice to forgo talking to the captured crew. Taylor knew that Kostas' detective brain was having trouble with a decision to ignore possible witnesses or accomplices.

"It is doubtful that the decoy crew knows anything," Taylor said. "They are just pawns, to be sacrificed when necessary. And, from everything we have seen, Ahmed is very good. He would not have let the crew of the other fishing vessel know anything they didn't actually need to know to perform their assignment, which is virtually nothing, except to protect the main vessel."

Kostas nodded in understanding, as Taylor explained. Mick rejoined the conversation.

"Someone needs to talk to the fishing crew, but it won't be us," Mick said. "No upside, but a great deal of potential downside. Because the chance of them knowing anything of value is so small, it is an unacceptable risk for us to let them know we even exist and are tracking Ahmed and Sofia. On illegal fishing charges, you will only be able to hold them incommunicado for so long. And once they have access to the outside world, we don't want them saying anything other than that they are being held by Greek authorities for fishing illegally."

Kostas drove them and their gear to the port of Piraeus. At the marina, a large yacht was waiting for them. Their kit had been pre-positioned, as they had requested. Taylor took Mick's gear bag, as well as his own, and went aboard to speak with the captain.

Mick and Kostas waited for the station chief. He arrived within ten minutes and handed Mick an envelope. Mick took the two blue tourist passports and the two wallets, one each for Mick and Taylor, out of the envelope. He then took all the money out of his and Taylor's wallets containing the credit cards in their real names. He placed their two diplomatic passports and wallets in the envelope and gave it to the station chief. Then Mick brought the station chief up to speed on the fishing vessel that got away and their belief that Ahmed and Sofia were on it.

Mick asked the station chief to pass the word to the team in Lebanon that it was time to move and to coordinate with the Lebanon team about what to do with Sami.

Mick turned to Kostas and shook his hand. "Kostas, you have been a tremendous help," he said. "We wouldn't have made it this far so quickly without you. Hope to see you again someday."

Then Mick boarded the yacht. He noticed that its name was Thor's Hammer, a good omen. As the yacht pulled away from the dock, Mick handed Taylor a passport and wallet. Then they went inside the cabin and went through their kit bags. There were also wet suits, scuba tanks, masks, and fins, which they checked over.

Back on deck, the sun was shining brightly and reflecting off the waves as they scanned the water, observing the various vessels they passed as they headed to open water. Mick decided to go to the cabin to check out the commo setup. When Mick went into the cabin, a crewman stood up from the radio desk and headed topside.

"I just made fresh coffee, if you want some," he said, as he left.

Must be the alternate captain. Or First Mate. Or the only mate, Mick mused as he poured himself a cup of coffee. Mick scanned through the radio frequencies. It was mostly commercial traffic. Occasionally, there was conversation between the radio operators of two ships from the same line, passing each other on their designated routes. Those conversations took on a more familiar tone, those guys clearly knew each other.

"Who uses Morse code, anymore," Mick said aloud, though there was no one to hear him, as he heard Morse code broadcast on the radio. Out of habit, and with his interest piqued, Mick grabbed a pad of paper and a pencil from the radio desk and began translating the message. It was from one vessel to another giving a location of where they were to meet up. Mick waited to hear the reply confirming receipt of the message but there was none. He thought that was strange. He wondered why someone would broadcast in Morse code unless they were sure the intended recipient was prepared to receive the message.

While he waited to see if there would be a reply or if the original message would be re-broadcast, Mick thought back to Pops and all the Morse code conversations they had together. As a radioman in his early days, Pops knew and had used Morse code often. When Mick was just a youngster, Pops had taught him Morse code. Pops had two telegraph keys, the mechanism used to type out the message, a series of dots and dashes. They would sit at the kitchen table, across from each other, without speaking. Pops would type out a message and Mick would translate the message. Then, Mick would type out the response. Back and forth it would go for hours. Both of them pounding out messages to each other in Morse code. Lots of information was shared between them without a single word being spoken aloud. Mick became so proficient that, as long as Pops kept each message brief, he did not need to write out the translation on paper. He did it in his head and immediately began his reply.

Mick had not heard Morse code since before Pops had died. He kept listening closely, hoping to hear the familiar dots and dashes again. He wondered about who was using Morse Code. Based on just the one message, it was a puzzle. It could be drug smugglers, he thought. Maybe the intended recipient was not within range yet or had been intercepted by law enforcement. It could be some type of real or training covert operation by any number of nations ringing the Mediterranean Sea, he thought. Now, that would be something. Defeating technological surveillance by good old retro Morse code, a dying art. No, he thought, there were still too many people around who did know Morse code. But probably not for too much longer.

His musings were interrupted by a radio message for him. He responded that he could hear the broadcast and was ready for traffic. He knew it would not be much. They were being sent the longitude and latitude of Ahmed's fishing boat. The longitude was sent. He confirmed receipt and then the sender signed off. Fifteen minutes later, he was contacted again. After he acknowledged that he could hear the broadcast and was ready for traffic, the latitude was sent. He confirmed receipt and the sender signed off. The longitude and latitude were sent separately fifteen to twenty minutes apart just to keep the curious guessing. Pretty low tech, thought Mick, but not as low tech as Morse code and certainly not as cryptic.

Mick went up topside to give the captain the coordinates to head for, which the captain programmed into the automated guidance system. As the fishing boat kept moving, they would get periodic updated coordinates. Mick reached for the compass on his belt and checked their direction. They were headed almost directly south.

The fishing boat had headed on a fairly straight line south, southeast, on a direct heading for the lawless waters of Libya, passing between the eastern end of the island of Antikythera and the western end of the island of Crete.

The vast majority of the hundreds of islands in the Aegean Sea between Greece and Turkey are Greek. Usually, nations claim territorial waters out to twelve nautical miles. However, Greece and Turkey both border the Aegean Sea and twelve nautical miles is not possible for both nations without significant overlap. As a result,

Greece and Turkey each claim six nautical miles of territorial waters in the Aegean Sea. Heading to Turkey would not defeat Greek authority unless the fishing boat pulled into a port in Turkey. But pulling into a Turkish port with Greek authorities in hot pursuit was not a smart move when holding a woman against her will. Turkish authorities would surely investigate the fishing boat under such circumstances and find Sofia. Heading south was the quickest and safest way out of Greek waters and the clutches of Greek authorities.

Given Mick and Taylor's current location south of Athens and just east of the Greek island of Hydra and the location of the fishing boat more than ten nautical miles south of Crete, Mick and Taylor had time on their hands. The fishing boat had a good head start. Knowing the fishing boat's location now and in the future should allow them to cut off some cruising time and catch up.

With night came darkness and there was nothing to see topside. Mick was relaxing while listening to the radio and holding out hope of hearing Morse code again. Taylor was sleeping. The latest position coordinates for the fishing boat showed that it was heading east toward Lebanon. Mick hoped they would catch sight of it in the morning

CHAPTER FIFTEEN

The headlines of the Tuesday morning Greek newspapers exclaimed, "Daughter of U.S. Ambassador Kidnapped." The papers had large photographs of both Ambassador Sopko and Sofia. Ambassador Sopko's photograph was a file photo, a professionally done head shot with the American flag in the background. The photograph of Sofia was also a head shot but not professionally done. It could have been from a driver's license, a passport, or a student identification card.

Early on Tuesday morning, Mick was standing next to the captain looking through binoculars in search of the fishing boat. The blue waters sparkled with reflections from the sunlight. It was tiring work because the reflections off of the water strained his eyes. The fishing boat was still too far away but since it had been a couple of hours since they had last received its position, Mick was watching. If the fishing boat stopped, they could run right up on it without warning. That was something Mick wanted to avoid.

Taylor came topside with three steaming cups of coffee and handed one to the captain and one to Mick.

"Four and a half days," Taylor said.

"Thanks for the reminder," Mick responded.

"No, it took four and a half days for the lid to blow off," Taylor said.

"What lid?"

"The press lid," Taylor replied. "I just heard a radio report down below. Apparently, it is all over the news in Greece and, soon, around the world that Sofia has been kidnapped."

"Well, it was only a matter of time," Mick said. "We shook enough trees in Greece, with the police search for Sami at the hotels. Sharing hot news is just part of human nature. Involve enough people in anything and soon the entire world knows about it."

Mick handed Taylor the binoculars and sat down to drink his coffee and rest his eyes.

"We can't let them get into Lebanese waters," Mick said, after taking a sip of coffee.

"Agreed," Taylor replied. "But unless we know for sure that Sofia is on board, what are we going to do to stop them?"

The conversation died there while both men thought through various scenarios for taking the fishing boat at sea.

When the fishing boat location coordinates came in again, it was clear that the fishing boat had altered course slightly. Before it had been headed straight toward Lebanon. Now it was headed slightly north of that on a direct line for Cyprus.

"It is too early to know if it is really headed to Cyprus," Mick said. "He could still turn toward Lebanon at any time."

"Let's hope he is going to Cyprus," Taylor said. "We can work with that. We may be able to get assistance from the Greek Cypriots. If he goes to Lebanon, we have to intercept before he gets close. Our odds of success go way down once he gets on his home turf."

Cyprus is an island south of Turkey. The majority of the inhabitants of Cyprus are of Greek descent, with a minority of Turkish descent. Cyprus is geographically in the Middle East, but Cyprus considers itself to be part of Europe and is a member of the European Union.

Mick knew all about Cyprus. He had studied its history years ago. In 1974, Greece was controlled by a military junta, called "the colonels." The colonels sponsored an overthrow of the elected President of Cyprus, with the aim of uniting Cyprus with Greece. The President of Cyprus had been elected by promising not to pursue a union with Greece so, as far as the colonels were concerned, he had to go. In July, in response to the attempted coup d'état, Turkey invaded Cyprus with 33 ships and 30 tanks. The Greek military junta collapsed and was replaced by a Greek democratic government. Peace talks began. The talks failed and the fighting continued. Peace talks began a second time in August. Those talks were abruptly aborted by Turkey. Minutes later, Turkey began a bombing campaign in Cyprus. Sixty hours later, Turkey had control of more than one third of the island, in the north, the prime agricultural area. Greece and Turkey were on the brink of full out war. And to make matters worse, both were members of the North Atlantic Treaty Organization.

Of course, the Greek Cypriots did not blame Greece for starting the mess. And they did not blame themselves for failing to prepare for their own defense. Instead, they blamed the United States for not defending them.

Hundreds of Greek Cypriots gathered outside the U.S. Embassy in the capitol of Nicosia to demonstrate against the United States for failing to stop the Turkish invasion of Cyprus.

The U.S. Ambassador's second floor office window looked out at an apartment building that was being built across the street from the Embassy. The building under construction had scaffolding set up on the exterior. During an anti-American demonstration on August 19, a gunman had scaled the scaffolding and fired into the U.S. Embassy. Two of the bullets went through a closed wooden shutter covering the Ambassador's office window on the outside of the Embassy, through the glass window, through two open doorways, and down a long hallway. The first bullet struck Ambassador Rodger Davies in the heart and killed him almost instantly. A Greek Cypriot secretary who went to aid the Ambassador was struck in the head by the second bullet and killed instantly.

Killing a U.S. Ambassador is an act of war and the shooter was believed to be a Greek Cypriot. Despite the Ambassador's murder, the United States immediately sent a replacement Ambassador to show that it was not blaming the Greek Cypriot authorities for the murder. It was not perceived as an intentional assassination. It was the right call by the United States at the time, replace the Ambassador and do not retaliate.

The Cypriots had wanted independence from British rule, and they got it in 1960. Independence means you are responsible for your own defense. Before you seek independence from a military powerhouse, you need to take a good hard look at your neighborhood. When Turkey invaded, independent Cyprus could not stop them. Turkey would never have invaded if by doing so they had to face the British military. The reality is that independence comes at a cost. Those not willing to pay the price for their own independence are subject to the whims of others. The price Cyprus paid was more than one third of their land mass.

The hostilities ended with a United Nations buffer zone splitting Cyprus into two areas; the internationally recognized Republic of Cyprus which is, practically speaking, the Greek Cypriot government-controlled area in the south, and the Turkish Cypriot administrative zone in the north. The split continues to this day. The only country that recognizes the Turkish Cypriot administrative zone as independent is Turkey.

"I have a feeling that he is not going to Lebanon," Mick said. "Still no ransom demand and no claim of responsibility means Hezbollah is not ready to publicly acknowledge its involvement. Going to Lebanon would be like putting up a neon sign declaring Hezbollah involvement."

"In Turkish Cyprus, if he is willing to spend some money, he could get whatever cooperation he needs with no questions asked," Taylor said.

Since the division of the island, the Greek Cypriot south had prospered while the Turkish Cypriot north had not. With little government control and a high poverty rate in the north, hard currency ruled. Only after Cyprus joined the EU in 2004 did things begin to pick up in the Turkish administrative zone as a result of increased access allowed between the two sides of Cyprus. However, increased access is a relative term. The number of authorized crossing checkpoints went from one to five, with some only for pedestrian crossing.

"They were willing to buy Sami a car just so he could ingratiate himself with Sofia," Mick said. "And they were willing to sacrifice a commercial fishing boat so they could get away with Sofia. I don't think money is a problem."

"Well, we might have a better idea of his probable destination after the next location coordinates," Taylor said.

Later in the morning, Mick received a radio message. It was sent in the clear, with ambiguous wording as a simple code, but the message was clear to him. During the darkness of night, a woman had been seen on the deck of the fishing boat for about forty minutes. From the surveillance photographs, the Agency had high confidence that Sofia was on the fishing boat.

A combination of satellite and aerial surveillance was being used to keep track of the fishing boat. Multiple satellites were overhead at various times of the day. Surveillance flights were being flown to cover the gaps in the satellite coverage. Given the amount of commercial air traffic in and around the Mediterranean, the surveillance flights did not arouse suspicion.

They must have been letting Sofia get some fresh air. Mick and Taylor were energized by the news. It was confirmation of their hunch. The one fishing boat had been running interference for the second fishing boat so that it could get away with Sofia.

Throughout the day on Tuesday, position coordinates for the fishing boat showed that it was maintaining a definite track for Cyprus. Mick and Taylor alternated taking turns to periodically watch for the fishing boat as they closed the distance. They wanted to get just within sight of it then drop back a bit so that the fishing boat did not suspect it was being followed.

"I am not comfortable yet that he is really going to Cyprus," Mick said.

"I know what you are thinking," Taylor said. "Is he really going to Cyprus or is he just steering well clear of Israeli territorial waters for now and he will swing back toward Lebanon once he clears Israeli waters."

"Exactly," Mick said. "The last thing he wants to do is come up against Israeli patrol boats."

Mick and Taylor discussed their options. Should they try to take the fishing boat at sea or wait for it to get to Cyprus. They were not SEALs. They were not as comfortable on the water as on land. And there was just the two of them. There was no way of knowing whether Ahmed would take to land or just stay on the water. And if he turned back toward Lebanon, they would have no choice.

CHAPTER SIXTEEN

David and Jason agreed that they would each make one of the two calls. They decided to wait to make the calls until the men went to work so that the men could give their employers excuses for leaving work early. If the men failed to show up for work, their employers might start calling around looking for them. An excused absence from work would give them at least twenty-four hours before their employers questioned their continued absence.

At nine o'clock in the morning on Tuesday, David called Mr. Musa's cell phone.

"*As-salaamu alaikum*," Mr. Musa answered.

"*Wa alaikum assalaam*," David replied, then continued in Arabic. "I am calling to confirm that you are satisfied with the delivery of your new refrigerator."

"Yes," Mr. Musa responded. "*Shukran.*"

Mr. Musa hung up the phone, told his boss that he had to leave because of a sudden illness in the family, and left work. On the sidewalk outside, Mr. Musa called his wife.

"I just called to remind you that it is time you left to meet me for our appointment," Mr. Musa said.

"I will leave now," Mrs. Musa responded, and hung up the phone.

Within minutes, Mrs. Musa and her son, Reza, were out of the apartment and on their way.

"*Salaam*," Layla said.

"*Salaam*," Jason replied, and continued in Arabic. "I am calling to confirm that you are satisfied with the delivery of your new refrigerator."

"Yes, the men were very professional, thank you," Layla said, and hung up the phone.

Layla immediately called her husband at work and told him that he needed to come home. Then she sat watching the children play in the living room while waiting for her husband to arrive home.

Mr. Musa arrived at the address he had been given first. He saw that it was a jewelry store. He pretended to be window shopping while he waited for his wife and son to arrive.

A taxi dropped Mrs. Musa and Reza just up the block from where Mr. Musa was standing. He waved to them, as his wife paid the taxi driver. When they were all together, Mr. Musa attempted to enter the store. However, the door would not open. It was locked. A fraction of a second later, Mr. Musa heard a click come from the door as the solenoid engaged and he pushed the door open. They all went inside the jewelry store.

Mr. Musa did not know what to do. There was only one man visible in the store standing behind the jewelry display cases and Mr. Musa did not recognize him. He hesitated as he considered whether or not he should address the man standing behind the display case. Before he could make up his mind, David appeared from a doorway behind the display area and motioned for them to come to him.

As they entered the back room, Mr. Musa saw a bank of computer monitors showing continuous surveillance all around the jewelry store, inside and outside.

"We have to leave now," David said. "We will leave out the back way. There is a white delivery van right outside. You will all get in the back as quickly, but calmly, as possible and I will drive."

"We have to wait for Layla," Mr. Musa protested.

"No," David said. "Layla and her family will go in a separate van."

"Now," David said, as he opened the back door.

They all went outside and got into the delivery van, without incident. David drove the van away, headed north, to a private boat docked in Jounieh, on the coast north of Beirut.

About an hour later, Layla and her family arrived at the jewelry store and were taken out the same back door by Jason and into a second white delivery van. Jason drove away from the jewelry store, headed north, up the coast, to a different boat also docked in Jounich.

The two families would not travel together. Small groups were key to moving around without attracting attention. The larger the group, the more people noticed the group. Each family would be placed on a different boat. They would not meet up until they were away from Lebanon.

While Jason was still on the coast road headed north, David arrived at a marina in Jounieh. He found a parking spot, pulled into it, and turned off the engine. Then he turned back facing the Musa family and gave them instructions. He described the private boat, provided the name of the boat, and told them where it was located. He instructed them on how to get out of the van, and how to walk calmly to the boat. He told them that he would be following behind them. Once they got on the boat, they were to immediately go into the cabin and stay there until they were told that they could come up on deck. David asked if there were any questions. Sixteen-year-old Reza raised his hand.

"You don't need to raise your hand, Reza," David said, as he held back a chuckle, but not a smile.

"Can we go fishing on the boat?" Reza asked.

"I'm not sure," David responded. "Probably not, but I will check for you once we leave the harbor."

Reza seemed satisfied with that answer. Seeing that the Musa's were ready, David climbed into the back of the van and opened the side door for them to get out. It went as planned. They walked calmly to the boat, which was a medium-sized yacht, got on, and went below. As soon as David was aboard, the yacht started up and headed out of the harbor and toward the open waters of the Mediterranean Sea.

About an hour behind, Jason pulled into a parking spot in the same marina in Jounieh. The scenario was the same, except there were no questions and Layla and her husband each carried one of the children to the yacht. The yacht carrying Jason and Layla's family was soon also out of the harbor and headed for open water.

Once each yacht left Lebanese territorial waters, they sent coded radio messages confirming their position. Then they headed for the one place Hezbollah could not roam freely, Israel.

The two yachts carrying the Musa families had reached the GPS coordinates they had been directed to during the afternoon on Tuesday, after skirting around Lebanese territorial waters and coming straight into the Israeli coast through Israeli territorial waters. They were off the coast of Tel Aviv. They both dropped anchor and waited.

A half hour later, an Israel Defense Force fast patrol boat came toward them. David and Jason both took up positions making themselves clearly visible on the aft decks. David held his right arm up in the air to indicate that his was the yacht to approach. The heavily armed patrol boat made a full wide circle around both yachts. Then the patrol boat pulled near David, shut its engines off, and drifted alongside David's yacht. Rubber bumpers were deployed over the side of the patrol boat. Next, a line was thrown from the patrol boat to David. He ran the line around a cleat and pulled the patrol boat in toward the yacht. The two boats were not touching but they were close enough that the bumpers occasionally brushed against the yacht.

A fit young woman jumped from the patrol boat onto the yacht. She walked the few steps over to David and stuck out her hand.

"Rachel," she said. "Institute."

David smiled as he reached for her hand to shake. Rachel, with no last name. The Institute for Intelligence and Special Operations, what most people commonly refer to as Mossad. David was sure it did not take much convincing to get Mossad to provide assistance, especially since they were taking the Musa family out of the reach of Hezbollah. No real downside for Israel as the families were willing participants and the upside was the possibility of messing with one of Hezbollah's operations.

"David," he said, as he shook her hand. "Agency."

Then, David pointed to Jason and said, "Jason."

Rachel nodded. "Is your cargo secure? No problems?"

"Yes and no problems," David responded.

With that, Rachel turned and went to speak to the captain. After a minute, the captain shouted down to David to disconnect the patrol boat. David untied the line and threw it back to the patrol boat. The patrol boat began to drift away and two of the crew pulled the rubber bumpers back aboard. Then the patrol boat started up and pulled away from the two yachts.

Both yachts pulled their anchors up and started their engines. The captain of David's yacht followed Rachel's directions and Jason's yacht followed David's yacht. The patrol boat followed Jason's yacht. Rachel directed them into two side-by-side berths in a marina.

As the yachts were being tied up, several men approached on the dock. Rachel went up to the men and signaled by hand gesture for David and Jason to join them. More introductions all around, two Agency guys and one Mossad guy.

Introductions over, Rachel pointed out a short white bus with deeply tinted windows in the parking lot. It looked like a small tour bus or perhaps a shuttle bus, like at airports to bring the passengers in from long-term parking. It looked like it could hold maybe 16 to 20 people. Rachel explained that David, Jason, and the cargo would walk to and get on the bus. They would all then go to the safe house and settle in. Two cars and one bus in a convoy.

Rachel asked if there were any questions. There were no questions. David and Jason walked back to the yachts and went below to get the two families.

Everything went without a hitch until everyone got settled into the safe house. The luggage for each family was already at the house. The women put the two little boys down for a nap in one of the four bedrooms and the adults and Reza were all back in the large, comfortably furnished living room. Then the questions started. It was as if the Musa family adults had finally stopped holding their breath and now wanted answers. The family members deferred to Mr. Musa.

"Where are we?" Mr. Musa asked.

"Tel Aviv," David answered.

"Is this where we will stay?" Mr. Musa looked very uncomfortable with that possibility.

"No," David said. "This is where you will stay temporarily until other arrangements can be made."

"How long?"

"Honestly, I don't know," David said. "It could be days or it could be weeks."

"Can we leave the house or are we prisoners?" Mr. Musa said the last part with a bit of humor, not rancor.

"You are not prisoners," David said. "You are temporary guests in a country willing to take the risk of helping us by harboring you. So, you might feel a bit like prisoners because you will have to follow the rules they set. I don't know all the rules myself right now. I will be leaving. Jason will be staying with you until you reach your final destination. But I promise you, everything done is done for a reason. And everyone involved wants to keep you and your family safe. You are not being punished. You are being protected."

Mr. Musa nodded, indicating that he understood.

"At least this is a very nice house and there are enough bedrooms," Mrs. Musa said, putting a cheerful spin on it.

That broke the tension. The two women went into the kitchen and started opening cupboards and the refrigerator. The men could hear their half-stifled surprise at the abundance of food and drink. They sounded relieved. The women sat together at the kitchen counter lining up meal menus for the next few days and checking cupboards to ensure they had the necessary ingredients.

David walked over to Reza who was sitting on the couch looking lost.

"Reza, I am sorry you didn't get to go fishing on the boat," David said. "But I have talked with Jason and he thinks that he can take you out to do some stuff while you are here. It may have to be just you and him, not your dad or your mom, but he will try to make sure you have something fun to do. Are you good with that?"

"Yes, thank you," Reza said, smiling tentatively.

"Don't be afraid of Jason," David said. "You can talk to him about anything. Tell him the things you like to do so he can see what he can arrange."

Reza's smile finally reached his eyes. He was happy, or at least hopeful.

When David stepped away from Reza, Mr. Musa came over to him.

"Thank you," Mr. Musa said. "This is hard on all of us. But for Reza it is the hardest because he really does not understand what is happening. We were not able to speak freely until we were on the boat. And then, even we did not know what was really going to happen to us."

"You don't have to thank me," David said. "No one wants to make this any harder on Reza than it has to be."

Mr. Musa lowered his voice, just above a whisper, and asked David, "What can you tell me about my son Sami?"

"Jason will get the details now that we are here," David said. "He will tell you whatever he can, as soon as he can. But know that Sami is safe, just as you are safe. He is not free to move around or to make telephone calls, just as you are not, but no harm has come to him."

"We have been so worried about him," Mr. Musa said. "Our imaginations run wild with what happened that would lead you to take us away from Lebanon like this. Just knowing he is safe is a big relief."

"I need to prepare you for what you will likely see as soon as you turn on the television," David said. "The daughter of the U.S. Ambassador to Greece was kidnapped. The news reported it in Greece this morning and, by now, it is probably on the news in every country."

Mr. Musa turned white, sank down onto a chair, and placed his hands in front of his face. Concerned and confused, Reza jumped up from his seat on the couch to go to his father, but David waved him back to his seat.

Reluctantly, he sat back down, while David kneeled down next to Mr. Musa.

"Sami, what have you done?" Mr. Musa whispered to himself. "Three sons lost to Hezbollah. My three sons."

"Mr. Musa, you need to pull yourself together for the others," David said quietly. "They need you to be strong. Reza needs you to be strong."

"Why are you helping us?" Mr. Musa asked bewildered, with his hands clasped tightly together in his lap. "You must hate us. Kidnapping an ambassador's daughter. You have known all along. Will I ever see my son again? What if they kill her?"

"I know this is a shock to you," David said. "But your family is safe. Sami is safe and you will see him again. Try to remember that Sami did what he did because your family was being threatened. It does not make it right. But Sami saw no other way to protect his family, your family. Jason will tell you more when he can. In the meantime, you must prepare your family. They will see the news and they know that Sami is in Greece."

Mr. Musa nodded. He sat silently on the chair trying to process what had happened to his family.

David flew out of Israel's Ben Gurion Airport and into the Larnaca International Airport in Cyprus. The flying time was just under an hour on a Cyprus Airways direct flight.

CHAPTER SEVENTEEN

Mick was standing on the deck of the yacht in the late afternoon. They had caught sight of the fishing boat. It was in Cypriot waters and had slowed down considerably. They had relied on the periodic GPS coordinates to keep pace with it. It was closing in on the island of Cyprus.

Mick was scanning the water ahead with binoculars between sips of coffee. Taylor came up from below and stood by Mick.

"Seems he came to Cyprus," Taylor said.

"Indeed, it does," Mick replied.

"He has to head to the north end of the island," Taylor said. "I can't see him pulling into the south end."

"He doesn't have to pull into a port," Mick replied. "He can stay on the water. But you are right, if he does enter a port, it will be on the north side."

"David is on the ground," Taylor said. "As soon as we know where Ahmed is headed, he will meet up with us."

Evening came and the fishing boat was laying offshore of Trikomo, on the southeast side of the Turkish administrative zone of Cyprus. It was not heading into dock. It was not moving, except with the current.

Mick had instructed the captain to move farther offshore to keep out of sight of the fishing boat. From their position, they had no eyes on it. Aerial surveillance was increased to keep a regular check on the fishing boat's location.

Taylor asked, "What is he waiting for?"

"My guess is darkness," Mick responded. "If he is going to pull into a dock, he wants as few eyes as possible on him as he transfers Sofia to land. Even if he is just going to refuel, he still wants as few eyes as possible on the vessel."

"Then we better get David to Trikomo as soon as possible," Taylor said. "He can be our eyes, if they transition to land."

Mick went below to send a message for David.

CHAPTER EIGHTEEN

Sofia's entire body was cramped in the small closet space. She could stand or sit down with her legs beneath her. However, there was no room to sit on the floor with her legs extended. She stood. Then she sat. Sometimes she kneeled. Sometimes she sat with her legs beneath her and off to one side or the other. Sometimes she sat Indian style but with her knees resting on the walls on each side of her. She periodically changed positions to keep her blood flowing and her legs from falling asleep.

There was no window in the closet. There was also no light in the closet. It was pitch black and Sofia could not see her hand in front of her face. She had a hard time keeping track of time. She slept leaning against the wall periodically to forget the discomfort and, more importantly, to forget her situation. When she was awake, she ran the scene at the church over and over in her mind. She had made a split-second decision and she was convinced it had been the wrong one. She should have screamed. She should have fought. They had offered no proof that they could have gotten to Peter or Matthew. She had let her emotions dictate her actions.

She paid a price for sleeping. When she awoke, some part of her body, usually a leg, was asleep. Then she endured the pins and needles pain as the blood returned to her leg and she regained use of it. Upon first waking, she was disoriented by the darkness, every single time. She knew her eyes were open, but she could see nothing. It panicked her until she remembered that she was in a closet.

She knew that she was on a commercial fishing vessel. They had come aboard at night, and she did not see much in the dark before they put her in the closet. At the time, she only knew that it was some kind of boat. But they had let her out of the closet several times, to eat and to use the bathroom, and once to stretch out and pace on the deck in the middle of the night. While on deck, even in the dark, she had been able to get a better look at the boat. She was sure that it was some kind of commercial fishing boat.

When she was let out of the closet to eat, she sat at a small wooden kitchenette type of table. The food was poor and bland. Lots of rice, some bread, and small pieces of fish. There was water in plastic bottles to drink. The only person she ever saw on the boat was the French speaking man. But she knew others were on the boat because occasionally she could hear them talking. They spoke in Arabic, she thought.

The French speaking man always insisted that she used the bathroom before he returned her to the closet. What passed for a bathroom was disgusting. It was dirty and it reeked of urine.

There was a loud knock on the wooden closet door. Sofia knew that the door would be opening soon so she scrunched as far back from the sound of the knock as she could manage, which was not much. The door opened, some light spilled into the closet, and the French speaking man was standing at the closet door, like he always was. But this time, he was not holding the handgun.

He told her to come out and she did. Then he told her to sit at the table and she did. Once seated, she saw the other man that had taken her from the church. He was holding the handgun pointed at her. Sofia could tell that it was night because it was dark outside the portholes.

The French speaking man told her to put her arms out and she did. He took a roll of duct tape and wrapped the tape around her arms, starting at her wrists and going up her arms a few inches, binding her arms tightly together. She asked him why he was binding her. He did not respond. Instead, he pulled a piece of duct tape off the roll and placed it over her mouth. The tape went over part of her hair. The hair had pulled and hurt her head as she had twisted trying to avoid the tape over her mouth. He then crouched down and pulled both of her legs out from under the table. He bound them together with duct tape at the ankles.

Sofia was scared. They had never bound her before. It was different and it was ominous. All she could think was that they were going to throw her over the side of the boat, and she was going to drown. She was panicked and she became short of breath. She could only breath through her nose. Since she was on the verge of tears, her nose had become moist and was inhibiting her breathing. She forced herself to calm down and to breath steadily. And she waited.

The man with the handgun stayed in the cabin, pointing it at her. The French speaking man left the cabin. The engine of the fishing boat started up and the boat began to move.

Sofia had no idea where they were or what time it was, only that it was night. After a while, the boat engine slowed. The boat was maneuvering, she could feel it changing directions. Then she felt it hit against something. A dock. Or maybe another boat, she thought. Then there was silence as the engine was turned off. Sofia waited.

The French speaking man came back into the cabin. He was carrying rolled-up plastic-looking fabric of some kind. He shook the fabric out and laid it on the floor. It was black, about seven and half feet long and three feet wide, and had a zipper on the front, going down the length of the fabric.

Sofia stared at it. Then comprehension dawned on her. It was a body bag.

The French speaking man unzipped the bag. Then he spoke to the man holding the handgun, who put the handgun down and walked toward Sofia. Both men grabbed hold of her upper arms and forced her to stand. Then the French speaking man reached down and picked up her legs. They laid her flat on the floor on top of the body bag.

Sofia was sure they were going to kill her. She began to scream but her screams were muffled by the duct tape on her mouth. She twisted from side to side to stop the French speaking man from zipping the body bag up.

The other man, the one at her head, grabbed the handgun and struck her in the head with the butt of the gun.

Sofia lost consciousness.

CHAPTER NINETEEN

David was dressed all in black -- black pants, black shirt, lightweight black jacket, black socks, and black boots. He had considered black grease on his face and hands but had decided against. It would help him while crossing through no man's land but, after that, it would draw attention to him.

He was on the Greek Cypriot side of the UN patrolled buffer zone, the Green Line, between Greek Cyprus and Turkish Cyprus. He was armed with two handguns. Two fully loaded Glock 19s with four additional magazines. One Glock was in a holster on his belt. One Glock was in a holster on his ankle. The spare magazines were divided between four pockets so they would not clink together as he moved. He could not take anything bigger and expect to remain stealthy in the Turkish zone.

He looked into the Green Line. On the northern side, there were barriers made of concrete wall and barbed-wire topped chain-link fencing. There were also watchtowers, two of which he could see. He had been told that there were also minefields. He studied the map he had been given for how to cross through the Green Line and into the Turkish zone undetected. He could travel into the Turkish zone by foot or in a car through one of the authorized gateways, but the firearms were a problem. The only reliable way to get the firearms in was to go in through an unauthorized route.

He watched the two watchtowers that he could see and plotted his route. He mapped his steps in his head. He was just east of the closest watchtower. He had to start the crossing through the cleared area when the watchtower guard was looking the other way. A diversion to draw the guard's attention to the west was being put together by others as he waited.

A small but loud explosion sounded from the west. David took off running across the Green Line while the watchtower guard's attention was naturally drawn to the direction of the explosion. As he closed in the on the Turkish wall, he slowed and carefully watched every step he took. He reached the wall, where the concrete wall ended and was replaced by a chain-link fence topped with barbed-wire. He grabbed the chain-link fence and scaled the joint between the two types of fencing. When he reached the top, he withdrew wire cutters from his jacket pocket and cut at the barbed-wire. A second small but loud explosion sounded in the west as he made the breach in the barbed-wire. The breach was only as big as he felt he needed to get through. Then he replaced the wire cutters in his pocket and crossed over the top of the fence and scaled down the other side as sirens sounded in the distance. He made it over with only one snag by the barbed-wire, on his left leg, the trailing leg. There was a small tear in his pants and a larger scratch on his leg.

David took cover behind an old wooden shed. He tucked into the side of the shed out of sight of the watchtower guards and out of the light from the nearest tower. He took a night-vision monocle from his jacket pocket and plotted his next move.

He walked at a normal pace to a one-story cinder block commercial building. Running would only draw attention now. Walking was normal. If a guard saw someone running away from the fence line and into the Turkish zone after the explosions, that would set off alarm bells. But people walk around from time to time, for all different reasons. And it was dark. The eye is more likely to see a fast movement in the dark than a slow movement.

Once David reached the farthest end of the commercial building, he walked casually, like someone with someplace to go but no definite time to be there. He was far enough beyond the fence that the guards could no longer see him in the darkness even if they looked in his direction. But the residents could see him. To any resident out and about, David wanted to look like just another guy also out and about.

He worked his way to about two miles into the Turkish zone, where he leaned into another small outbuilding structure, made of cinder blocks, and waited. Within minutes, a four door Renault drove up and stopped near him. The driver rolled down his window and tapped the top of the car twice. David walked out of the shadows, crossed the road behind the car, to avoid the headlights, and got into the front passenger's seat. The car drove off for Trikomo.

The driver was a Turkish Cypriot on the payroll. He handed David a cell phone. It was a cheap cell phone, but it was a smart phone, not a flip phone. The driver said to call him Attila and that his number was in the contacts as "A." David saw that there were also contacts "B," "C," and "D."

David pressed the button for "A." Attila's phone lit up and began to vibrate on the console between the front seats. David disconnected the call and checked and saw that the phone was fully charged. He placed the phone in vibrate mode and put it in his pocket.

On the way to Trikomo, they passed through villages and countryside. But David did not see much of Turkish Cyprus because it was dark.

They arrived at Trikomo just before midnight. The town sign announced that they had entered Iskele. The town was asleep. There were scattered lights on in some windows, but David saw no one on the streets. The town was situated well back from the lowland by the sea.

Before the Turkish invasion, Trikomo was almost exclusively a Greek Cypriot town. The Greek Cypriots fled south during the invasion. The Turkish Cypriot residents of Larnaca, in the Greek Cypriot-controlled south, moved in mass to Trikomo after the invasion, and the Greek town of Trikomo became a Turkish town called Iskele. However, the town was still Trikomo to the officially recognized government of Cyprus, the Greek Cypriot government in the south.

The driver pulled up to the area of a marina and pointed to a radio or cell tower a short distance away. David thanked him and got out of the car. He walked to the tower. There was an advertising sign hung on the tower. It was located at about the height of a two-story building, more than twenty feet up the tower. David climbed the tower and snugged in behind the sign to conceal as much of himself as possible.

From his vantage point, David could see the marina. He did not need the night-vision monocle to see the boats docked at the marina. But he used the monocle to get a good look at each of the boats in the darkness. There were no streetlights at the marina. David's eye was drawn to two men at the marina, just standing next to the rear of a cargo truck. One of the men was smoking a cigarette and not cupping the ember with his hand. They appeared to be waiting for something.

Just after one o'clock in the morning, David watched a commercial fishing boat enter the marina area and pull up to a dock near where the two men were waiting by the cargo truck. He watched the fishing boat maneuver into position at the very end of the dock then he watched as two deck hands tied the boat to the dock and returned to the boat. There was a light on in the cabin. David watched and waited.

After about fifteen minutes, the light in the cabin blinked off and back on several times. The two men by the truck walked down to the fishing boat and stood on the dock next to the boat. Two men came out of the cabin carrying a long dark object between them. They handed the object over to the two men on the dock and got off the boat.

All four men walked to the cargo truck together. The back door was opened, and the long dark object was placed in the cargo bay. The two men from the boat jumped up into the cargo bay and the other two men closed the door then got into the cab of the truck. The truck drove off.

David called Attila. He told him where the truck was leaving from and what it looked like. He told Attila to follow the truck, find out where it goes, then come back and pick him up. David watched the truck from the tower as long as he could. Just before he lost sight of it, he saw headlights at a distance on the road behind it.

As David climbed back down the tower, he saw the fishing boat leaving and heading back out to sea. He walked up to the street to where Attila had dropped him off. Then he waited in the shadows again.

Attila returned about an hour later. David got into the car and Attila told him what he had seen. The truck had gone to the southern outskirts of a village, to the northeast of Trikomo, not far away. It had pulled into an enclosed walled compound. Attila drove on, without stopping. He waited twenty minutes then he drove back. On the way back, he could see through the gate that the truck was still in the compound.

David asked Attila where there was another marina or dock nearby that they could use. Attila took David to a different marina in a town north of the compound. They drove by the walled compound on the way so that David could see it for himself.

While standing on the dock, David retrieved a radio from his thigh pocket and called out to Mick and Taylor.

"I think it is time you come home now," David said, over the open airwaves.

"Copy," Mick said.

"Go northeast from your position and watch for a signal."

"Copy," Mick replied.

David waited in the darkness on the dock. When he heard the engine of a boat, he turned on a high-powered flashlight and swung it gently back and forth through a six-inch arc facing out to sea. The captain used the light to guide the yacht into the dock.

Mick and Taylor jumped off the yacht and on to the dock, where they met up with David. Attila was waiting in the car. The first mate secured the yacht lines to the dock and got back on the yacht.

Mick asked, "What is the situation?"

"I think that they have taken her to an enclosed compound nearby," David replied. "I watched a commercial fishing boat pull into a marina at Trikomo. Two men and a cargo truck were waiting for the fishing boat. Two men got off the fishing boat with a long dark object between them. It was the right size and shape for a person wrapped up. The two men from the fishing boat and the long dark object went into the cargo bay. The other two guys drove the truck away. My driver, Attila, followed and knows where the truck went."

"We have full kit," Mick said. "Do you need anything?"

"That depends on what we are going to do," David responded. "If we are going to take it down tonight, I would rather have better firepower and full night-vision goggles, not just a monocle."

Mick and Taylor laughed quietly.

"Full kit for us," Taylor said. "Two of everything, not three."

David shook his head and asked, "How did I pull the short end of the stick, again?"

They all laughed. It relieved the stress, a little. They all went back onboard the yacht. David examined and bandaged the scratch on his leg, while Mick and Taylor sorted through the kit and gear bags.

Mick and Taylor each took an AR-15 with four extra loaded magazines, to add to their nine-millimeter Glock semi-automatic handguns and extra pre-loaded magazines. Too many magazines meant rattle. So, they both took bendable, soft, quarter inch thick plastic squares out of their gear bags and put them in their pockets. One magazine on one side and one magazine on the other side. No rattle. But a plastic square to deal with. Stealth trumped convenience of access. David added extra pre-loaded magazines for his Glocks and plastic squares to his pockets. Mick and Taylor each took night-vision goggles for themselves and one night-vision monocle for Attila. All three of them strapped knives to a lower leg. Mick grabbed a small pair of binoculars and stuffed them in his thigh pocket.

Finally, they took out five portable radios. Mick checked each one. They were all fully functional. He set them all to the same frequency. They each had one and there was one for Attila.

They left their tactical carrier vests and portable water system packs in the bags. They might have to blend in, particularly to exfiltrate, and exterior vests and water systems was no way to blend.

Mick took the fifth radio to the captain, with instructions to stay offshore but within range.

"I am going to need to refuel," the captain said.

"Then sit here tonight," Mick said. "If we don't call you before dawn, fuel up here then stay offshore but in close.

If we do call you tonight, we will need to head out to sea in a hurry with whatever fuel you have."

"Okay," the captain said, as he nodded his understanding.

"Can we get to the Greek side with the fuel you have?"

"Yes," the captain answered.

"Good, then that is the plan," Mick said, as he turned and returned to Taylor and David in the cabin.

When Mick walked in, he saw that David still did not have an AR-15. Mick reached into his gear bag and pulled out his spare AR-15.

"Two is one, one is none," he said to David, as he handed him the rifle.

"Watch and learn, David," Taylor said. "There are no short sticks when Mick is around."

David checked the AR-15 over and began piling extra pre-loaded magazines for it into his pockets. He had to put some of the Glock magazines back in the bags, but he was happy to do it.

Mick, Taylor, and David went to Attila's car. They put the rifles in the trunk and got in the passenger compartment with Attila. Attila began driving.

CHAPTER TWENTY

Attila drove south to the walled compound, but he did not stop. He told the men well in advance that it was coming up on the left and they were prepared to get the best look they could as they drove by.

The compound was surrounded by a cinder block wall, which looked to be about six feet tall. There was a metal gate in the front wall, big enough for trucks to drive through. The gate had full metal covering on the lower half and see-through bars on the top half so drivers coming and going could see through the gate when it was closed.

Inside the compound was a tall one-story cinder block building with two loading docks and two personnel doors. The loading docks were to the right side of the building. One personnel door was near the loading docks, the other was at the far-left side of the front of the building. There were windows at the top of the building, near the roof. Light was shining through the high window on the left side. The men could not see if there were any other structures in the compound. But the cargo truck was still parked in front, parallel to the front of the building, near the personnel door to the left.

Mick asked Attila, "Is there anywhere where we can get a view down into the compound?"

"I don't think so," Attila replied. "There are only one-story buildings out here and there is no high ground near enough. We are away from the seashore. This is largely agricultural land. And the mountains are north of here, by the northern coast, too far away."

"Okay, find us somewhere discrete to park and plan," Mick said.

Attila drove on for a little while and then turned off onto a dirt farm road and parked the car. Everyone got out of the car and stretched. Then they huddled by the trunk, in the dark.

"It is almost four o'clock in the morning," Mick said. "And we don't have enough information to try a rescue right now."

"We need aerial surveillance to give us a look inside the compound," said David. "We would need a drone to get a look inside ourselves."

"It would be nice to know how many people are inside," Taylor added.

"Then we are agreed that we are not prepared to go in tonight?" Mick asked.

Taylor and David both agreed that they did not have enough information about the compound. They decided that Mick would be dropped a couple miles southwest of the compound and he would find a good spot to set up surveillance for the rest of the night. Taylor and David would go into Trikomo and get two hotel rooms. Attila would stay in one room and they would stay in the other room. Taylor and David would arrange for aerial surveillance of the compound and get back with Mick midmorning, sooner if they had new information.

Attila opened the trunk of the car. He pulled out two cell phones. They were identical to the one he had given David. They had the same four numbers pre-programmed in the contacts as "A," "B," "C," and "D."

"I am A." Attila advised them. "You need to see which of you is which letter."

"Easy enough," Mick said, as he called B.

The cell phone in David's pocket vibrated. David reached into his pocket and pulled out the phone, but he did not answer it. He just held it up, so everyone saw that it's face was lit up and it was his phone that had been called. Mick disconnected the call.

When Mick called C, the cell phone in Taylor's hand lit up and rang. Taylor answered the call to silence the ringing. Then he disconnected the call and put the phone in vibrate mode.

"I guess that makes me D," Mick said. "Taylor, call me."

Taylor called D and the cellphone in Mick's hand lit up and rang. Taylor quickly disconnected the call and Mick's phone went silent. Mick placed his phone in vibrate mode.

"Excellent," said Mick. "We have two forms of communication, phones and radios."

They got back in the car and headed northwest, back toward the compound. A couple of miles before the compound, Attila stopped the car and he and Mick got out. Attila opened the trunk again and rooted around in a bag behind the rifles. He took out three plastic bottles of water and offered them to Mick.

Mick could only find room in his clothing for two of the bottles of water, so he drank the third bottle of water right at the car and threw the empty bottle back in the trunk. Then he picked up the night-vision monocle originally intended for Attila and placed it in a pocket. He left his rifle and his night-vision goggles in the trunk. Not knowing who he might encounter, nothing out of the ordinary could be visible. Mick tapped the top of the car and set off into a field to find a spot to watch the compound.

Attila pulled into the parking lot of a four-story high-rise hotel in Trikomo. It was part of a chain, Attila said, but it was not any hotel chain that Taylor or David recognized. Attila stayed in the car while Taylor and David got out.

They walked into the hotel lobby at a few minutes before five o'clock in the morning on Wednesday. The lobby was of modern design. Modern being 1970's modern. It was big, clean, and brightly lit. They walked up to the reception desk where a young woman was waiting to assist them. She had seen them enter the hotel and had positioned herself behind the reception desk, looking attentive.

Taylor asked the woman, "Do you speak English?"

"A little," the young woman responded.

"Two rooms," Taylor said. "With two beds in each room."

The young woman asked, "For how long?"

"Two nights for now, maybe longer," Taylor replied.

The young woman struggled to explain, in English, that check-in was at three o'clock in the afternoon and they would be charged for last night if they wanted the rooms now. Taylor understood what she was trying to say.

"Okay," he said, while nodding his head affirmatively. Practically everyone in the world understood the word okay.

The young woman asked for payment and David produced a credit card in his alias name to pay for the rooms. The woman entered the information into a computer then asked David to sign a form that he could not fully read. David signed his alias name.

The woman handed keys with room numbers on them to David and said that they were on the third floor. They thanked her and crossed the lobby to the elevator to go up to their rooms. David took out his cell phone and called Attila and told him to meet them on the third floor.

The rooms were adequate. They both had two beds and a nice large bathroom. The rooms had a seventies modern look, but the bathrooms seemed to have been remodeled fairly recently. They had views of part of the town of Trikomo and the sea far off in the distance.

Attila gave David his best description of where the compound was located and went to his room down the hall to get some rest. Taylor and David stayed in their room.

While David used his cell phone to place a call to the U.S. Embassy in Nicosia, Taylor went into the bathroom, closed the door, and took a long hot shower. He emerged from the bathroom clean and refreshed. The towels had been a bit disappointing, a little small and not as soft as they looked.

David had to wait for the bathroom to clear of steam before he also took a shower. While David was showering, Taylor called down for room service and ordered three large breakfasts, a platter of pastries, two large pots of coffee, and several bottles of Coke, to be delivered to their room at seven o'clock. Taylor knew from experience that, in countries other than the United States, large is not always what he expected large to be. One of the breakfasts was for Attila. But still, he ordered a lot because they did not know how long they would be waiting in their room, and they would take some of the pastries to Mick later in the morning. Mick would be starving by then. Taylor and David both laid on their beds to rest and wait, fully clothed, except for boots and jackets.

CHAPTER TWENTY-ONE

Mick had found what he considered a reasonably good place from which to watch the compound. He was lying flat on the pitched roof of a wooden equipment shed, just below the roof crest. There was an old tractor inside the shed. There were no other structures nearby. It was a good location in that he was elevated and had a clear line of sight facing northeast to the compound. It would not be so good when the sun rose. There would be no shade. And he would be clearly visible to anyone in the field behind the shed.

Mick watched the compound through the night-vision monocle. It was about a half mile away. He could not see much inside the compound due to the wall, but he could see the high windows near the top of the building. The windows were wide but not tall. About five or six feet wide and only two feet tall. Mick could see the windows in the front of the building were replicated on the southwestern side. They probably went all the way around the building to let in natural light during the day, he thought. The window farthest left on the front of the building still had light showing through to the outside from inside. The other windows that he could see were all dark. Obviously, there was a wall inside the building between the farthest window on the left and the remaining windows in the front. Otherwise, there would have been light bleeding out at least through the next closest window as well. His view of the metal front gate and the road that ran by the compound was unobstructed.

The local population were early risers. As the sky began to lighten with the pre-dawn, Mick observed the occasional headlights of traffic on the road, mostly heading southwest toward Trikomo but periodically heading northeast. As the sky brightened, Mick turned the night-vision monocle off and put it in his pocket as it was of no use anymore. Instead, he retrieved the small pair of binoculars to continue his observation.

He scanned the compound through the binoculars. He could just see the top of the box of the cargo truck over the compound wall. It was still where it had been parked when they drove by during the night. There was no movement inside the compound. If the place was a functioning business, he expected to see employees coming to work. No one came to the compound in the early morning.

At around nine o'clock in the morning, Mick saw a car come up the road from Trikomo and stop at the closed metal gate. The driver got out of the car and banged on the lower part of the metal gate with his hand. A man came to the gate from inside the compound. He opened the gate and stepped outside the compound. He talked with the driver for a minute and they both went to the trunk of the car. The trunk was opened, and the driver lifted out a mid-sized cardboard box, about eighteen inches square, and several blue plastic bags. The other man took it all. He held the box with both hands in front and the bags dangled off his fingers below the box. The driver got back into his car, turned southwest, and drove away, leaving the man standing at the metal gate.

The heavily laden man walked through the gate, back into the compound. He shut the gate with his shoulder and struggled with the locking mechanism. Eventually, he walked back toward the building and out of Mick's field of vision. Within five minutes, the man was back at the metal gate properly securing the locking mechanism. Then he was gone again, back into the interior of the compound.

Grocery delivery, Mick thought. The guy in the car was just a delivery person, not a trusted associate who could be let into the compound. With the cargo truck still inside the compound, Mick had to assume that there were at least five people inside the building. Sofia and four men, two of whom came off of the fishing boat and two of whom came with the cargo truck. There could be more but no less than four men inside the building with Sofia. If they needed groceries to be delivered, that meant they did not put a lot of prior planning into this location.

Mick had a lot of time to think on the rooftop. At noon, it would have been six full days since Sofia had been taken. No ransom demand and no claim of responsibility bothered him. Why take Sofia if not as a bargaining chip or to instill fear of Hezbollah. Going to Cyprus and not Lebanon or Syria bothered him too. A Hezbollah stronghold would be a safer place to keep a hostage, surrounded by people who held Hezbollah in high esteem and would sound the alarm at the approach of strangers into the area. And there would be plenty of manpower.

The beginning of the operation had seemed so organized. Using Sami to ingratiate himself with Sofia at the university. Getting Sami a car so he could drive Sofia around and become familiar with her and her routines. Pre-positioning the delivery van near the Byzantine Catholic church in the Plaka. Knowing ahead of time that Sofia would be alone in the church. Communicating with Sofia in French. A quick and efficient exit out of Athens. Two waiting commercial fishing boats off the shore of Greece. Being prepared to leave one fishing boat to be intercepted by the Greek authorities while the second fishing boat left Greek waters. All very organized.

Now it appeared that the compound in Cyprus was a fallback position. Available, but not fully set up to house them in advance. The operation was not falling apart but it had definitely taken a turn away from organized and efficient.

Mick thought about Sami. Sami was clearly supposed to be bait to lure Sofia somewhere where they could grab her. For them to have brought him to Greece, he could not have been a backup plan. Sami was the main attraction. But they did not use Sami. His presence in Greece had been useless to them. In the end, they ditched him. They left him alone in Athens to fend for himself because they did not need him after all. The plan changed at the spur of the moment. They must have been conducting surveillance of the Ambassador's residence while Sami sat in his hotel room. They could not have known in advance that Sofia would go to the Plaka on that Thursday. It had only been decided the night before. They had to have followed the Embassy car to the Plaka that morning then the kids on foot throughout the Plaka.

They sent Sami to watch the Embassy car in the morning after it arrived at the Plaka and parked. So, they still had to have been planning to use Sami then. But they saw the kids split up, the driver leave Sofia at the church, and Sofia go into the church alone. They knew from Sami's reports that she would be in there for some time, alone. They saw an opportunity and they took it. A snap decision based on their observations on the ground.

Then they followed the original plan and took Sofia to the fishing boat which was waiting offshore. Everything was still going according to plan, only earlier than they had perhaps anticipated. Even the sacrifice of the second fishing boat was part of the original plan. Then they were headed for Lebanon, their home base, as planned.

So, what had changed, Mick wondered. The story breaking in the media was the only answer he could come up with. They had been willing to go along with the media blackout for as long as the United States and Greece blacked it out. They made no contact with the United States and made no public claim of responsibility. They did nothing to draw attention to themselves or Hezbollah. But then the story broke in the news and they changed course. Turkish Cyprus became the fallback destination.

Hezbollah must have determined that Lebanon was no longer a politically safe destination. If Sofia were seen or found in Lebanon, no one would believe any Hezbollah denials of responsibility. Lebanon, and Hezbollah in particular, could not afford another war like the July War with Israel. Hezbollah must have determined that their hold on power in Lebanon could not withstand the anger generated by such a brazen breach of diplomatic protocol. They could deny involvement but not if Sofia was taken to Lebanon, or even Syria, given Hezbollah's involvement in the Syrian Civil War.

So, they changed destinations to Turkish Cyprus. And they were not entirely prepared to do so, Mick thought. The team had to strike now, tonight, before the kidnappers burrowed in, before they could assemble a proper protective force. Or before they moved Sofia to a better fortified and defensive location.

The sun was beating down on Mick's back and he was beginning to sweat at ten o'clock in the morning when his cell phone began to vibrate in his pocket.

"Go," Mick said, as he accepted the call.

"We have new information and planning to do," Taylor said.

"Pick me up near where you dropped me off," Mick said.

"On our way," Taylor said, then disconnected the call.

Mick took one last good look at the compound through the binoculars. Then he took a good look at the area immediately surrounding him. He could see no one in the fields. He backed away from the crest of the roof toward the edge of the roof. He let his legs go over the edge of the roof and hung at the edge, bent as his waist, with his torso on the roof and his legs hanging down off the roof. After a momentary pause to steady himself, he pushed off the roof and fell to the ground, landing hard on his feet.

Mick moved in next to the shed, facing outward, and looked around again. He looked at the ground around him and checked his pockets. Nothing had come out, nothing was missing. Leave no trace ran through Mick's mind. The empty water bottle he was carrying under his shirt had shifted to his side. He shifted the bottle under his shirt to the back, out of his way. Then he headed directly west through the field, walking at a normal pace while looking around like he was studying the field. He occasionally reached down to grab a handful of dirt and stood still while he pretended to analyze it. He walked for thirty minutes and made his way to the shoulder of the road, a bit closer to Trikomo than where he had been dropped off during the night.

Taylor and Attila were parked on the side of the road, heading southwest. The hood of the car was up and both men were looking in at the engine when Mick walked up to them. Attila immediately closed the hood and they all got into the car. Taylor handed Mick two pastries wrapped in a napkin and a large bottle of cold water as Attila started the car and headed for the hotel.

CHAPTER TWENTY-TWO

Once in the hotel room, Mick reached into the closet and grabbed a hanger and hung up his jacket. He removed his Glock and his knife and placed them on the top shelf in the closet. He took all of the spare magazines out of his pockets and piled them next to the Glock. He unclipped the compass from his belt and put it next to the knife. Then he took a second hanger and went into the bathroom and closed the door.

He stripped off his clothes, hanging his pants and shirt on the hanger. He beat his clothes with his hand to knock any loose dirt off. Then he hung the clothes hanger from the towel rack closest to the shower.

He took a long hot shower, scrubbing the dirt and sweat from his body and his hair. His clothes simultaneously got steamed to freshen them up and to pull the wrinkles out of them. He dried off and wrapped a towel around his waist. The towel should have been bigger but it worked. He grabbed his clothes and walked out into the room. He hung the clothes on the hanger in the closet. He hung his underwear and socks, which he had handwashed in the sink, over an empty hanger to dry. He placed his boots on the floor of the closet.

Mick started picking at the left-over food on the desk while Taylor called down to room service for lunch meals and drinks. There was less than a full cup of coffee left in the two carafes and it was cold. Mick drank it anyway, for the caffeine.

David called Mick over to one of the beds. There were twelve, fourteen by eleven-inch photographs on the bed, some taken just after dawn and some thermal imaging taken during the night. They had been delivered by a courier shortly before Taylor and Attila had gone out to get Mick. David had studied the photographs while they were gone.

"The only outbuilding in the compound is a roofed but not walled area in the front right corner of the compound," David said, while pointing first at one of the photographs then at the same position on another. "You can just see it has a table and chairs inside. Probably an outside lunch area or a driver waiting area out of the sun."

"There are two gates into the compound," David continued, while alternately pointing at several photographs. "There is the main gate in the front, wide enough for trucks to drive through, and there is a smaller pedestrian gate at the rear of the compound, towards the back left corner. As you can see, there is a car parked behind the compound, near the back gate."

"That is behind the left side of the building," Mick noted. "The building has to be divided into at least two sections, an office section where the pedestrian door is on the left front of the building, and a working area which goes to the right front of the building, where the second pedestrian door and the two loading docks are located. Light bleeding out from the far-left window did not also bleed out from any of the other windows in the front."

"Makes sense," David said. "An office area and a larger work area. There must also be an interior door between the two spaces."

"It also makes sense on the thermal," David said, as he moved over to the thermal images. "No heat showing in more than two-thirds of the building, from left of center all the way to the right wall. All of the heat is showing on the far-left side of the building."

Mick and Taylor each picked up one of the thermal images and studied them. After a minute of silence, David continued.

"By my count, there are six people in the building, all on the left side," David said. "I think the heat spot all alone in the far-left rear corner area is Sofia. That one heat spot does not move from photograph to photograph. It is static while the others change positions, even if only a little."

"The others are the two men from the boat, the two men from the cargo truck, and a new person," David continued. "You can see that there is one guy who stays near the front door. The rest move around in the center area. And in one photograph, there is a guy outside the building, at the rear, between the back wall of the building and the pedestrian gate in the back wall of the compound."

"Taking a smoke break," Mick said. "That means that there is a rear exit from the left side of the building. The guy goes out, has a cigarette, and comes back in, all at the rear of the building. That area was out of sight from my observation position. But he is not patrolling the perimeter."

Mick explained his thoughts about this location being a fallback location, which they had headed to only after the news of Sofia's kidnapping had broken. It was available but not prepared ahead of time to accommodate the men from the fishing boat and Sofia. With only five men at a fairly remote location, there would probably never be a better time to go in, he concluded. Taylor and David agreed.

They spent the rest of the day planning the rescue of Sofia at night, while they had the advantage of night-vision to get up close to the compound, preparing their equipment, and resting. Because they were going to go in at night, they knew that there was no way they could guarantee that they would be able to properly police their brass. They unloaded every magazine that they were taking. They put their gloves on and thoroughly wiped down every cartridge individually with a soft cloth as they reloaded their magazines. They all needed sleep but their own security came first and they had the time. They could not afford to leave their fingerprints behind on spent cartridges.

Attila came over to their room for lunch and brought the local newspaper. The story of Sofia's kidnapping was front page, above the fold news, not that they could read Turkish. Attila summarized it for them. There was nothing they did not know in the newspaper article. But at least it was proof that all of Cyprus, both the Greek and Turkish sides, were aware of the kidnapping and had seen photographs of Sofia.

Additional aerial photographs were delivered in the afternoon and again in the evening, but nothing had changed. The cargo truck was still parked where it had been and the car outside the rear pedestrian gate had not moved.

CHAPTER TWENTY-THREE

Mick, Taylor, David, and Attila arrived a half mile southwest of the compound a few minutes before midnight. Attila had pulled on to a dirt farm road and gone away from the main road. When the car stopped, they all got out.

Attila opened the trunk. Mick, Taylor, and David put on their gloves. They reached into the trunk and picked up their AR-15s. They all checked their rifles over. They hung the rifles on two-point slings. They had checked and rechecked their Glock handguns at the hotel. A silencer for the AR-15 had been delivered to their hotel room late in the afternoon. David affixed the silencer to his AR-15.

Mick and Attila went over Attila's role one last time. Attila assured Mick that they could depend on him. Mick gave Attila a night-vision monocle and showed him how to use it. Mick and David put night-vision goggles on their heads. David handed his night-vision monocle to Taylor.

At ten minutes after midnight on Thursday, twelve hours short of one week from when Sofia was taken, Mick, Taylor, and David set out walking through farmland toward the compound. Taylor walked immediately behind Mick because Mick had the night-vision goggles on.

When they got to the compound, Mick separated from Taylor and David. Mick went to the rear of the compound, toward the rear pedestrian gate. Taylor and David went to the front right corner of the compound.

David and Taylor swung their AR-15s from their chests to their backs. Taylor crouched down next to the outer wall of the compound and laced his gloved fingers together. David put his left foot in Taylor's hands and Taylor pushed up as David swung his right leg over the wall. David crawled onto the roof of the outside seating area and snaked his way to the corner closest to the main building. Then got comfortable in a prone position and he waited.

Taylor swung his AR-15 back around to his chest. He turned the corner and followed the front wall to the metal gate where he also waited.

Mick stayed close to the rear wall and crept to the rear pedestrian gate. The car that had been parked outside the compound by the rear pedestrian gate was not there. He checked through the rear gate for anyone outside and saw no one. Backing away from the gate, he slung his AR-15 behind him. He reached up and grabbed the top of the rear wall and climbed up. He stopped on top and looked again into the rear of the compound. Still, no one outside. He swung both legs over the wall and jumped down. He moved quietly up the short flight of stairs to the pedestrian door at the rear of the building. Then he waited.

Exactly ten minutes after Taylor had lifted David up at the wall, Taylor began banging on the bottom part of the metal gate. The sound was loud and insistent in the stillness of the night. No one responded initially. Taylor kept banging on the gate, demanding attention.

A light came on outside the far-left pedestrian door at the front of the building. The door opened and a man stepped out. He looked toward the gate. Then he closed the door and walked down the short flight of stairs and headed toward the gate. As soon as the man was outside of the half circle of light coming from the outside doorway light, David fired his silenced AR-15, a single shot. The man was struck in the head. In one side and out the other. He dropped to the ground instantly. One down. The shot was not completely silent but it was not loud. The men inside would not have heard it.

Taylor moved left, away from the gate, turned right at the corner, and ran down the wall until he was past the beginning of the building inside. He slung his AR-15 behind his back and reached up and climbed up the wall. He used the night-vision monocle to check for people outside in the compound. He saw no one. He put the monocle in his thigh pocket, jumped into the compound, and brought his AR-15 back around to the front. He crept quickly to the left front corner of the building and again used the night-vision monocle to check for people outside in the compound. The outside doorway light interfered somewhat with the night-vision monocle but he saw no one, except for David still on the roof of the outdoor seating area covering Taylor. Taylor acknowledged David then Taylor put his night-vision monocle in a thigh pocket.

David slid over the side of the outside seating area roof and came toward Taylor. He removed the silencer on his AR-15 and put it in a thigh pocket before reaching Taylor. There was no further need for a silenced weapon and he wanted better maneuverability. David had pushed the night-vision goggles up on his head. Taylor and David climbed the short flight of stairs and each took a position on the landing at the sides of the doorway. Seconds later, the door opened. David shot the man in the doorway. A three-round burst directly in the chest, at point blank range. Two down. The shots were loud. The man fell to the floor. Taylor rushed into the building and fired at the only person he saw, a man with his hand on the handle of a door to the right, most likely leading to the other side of the building, the work area. The man was hit with a three-round burst to his upper back, between the shoulders. He dropped like a rock. Three down.

At the sound of David's unsilenced shots, Mick kicked in the wooden rear door of the building. It was a fairly solid exterior door, but the lock and hinges were not strong. It gave way with just one kick and swung inward as Mick moved to his right out of the line of fire through the doorway and pushed his night vision goggles up on the top of his head. Someone shot at the doorway, but the shots went wide and into the wall beside the door. Plaster dust fell to the floor. Mick entered the building in a crouch, saw a man clearly in the light at the end of a short hallway, and fired a three-round burst. The man fell to the ground. He had been shot through the neck and the face. Three-round bursts tend to climb. Four down. Mick stayed in a crouch near the back door and listened. After a minute of silence, Mick took charge.

"Delta, rear, one," he yelled loudly.

"Charlie, front, one," Taylor responded in kind.

"Bravo, front, two," David yelled.

"Clear it," Mick yelled.

Mick saw two doors in a short hallway in front of him. He believed Sofia to be in the room on the right, so he opened the door on the left first and pushed it in while staying in the hallway off to the left of the door. As the door swung in, Mick could see that it was a bathroom and that it was dark. He moved to the other side of the doorway and reach around inside the bathroom and felt for the light switch. He turned the light on. Two stalls, no feet beneath. He entered the bathroom and checked the stalls for anyone crouching on the fixtures inside. Both were empty. He left the light on and went back into the hallway.

Taylor and David went through the doorway to the large work area. David put his night-vision goggles back on and went through the doorway first. Nothing.

"Find the light," David said to Taylor.

Taylor found a light switch on the wall and turned the light on. David's night-vision goggles whited out and he reached up with his left hand and pushed them up on his head while Taylor scanned for targets. It took no time to clear the work area as it was mostly empty, with just a forklift inside. They left the work area and headed for the hallway at the rear of the office area. As they approached the hallway, they stayed well away from the opening.

"Bravo and Charlie, all clear," Taylor called out.

"Come," Mick called back.

Taylor and David entered the short hallway, stepping over the dead man. Mick pointed to the door to his right and Taylor and David posted up on either side of the door, with David behind Mick. Mick reached over to the door handle and pushed the door open. Taylor went left and Mick went right in the room. David stayed in the hallway, watching both the front door and the back door.

"Clear," Mick shouted.

It was a small office with a desk along the rear wall and filing cabinets along the doorway wall. A blonde woman was duct taped to a desk chair in the middle of the room. Sofia. Mick let go of his rifle and let it hang from the sling. He approached Sofia slowly.

"We are Americans," Mick said in a calming tone of voice. "We are here to take you home. Do you understand?"

Sofia nodded her head up and down vigorously, while tears streamed down her face.

"I am going to get my knife out to cut you loose," Mick said. "Okay?"

Again, Sofia nodded her head up and down vigorously.

Mick took his knife from the sheath at his ankle. He approached Sofia slowly and cut the tape holding her lower arms to the arms of the chair first. While Sofia worked the duct tape off of her mouth, Mick bent down and cut through the duct tape binding her legs to the legs of the chair.

As Mick began to rise, Sofia flew out of the chair at him, knocking him backwards. He scrambled to recover his balance. Sofia grabbed him around the waist and held on to him tightly and sobbed. His AR-15 was digging into his chest. He ignored it and put his arms around Sofia.

"It's okay," Mick said. "We are going to get you back to your family."

Mick turned his head to Taylor and said, "Call A and clean up."

Taylor called Attila and walked out into the hallway. He took two photographs of each dead man, one of their full body and one of their face. He went through their pockets, taking everything they had by way of identification, and putting it in a plastic bag. One bag for each man. Taylor took every set of keys he could find, off of the dead men and in the office. David kept watch on the front and rear doors.

When Sofia's sobs began to lessen, Mick asked, "Are you okay?"

Sofia nodded her head affirmatively.

"Are you hurt?"

Sofia shook her head negatively.

"Can you walk?"

"Yes." Sofia said, quietly.

Mick was judging Sofia's condition by her answers. The questions were designed to elicit the same information through both positive and negative answers. Sofia had to understand each question in order to know which answer to give, yes or no. Mick was satisfied that Sofia was functioning well enough to understand his directions to her.

"Do you need to use the bathroom?"

Sofia nodded her head yes. Mick walked Sofia over to the bathroom doorway. She did not let go of him.

"I'll wait for you here," he said.

"No, no," Sofia cried. She did not let go of him.

Mick walked her into the bathroom and to the stalls.

"I'll wait right here," he said.

Sofia looked up at him and did not let go initially. Slowly, she began to release her grip on Mick. Then she went into one of the stalls. Mick turned his back on her, to give her privacy while she could still see him. She did not close the stall door. During the short walk across the hallway to the bathroom and in the bathroom, Mick had satisfied himself that Sofia could walk and did not need to be carried out of the building.

When she was finished, she came out of the stall and took Mick's arm. He walked her over to the sink and she washed her hands while he stood right next to her. She wiped her hands on her jeans. There were no paper towels. She looked in the mirror and reached up to the side of her head where blood and hair were matted together. Mick could tell that it was a superficial wound that was no longer bleeding. If she touched it, she would probably open the wound again.

"Leave it," Mick said gently. "We don't have time now."

Sofia turned to Mick and grabbed his arm. As they came out of the bathroom, Taylor came up to Mick.

"Still need to ID the guy out front," he said.

"Okay," Mick said. "David, go cover Taylor. I'll cover the rear and watch Sofia."

David and Taylor went to the front door. David took the night-vision goggles off of his head and handed them to Taylor. Taylor put them on then flipped the wall switches to turn the outside light and the front office light off. Then he opened the door and waited a moment. Nothing. Taylor stepped outside, went down the short flight of steps, and over to the dead man in the dark. He took the two photographs, using the flash on his cell phone. Each time, his night-vision goggles whited out and he had to wait for them to readjust. Then he went through the man's pockets and bagged the contents. When he was done, he walked back to the stairs, pushed the goggles up on his head, and went up the stairs and into the office. David closed the door behind Taylor and locked it by turning the deadbolt. David and Taylor walked back to Mick in the hallway.

"Sofia, we are going to leave now," Mick said. "You can hold on to my belt loop, but I need to have my arms free. Do you understand?"

"Yes," Sofia said softly, and she switched her grip from his arm to one of his rear belt loops.

"Get the gate open," Mick said to Taylor.

David and Taylor went to the back door. David opened the damaged door and they waited a moment. Nothing. Taylor stepped outside as he lowered the night-vision goggles. He looked around the outside of the rear of the building and saw no one. He went down the short flight of stairs and walked to the back gate and tried to open it. It was locked. He went through the keys he had taken from the office first. One of the keys opened the gate. He opened the gate and saw Attila waiting in the car, parked next to the rear gate. He signaled to David.

Attila had taken the light bulb out of the interior light in the car and had turned the dash lights off. He had used the night-vision monocle to get into position at the rear gate of the compound without turning the headlights on. He had used the handbrake to come to a stop at the rear gate, ensuring that the brakes lights also did not come on.

"We're good," David said to Mick, then he turned off the last remaining light in the building.

Mick lowered his night vision goggles and walked to the door with Sofia clinging to his belt loop. He went out the door, down the short flight of stairs, across the short area between the building and the wall, through the gate, and to the rear passenger door of the car. He opened the car door. He did not even ask Sofia to get in the car, he just got in himself and she followed behind him. She was half on and half off of his lap. David got into the rear passenger seat on the other side. There was not enough room for the three of them.

"You are going to have to sit on my lap, Sofia," Mick said.

Sofia got on Mick's lap and David was able to get all the way in and close the door. Three people and two rifles in the back seat was a very tight fit. Taylor locked the gate, closed the rear passenger door where Mick and Sofia were sitting, and got into the front passenger seat of the car.

Taylor pulled out his radio and called the captain of the yacht, requesting that he meet them at the same location where he had dropped them off. Attila started the car and drove back to the road, with Taylor using the night-vision to see and directing Attila where to turn. Once the car was back on the main road, Attila turned the headlights on and headed northeast toward the marina.

Mick struggled to reach into his thigh pocket and retrieve a foil pouch. The pouch contained a slurry, not a solid and not quite a liquid, designed to be easily ingested by a person in a diminished physical condition. Mick handed the pouch to David to open. Then Mick handed the open pouch to Sofia.

"Please eat this," Mick said to her. "It is vitamins and electrolytes, things that will help you."

David opened a bottle of water and handed it to Mick. Sofia alternated between the slurry from the foil pouch and water from the bottle.

CHAPTER TWENTY-FOUR

Attila pulled into the marina. The yacht was waiting at the end of the dock. Mick, Taylor, David, and Sofia got out of the car. Sofia was still clinging to Mick's belt loop. He gently moved her hand to another belt loop so he could reach into his back pocket. He took out his wallet and pulled out two thousand euros.

"You are a good man," Mick said to Attila, as he handed him the money.

"There is no need," Attila said, rejecting the money.

"You deserve it," Mick said, as he forced the money on Attila and shook his hand.

Everyone, except Attila, walked down the dock to the yacht. Taylor and David at the ready, prepared for anything to happen, and Mick focusing on getting Sofia to the yacht. As soon as all four were aboard, the first mate cast off the lines tying the yacht to the dock and jumped onboard. The yacht headed out to sea.

Mick took Sofia into the cabin and Taylor and David followed. Mick sat Sofia down at the table and tried to disengage from her.

"Don't leave me," Sofia begged quietly.

"Okay," Mick said. "I won't leave you. But you are safe now. You need to process and accept that."

"Taylor, make the call," Mick said.

Taylor went to the radio and made the call, while David rooted around in the overhead cupboards and in the small refrigerator. He placed crackers, peanut butter, a butter knife, and several bottles of Orangina on the table.

"Eat and drink, Sofia," Mick said, as he opened two bottles of Orangina and gave one to Sofia.

"Are my brothers okay?" Sofia asked.

"Yes," Mick replied. "I spoke to them myself a few days ago. They miss you."

"They want us at Larnaca at first light," Taylor said. "Apparently, the captain already knows where."

Then Taylor went to tell the captain.

"David, how about some coffee," Mick said.

David laughed. "You hate my coffee," he said, as he went to start a pot of coffee.

At first light, on Thursday, the yacht pulled into dock at a private residence in Larnaca, on the Greek Cypriot side of Cyprus. Mick, Taylor, and David had stowed their rifles, extra magazines, knives, and night-vision devices back in the kit bags. They were each still armed with their Glocks.

They needed to interview Sofia but now was not the time. Ali had died at the compound. Ahmed had not been at the compound and they needed to find him.

Mick had tried to prepare Sofia for their coming separation, but she was still holding onto him. She was alternating between his forearm and his belt loop. Mick got up from the table and Sofia followed. They all went up on deck.

The back yard of the residence, including the dock, was filled with people. Most of them were heavily armed. Marines, wearing utilities and carrying M-16s, were on the dock. An Embassy photographer was taking pictures discreetly. Mick knew that the price of keeping regular journalists away was letting the Embassy photographer take the photographs. The photographs would be cropped to conceal his team's identities before being released to the press. Sofia's recovery was big news, and nothing was going to stop the United States government from promoting its victory over terrorism.

The U.S. Ambassador to Cyprus came aboard the yacht to speak to Sofia. He introduced himself and told her that her father would be arriving soon at the airport and she would be reunited with him. Silent tears ran down Sofia's cheeks at the mention of her father. She did not wipe them away.

Sofia asked, "My brothers too?"

He told her that he thought that they would be with her father.

Then the Ambassador made a mistake. The Ambassador had not noticed that Sofia had attached herself to Mick. He moved to get between Sofia and Mick to take Sofia off the yacht. Sofia reacted instinctively. She had been holding Mick's belt loop with her left hand and she grabbed him around the waist with her right hand.

The Ambassador had a pained looked on his face as he realized that Sofia was literally clinging to Mick.

"Ambassador, I'll stay with Sofia until her father arrives, if that is alright with you," Mick said, politely.

"Of course," the Ambassador said, not wanting to make the situation worse. He graciously waved his arm in a motion indicating that Mick and Sofia were to go ahead of him. Mick walked Sofia off of the yacht and on to the dock. The Ambassador followed them, and Taylor and David followed the Ambassador.

On the dock, the Marines formed up on either side of Mick and Sofia and they all walked around to the front of the residence where black Embassy vans with diplomatic license plates and heavily tinted windows were waiting. Mick let the Marines guide them to the correct vehicle. Then he got inside with Sofia. Taylor and David followed them. One of the Marines got into the front passenger seat. The Ambassador went to his own black luxury sedan.

It took a few minutes for the convoy to form up and the van to begin to move. Mick could see that the convoy had a Greek Cypriot police escort and was, therefore, able to blow through red lights. They drove straight to a private aviation hangar at the Larnaca airport. Mick took Sofia into the private lounge and sat down beside her. Two Marines took up positions at each of the doors to the lounge, the general entry door and the door leading to the tarmac. Taylor and David found seats nearby. The Ambassador to Cyprus sat across from Sofia. To his credit, he did not try to engage her in small talk. He just waited with her.

Mick watched as the Embassy photographer quietly entered the lounge and took an unobtrusive position near the wall. He would not intrude on the family reunion, but he was certainly going to document it.

It was not long before Ambassador Sopko's jet touched down and taxied to the hangar. Mick could tell the jet had landed by the increased activity in the lounge. Sofia seemed oblivious. In fact, she looked exhausted. Her head was laying on his bicep. Her eyes were closed but Mick knew she was not asleep because her two-handed grip on his forearm was still tight.

As people began filing out to the hangar, Mick gently roused Sofia. He wanted her to be ready to greet her father when he walked into the lounge.

"I think your father is coming soon," he said softly.

Sofia perked up immediately and started looking around the lounge. Mick stood up and Sofia did too. He walked her over to the area near the doorway into the lounge from the tarmac. Two men in black suits came into the lounge. Part of the Ambassador's security detail. Moments later, Ambassador Sopko walked through the doorway.

"Daddy!" Sofia cried out but she did not leave Mick's side.

Ambassador Sopko ran the few steps to Sofia and hugged her tight. Sofia hugged him back with one arm. Her right hand stayed firmly attached to Mick's forearm. Seconds later, Peter and Matthew came into the lounge together. Sofia saw them and let go of Mick. She grabbed them both and hugged them together.

Mick moved away to let the family have some privacy. He stood by the Ambassador to Cyprus and waited, like everyone else in the lounge. The Ambassador to Cyprus turned to Mick, put out his hand to shake hands, and said, "Thank you." Mick shook his hand.

When the family was reunited and feeling a little more at ease, Ambassador Sopko detached himself from his children and came over to where Mick, Taylor, and David were standing.

"Thank you," he said, over and over as he shook their hands, one by one. "I will never forget what you have done for me and for Sofia."

After waiting for the Ambassador to finish his thanks, Mick turned to business.

"Sir, what are your plans? We need to interview Sofia. Ahmed got away. He wasn't at the compound."

Ambassador Sopko turned his head and looked at his children. Then he turned back to Mick.

"I am taking the children to Edelweiss, in Germany," he said. "We are flying there directly from here. I can't take her back to Greece just yet. We would be hounded by the press. I have been advised that she needs to be evaluated by medical doctors and that she needs a safe and secure environment while that happens. Come with us. You can interview her when she is ready."

"That works," Mick said. "Sir, I must ask you not to disclose anything you know from our investigation to Sofia."

"Yes, I understand," the Ambassador said. "It was already explained to me that the psychiatrists do not want Sofia to be given any outside information about her kidnapping."

"You have been given good advice," Mick said. "The cut on her head is superficial, the blood in her blonde hair makes it look worse than it is. But she does need to be evaluated by doctors. The trauma of being held captive can be long-lasting and needs to be addressed as soon as possible. Our military doctors in Germany are experienced in dealing with this type of situation."

The Ambassador did not respond. He stood silently for a moment, thinking. Mick had only confirmed what he had been told by the experts he had consulted. As he turned to rejoin his children, he made one final remark.

"Find that bastard and make him pay. If you need anything, just ask."

CHAPTER TWENTY-FIVE

It was late afternoon on Thursday when they arrived at Edelweiss, in Garmisch, Germany. It had taken longer than Mick had expected to prepare to leave Cyprus. Food had been delivered to the private aviation hangar in Larnaca. The Ambassador had encouraged Sofia to eat as the family sat closely together. She had picked at some fruit. She had not eaten anything close to a meal. Sofia had sat between her brothers, one hand on each of them most of the time. She had looked physically exhausted and emotionally drained. Matthew never left her side.

Mick had been careful to stay within her forward field of vision, not intrusively close but always within her sight. He had delegated most of his responsibilities to Taylor and David. They had reported in to Bronwyn Richards, arranged for the team to accompany Sofia to Germany, and arranged for their kit and gear to be transferred from the yacht to the plane.

The Ambassador's plane had flown from Larnaca to Munich. The plane was a luxury jet with large leather seats set up in groupings of four. The family sat together, with Sofia in the backward-facing aisle seat and Matthew next to her in the backward-facing window seat. The Ambassador's security team sat in the seat group directly across the aisle from the family. Mick and his team sat in the seating group directly behind the security detail, with Mick in the forward-facing aisle seat. Sofia could see him.

The plane had been met at the Munich Airport by two German officials who boarded the plane and welcomed the Ambassador and his family to Germany. The normal immigration process was waived. No one had to show a passport which was a good thing because the team only had their alias passports.

They had transferred to United States Army helicopters at the airport. Mick went with the family, Taylor and David rode in a separate helicopter. They were flown to Edelweiss.

The Edelweiss Lodge and Resort is a limited access U.S. Armed Forces Recreation Center in Bavaria. It has a hotel, a main dining facility and other smaller eateries, a bar, a gym, and other recreational facilities. It offers the ability to take tours of tourist attractions in the surrounding area, both in Germany and in other nearby countries, scheduled through the hotel with English speaking tour guides. A place designed to provide vacationing military personnel and their families with a safe, comfortable, enjoyable, and relaxing environment. Not exactly a four-star luxury place but a slice of home in a foreign country for those serving overseas.

It was the right place for Sofia and the Sopko family. The primary benefit was that it was not in Greece or the United States, where the family could be expected to be hounded by the press. It was a secure little slice of America in southern Germany, with self-contained amenities. America without actually being in America and Germany without actually having to deal with the natural difficulties of navigating your way around in a foreign country.

Ambassador Sopko's entourage took over a whole wing of the second floor of the hotel. Ambassador Sopko had two rooms for his family and two rooms for his security detail. Mick was given his own room, while Taylor and

David shared a room. Each room was a small suite and had two queen sized beds and a seating area.

Sofia stood in the hallway and watched Mick open the door to his room before she would enter one of the rooms assigned to her family. Her brothers had gone into the room first. Ambassador Sopko locked eyes with Mick as he waited patiently with Sofia in the hallway until Mick went into his room. Mick nodded to both of them, conveying the message to both that he was right there, close by, before he entered his room.

Inside his room, Mick stripped out of his clothes, went into the bathroom, and took a long hot shower. He came out of the bathroom with a large, soft towel wrapped around his waist. He went directly to the nearest bed and fell into it. He was exhausted and was asleep within minutes.

Mick was awakened by the ringing of the telephone on the nightstand Friday morning. He had slept like a rock and it took him a moment to recognize his room. He answered the phone. It was Ambassador Sopko. He wanted to know if Mick would accompany them to breakfast. It was phrased like a polite invitation. But Mick understood that he was needed to get Sofia to go down for breakfast. He asked them to wait ten minutes and hung up the phone.

Mick got out of bed and walked to the door. He opened his door and saw his gear bag sitting in the hallway next to the door. The Agency had secured the team bags upon their arrival at Edelweiss. Mick had fallen asleep before his gear had been delivered. He grabbed the bag and brought it in to the room. He set the bag on the bed and opened it up. All the firearms, ammunition, and tactical items had been removed. The bag now held mostly clothing.

Mick called the operator and was connected to Taylor and David's room. He quickly told Taylor that he was going down to breakfast with the Sopko family in ten minutes. Taylor said they would see him down there.

Mick took his ditty bag into the bathroom and quickly brushed his teeth and shaved. He dressed in fresh underwear, tactical pants, and a polo shirt. He put on clean socks and his black boots. He put his wallet in his pocket and his compass on his belt. He debated momentarily with himself about wearing his jacket to conceal his Glock, which he had been wearing when he arrived. He decided against taking it and walked over to the wall safe in the closet. He set the combination then retrieved his Glock and spare magazines from his pile of clothes on the floor. He placed the Glock and the magazines in the safe and closed the door.

The Ambassador's security team would be armed and Sofia was in no real danger while in the recreation center. Mick's job protecting Sofia, physically, was officially done. He mentally shifted back into investigator mode. His job now was to stay relatively close to Sofia and to evaluate her until he felt they could interview her.

After stretching out his body and loosening his muscles, he walked out into the hallway. He walked two rooms down the hall. The security man standing in front of the door knocked on it as Mick approached. The Ambassador opened the door.

"Good morning, Mick," he said, a little too exuberantly. "We are ready to go."

He called back into the room for his children.

Peter came out first, then Sofia came out holding Matthew's hand. She looked a lot better, but she still had a tiredness about her. She had showered and changed into clean clothes. The cut on her head was largely concealed by her clean hair. She was wearing clean jeans and a clean T-shirt. She had the same running shoes she had been wearing when Mick had first seen her.

"Good morning," Sofia said softly. She reached out and gently touched Mick's arm briefly, but she did not hold on to him.

"Good morning," Mick replied, as he stepped back to allow Sofia and Matthew space to pass him together. "Looks like someone forgot to pack shoes for you, Sofia."

Sofia glanced down at her feet and then looked back into Mick's eyes. There was no smile to match Mick's smile. Peter led the way to the elevator, followed by Sofia and Matthew, then the Ambassador and Mick, and finally the security man.

Breakfast was served buffet style in the dining facility, with two main service lines. One for hot foods and one for cold foods, with drinks at an island between the two lines. Matthew picked up a tray and handed it to Sofia. Then he picked one up for himself. Matthew headed for the bacon and eggs hot line. Sofia went with him. The Ambassador and Mick followed behind. Peter was already ahead of them in the same line.

At the end of the line, Sofia had nothing on her tray. The Ambassador looked at Mick concerned. Mick looked around, saw an employee, and signaled for the employee to come to him. He handed the young woman his tray and asked her to follow Matthew and to put the tray on his table. The young woman took the tray from him and listened to him but her eyes kept darting over to Sofia. The young woman hurried away to follow Matthew with the tray.

"Let's go look at the cold line," Mick said to Sofia, as he gently touched her forearm.

She looked up at him, relief apparent in her face. They walked over to the cold line and Sofia choose a pastry and a banana. Then Mick guided her over to the drink island. Sofia and Mick both got cups of coffee and glasses of orange juice. They walked through the dining room to a large round table in the corner, where Sofia's family was seated. Two seats had been left empty between Peter and Matthew. Mick's tray had been placed in the seat next to Peter. Mick nodded to Taylor and David seated at a table nearby with one of the security men.

When everyone was seated at the table, Ambassador Sopko said, "Let us give thanks." And he led the family in prayer.

After the prayer, breakfast began in awkward silence, with everyone eating and no one talking. Ambassador Sopko tried twice to get a conversation going, to no avail.

"Can we go to see Neuschwanstein Castle, Sofia?" Matthew asked Sofia. "It looks great on the posters. Like a real fairy tale."

For a moment Sofia did not respond. But then she turned to Matthew, put her arm around his shoulder, and pulled him in close to her.

"Of course, we can go to see a fairy tale castle," she said, while smiling at Matthew.

Sofia's smile appeared forced but focusing on her brother distracted her from the harrowing events of the last week, at least for a little while. The three children continued to talk about the castle and other sights they wanted to see. Sofia's participation was limited but it was there. She was trying.

When breakfast was over, they headed back to their rooms. Sofia did not hold on to anyone. In the hallway, Sofia did not hesitate to see where Mick was going before entering her room. Ambassador Sopko stopped Mick before he returned to his own room.

"We won't be going anywhere today," he said. "The doctors would like to spend time with Sofia. It will probably take most of the day. Thank you for coming to breakfast with us."

"It is too early to make any long-term assessment," Mick said. "She has been through a lot. Being a captive is dehumanizing. She believes she survived by being compliant, subject to the will of others. It has temporarily stripped her of her capacity to exercise her own will. That is why she clings to others, me because she feels safe with me, and Matthew because she feels a compelling need to protect him, which supersedes even her own need for protection. It will take some time, but she is a strong woman."

"I can't thank you enough for what you have done for Sofia," the Ambassador said. "I did not realize until we were on the plane coming here that you were intentionally positioning yourself to always be within Sofia's view. I watched her seek you out with her eyes every few minutes. Had I realized earlier, I would have had you sit next to her. I feel like I am blundering my way through this."

"You are doing fine," Mick replied. "Being with you and the boys is the best thing for her right now."

"May I impose upon you to eat with us the rest of today and tomorrow?" The Ambassador asked Mick. "I want Sofia to feel as safe as possible when we are out among other people."

"Absolutely," Mick said. "Not a problem."

Mick went to Taylor and David's room. He knocked on the door and Taylor opened it. Mick went into the room and called both Taylor and David over to him.

"Good job, guys," he said. "You both did fantastic work. Jason is going to be pissed that he got stuck with babysitting the Musa family, while we are here at Edelweiss."

They laughed and congratulated each other on the successful rescue of Sofia. Then Mick turned the conversation back to work.

"Have we heard anything from Bronwyn?" Mick asked them.

"No," Taylor replied. "Everything we took off of the dead guys was sent back to Bronwyn as were the photographs of the dead guys. So far, no word."

"Any idea when our real passports and credit cards will catch up to us?" Mick asked.

"They should be arriving sometime today," David said. "In the meantime, all of our expenses, hotel, meals, whatnot, have been taken care of. Charge everything to the room."

Mick then asked, "How are we for money?"

They each reached into their pockets, took out their wallets, and took out their cash. They counted out the money. They had over eleven thousand euros and six thousand dollars, combined. Taylor handed Mick a thousand euros so that they each had roughly the same amount.

"Who is volunteering to write the report?" Mick asked.

Taylor and David laughed. No one was ever lucky enough to get out of writing the report. Each of them had to contribute because each of them had a unique role, which came with unique vantage points and unique observations. Standard operating procedure was that only one final report would be submitted. The reality was that they would each write out their portion of the report, recalling as much significant detail as possible, then they would work together to combine the three into one cohesive narrative. A detailed mission summary. Detailed in the relevant parts. Detailed enough to answer the most obvious questions that would surely be asked. A summary because it was impossible to include everything. One report that they all agreed on. Better than three disjointed and possibly conflicting reports. One report that would be read by very few people. One report that would quickly be filed away, possibly to never be seen by human eyes again.

"Today is a down day," Mick said. "No word yet from Bronwyn and Sofia will be with the doctors all day. Let's get some preliminary observations written out while our memories are still fresh then we can chill."

"Drinks tonight in the bar after dinner," Taylor said.

Mick and David agreed. The mention of dinner reminded Mick to tell the others that he would be eating with the Sopko family for a couple of days.

Mick ate lunch and dinner with Sofia and her family. Taylor and David ate at a table next to them each time. Otherwise, the team did not leave the room. They worked on the report and they reviewed the mission together. Their passports and credit cards arrived in the late afternoon.

After dinner, Mick, Taylor, and David walked together into the bar at Edelweiss and took seats at the bar. It was not a big place, and it was not full. It was early yet. Mick ordered three beers and gave the bartender his room number.

"No need," the bartender said. "For you three, the drinks are on the house all night."

The bartender placed three bottles of beer on coasters in front of them and they thanked him.

"We have to stop dressing alike," Mick said to Taylor and David.

They all laughed. There was no secret as to who they were at Edelweiss. The rest of the world would never know, but the American military at Edelweiss had quickly figured it out. They had seen and heard the news of Sofia's rescue being reported all day long on AFN, the Armed Forces Network, and on AFRS, the Armed Forces Radio Service. Many of them had seen Sofia and her family at the large table in the corner of the dining room during meals. Yet, not a single person had approached the Sopko family, at least while Mick had been with them. The family was politely being given space in the midst of the military community. The Ambassador's security personnel were obvious to anyone who cared to notice. Many noticed then politely ignored the alert and observant armed men in suits attempting to be discreet. It had probably taken a little longer to put Mick's team into context but not too much longer. The team had an unmistakable look about them. Unmistakable in a community where that particular look had been born.

They had just finished their beers and ordered another round when a man, dressed in a suit, came into the bar and walked over to them. He was carrying an extra-large manila envelope and he had searched them out. It was time to go back to work.

Mick took the envelope from the man, cancelled their just placed re-up order, and they went up to Mick's room, while the man in the suit left. Once inside the room, Mick opened the envelope. It contained papers and aerial surveillance photographs of the area in and around the compound in Cyprus, many of the photographs were thermal images, some were not. There were date and time stamps on the photographs. Mick laid the photographs out and they all studied them.

"Ahmed left in the car parked out back shortly before we started hiking in to the compound," Mick said. The thermal photographs confirmed it. Only one person had left in the car. Ahmed had been there when the team left Trikomo but had left in the car before they got to the compound. He had turned right on the main road, heading northeast away from the compound.

"He couldn't have known we were coming," Taylor said. "He left to do something. It had to have been important to him for him to leave the compound."

"In the middle of the night, he was probably going to get more men," David said. "The compound was not well defended. He knew he needed more men."

"You are probably right," Mick said. "If the compound was a fallback location like it appears to have been, it may have taken him that long to get more personnel. And he would have wanted to see them personally before letting them know where the compound was located."

"Water under the bridge," David said. "Where is Ahmed now?"

The photographs had no answer to that question. Mick divided the reports amongst them, and they read through them.

"Of the four dead guys, two were Lebanese and two were Turkish Cypriots," Taylor said. "Mick shot Ali, he was at the back, closest to Sofia. David shot the other Lebanese guy at the door. He also got one Turkish Cypriot guy headed for the gate. And I shot the Turkish Cypriot guy trying to get out of the office and into the work area side of the building."

"Still no further substantive information about Ali," Mick said. "Lebanese, with a Syrian passport. The passport is genuine, not forged, but the identity is false. It's confirmed that he flew from Larnaca to Athens on the same flight as Ahmed. And we know he was the one with Ahmed when Sofia was taken. The only new information is that he and Ahmed also flew from Syria to Cyprus the same day and passed through EU immigration control upon entry to Cyprus. There was nothing personal in his pocket items. His phone communicated only with one number, Ahmed. It was a throw away phone, just like Sami's phone."

"Ahmed's Syrian passport identity and phone are long gone by now," Taylor said. "So, none of that information helps us."

"The two Turkish Cypriots were nobodies," David said. "Young guys in their mid-twenties, with valid local identification. Their pocket items were all everyday junk. Nothing of value. Neither had a cell phone on them."

"Probably temporary help to deal with locals, when necessary," Taylor said. "If we had not killed them, Ahmed would have done so eventually. He couldn't leave local witnesses."

"The last Lebanese guy was in the import/export business in Nicosia," Mick said. "He had valid identification. No known connection to Hezbollah but he was originally from south Lebanon. His pocket items were junk, nothing useful. His cell phone is still be analyzed. Big download. Apparently, he never deleted anything. But no results from the phone dump yet."

"Just because we don't know about a connection to Hezbollah doesn't mean there isn't one," David said. "He was perfectly situated. A useful asset living in Cyprus. He could find the compound and rent or get access to it. Maybe he owned it. And they had to contact him somehow. Maybe the phone dump will have something of value after it is analyzed."

"In any event, all of this tells us nothing about where Ahmed is now," Mick said. "The only things we know for certain are the connections to Lebanon and Syria."

"It also tells us we made our move at exactly the right time," Taylor said. "Four men to deal with, not five. And the leader, Ahmed, was gone at the time. He would have put up more resistance and maybe even tried to kill Sofia, just to deprive us of the rescue."

"Yes," Mick said. "Luck was on our side this time. But now we still have to find Ahmed."

CHAPTER TWENTY-SIX

Saturday morning Mick was awake and fully dressed when Ambassador Sopko's call for breakfast came. Mick went into the hallway and the family was already coming out of one of their rooms. The two boys walked out of the room together.

Good morning, Mick," Sofia said, with a small shy smile as she walked out of the room. She came over to him but did not touch him. She just walked down the hall beside him.

"Good morning to you, Sofia," Mick said. "You look more rested today. Are you feeling stronger?"

"Yes," she replied. "Thank you. I need to thank you for saving me. I am sorry I didn't say it before."

"You are welcome," was all Mick said in reply.

They got in the elevator and went downstairs to the dining facility. Mick walked over to the cold line and Sofia followed him. Mick caught Taylor's attention. Taylor was already in the hot line. Taylor nodded his understanding.

Mick and Sofia were each selecting items from the cold buffet then Sofia stopped and turned to Mick.

"I made a mistake," she said, very quietly. "I should have screamed and ran but I didn't. My mistake caused you to have to risk your life. I'm sorry."

Mick reached over, took her hand in his, and gave it a light squeeze before letting go. "You are not responsible for this," he said. "No one blames you. Don't blame yourself."

Sofia looked up at him with a small smile of relief on her face. There were tears in her eyes but only one tear fell, and she quickly wiped it away.

When Mick and Sofia were about to pass the table Taylor and David were sitting at, Sofia stopped abruptly. Mick almost ran his tray into Sofia's back because he had been looking at the tray of bacon and eggs that Taylor had gotten for him which was sitting on their table.

"Dad," Sofia called to her father. "I'm going to eat over here, if that is okay."

Ambassador Sopko looked to Mick first. Mick nodded affirmatively.

"Fine, honey," he said to Sofia. "Whatever you like."

Sofia took the empty place at their table between David and Taylor. Mick consolidated his cold items with the items on his hot tray, then placed the empty tray under the full tray, and sat down opposite of Sofia. Then he began to eat his bacon and eggs. He took the first mouthful. He stopped mid-chew when he heard laughing. He looked up. Sofia was laughing at him.

"You went through the cold buffet just for me," she said. "Thank you. Again."

The Sopko family table had gone silent and the family had all turned to look at Sofia when they had heard her laugh. Mick finished chewing and swallowed his mouthful of food.

"I do like bacon, eggs, and toast for breakfast," Mick said sheepishly, pointing to his overflowing tray. "As you can see, I am not missing out this morning."

He smiled at Sofia while Taylor and David started laughing.

"And coffee," Taylor said. "Mick drinks coffee twenty-four hours a day. You should see him when there is no coffee in the morning."

The whole table laughed. When the laughter died down, Mick introduced Sofia to Taylor and David. She knew who they were but now it was different. She was having breakfast with people she did not really know.

They ate and they all talked, Sofia included. They talked about trivial things, mostly where they had each gone to school, what they had majored in, and what languages they spoke. Safe topics. It was a relaxed breakfast.

When they were done, they all headed out into the lobby. Matthew took Sofia by the hand and led her over to the tourism information area to see what there was to see and do nearby. Matthew was speaking excitedly. Sofia was attentive. Ambassador Sopko waited with Mick.

"Thank you, again," the Ambassador said. "You are doing her so much good."

Mick chuckled. "That wasn't me," he said, referring to breakfast. "That was all her."

"But she trusts you," the Ambassador responded.

"I admire the way she is fighting back," Mick said. "She is fighting her fear. She wants to conquer it. I think that she will. And it will be all her, because no one else can do it for her, it has to be all her."

The Ambassador's gaze turned back to Sofia. "She will be with the doctors this morning," he said. "But I would like to get her and the boys outside to do something this afternoon. Would you be able to accompany us?"

"Sure," Mick replied. "If the doctors think Sofia is ready to go out, I will be available."

Mick, Taylor, and David spent the morning in the gym then relaxing. At lunch, Sofia insisted that they all join her family at the large circular table, which could comfortably seat eight.

The lunch talk was all about the sights available to see in the area over the next several days. Both Peter and Matthew had clearly been studying the tourist brochures. Peter's top choice was Kehlsteinhaus, Hitler's Eagle's Nest, near Berchtesgaden. Matthew's top choice was still the Neuschwanstein Castle, which he called the fairy tale castle. Sofia expressed no preference but was agreeable to anything. Toward the end of lunch, Ambassador Sopko announced that, today, they would go to Zugspitze, the highest mountain in Germany, and they would look down into Austria. It was close to Edelweiss and he had been able to arrange last minute transportation late that morning. They would make arrangements to see the other sights over the next few days when they returned from Zugspitze. He invited Taylor and David to come along on the Zugspitze trip as well and they accepted the invitation.

After lunch they all went up to their rooms to get jackets. It would be a lot colder at the top of the mountain. There was a private tour bus waiting for their party outside the lobby, with a driver and a tour guide. The party included the Sopko family of four, the team of three, and four security personnel.

The boys were excited to be going somewhere. Sofia was happy that the boys were happy but there was a tenseness in her posture. The way she held herself was stiff and formal, not casual. She was clearly a little apprehensive about leaving the safety of Edelweiss.

There were more than enough seats on the bus. Everyone took two seats to themselves. Two security men had the seats in the front row, then the family, with the team behind. Finally, two security men sat the farthest back in the bus. Mick made sure he sat on the side opposite of the side Sofia had chosen. Mick was directly behind the Ambassador and across the aisle and one row back from Sofia.

They rode to the Eibsee-Seilbahn cable car, which they took to the top. The views of the mountains from the cable car were amazing. The mountain peaks were snow covered, with greenery running down the lower sides of the mountains. The cable car ride took about ten minutes.

When they arrived at the top, it was like being in another world. The sun was shining down on the snowy mountain peaks and the eternal high glaciers. The terrain below alternated between rugged mountain, brilliant snow-covered glaciers, and greenery. Every view was spectacular. The guide informed them that the mountain was the tallest in Germany at 2,962 meters high, almost 10,000 feet.

Taylor and David went with Peter and Matthew while they climbed out to the golden cross at the summit. The boys posed for Sofia while she took photographs of them at the top of Germany with the camera feature in a cell phone. They spent a little less than an hour walking around at the top, just looking out at the views.

The tour guide had said that they could see other countries from the top of the Zugspitze. Mick used the compass clipped onto his belt to orient himself. He looked out into Austria and further out into Italy to the south. Then he turned to the southwest and looked out to Switzerland and Liechtenstein.

They stopped into the restaurant where they had desserts before heading back down on the cable car to the bus. The Germans know how to make cakes and other desserts. Even in a restaurant catering to tourists, the desserts were delicious, tasty and moist, like freshly made cakes should be.

While there were some other tourists at Zugspitze, they were not approached by anyone. There were a few double takes at Sofia and the Ambassador. That was to be expected. Their photographs had been shown wall to wall on the news for days. They were not hard to recognize, particularly since they were both together in the same group. Mick had seen several people take pictures of Sofia. But it seemed to Mick that the other tourists were going out of their way to keep their distance from Sofia, to give her space. Having an obvious security detail probably helped.

On the bus ride back to Edelweiss, the children talked and laughed together. They all looked happy. Sofia looked relaxed. When they arrived back at Edelweiss in the late afternoon, Sofia went with Peter, Matthew, and her father back to their room, without a backward glance at Mick. Taylor saw Mick watching Sofia walk away.

"She's over you, buddy," Taylor said, while laughing. "Next, you won't be invited to dinner."

"You think?" Mick replied, as he smacked Taylor lightly in the abdomen, while laughing too. Mick was amazed at how quickly Sofia seemed to be coming back from her experience. It was time. She could handle being interviewed.

Mick was invited to dinner that night. They all were. They sat at the large circular table with family again.

After dinner, Mick asked the Ambassador if they could talk privately. The Ambassador sent his children back to their rooms with the security detail. Mick and the Ambassador went into the bar, just the two of them, and sat at a table in the back corner. A waitress came over to them, they ordered drinks, and the waitress left.

"We need to interview Sofia," Mick said. "I think it's time."

The Ambassador asked, "When do you want to do it?"

"Tomorrow morning, after breakfast," Mick said.

"I know you need to do it," the Ambassador said. "I just didn't want to think about it. I didn't want to think about her having to relive it."

"Maybe you could take the boys somewhere while we do it," Mick suggested. "Or at least send the boys off with your security team to do something."

"I can't leave her alone yet," the Ambassador said. "But I'll send the boys."

They stopped talking while the waitress delivered their drinks and left.

"She won't be alone," Mick said. "I'll be with her."

"Thank God for that," the Ambassador said. "She trusts you. Hell, I trust you. You found Sofia and brought her back to me."

"Thank you for saying so but that is my job," Mick said. "And I had a lot of help."

"And now your job is to find the ringleader, not to keep holding Sofia's hand," the Ambassador said. "Holding Sofia's hand is my job. I understand. But you will probably leave after you interview her. Please, promise me you won't leave Sofia a mess. I don't think I could handle it."

"Tomorrow is Sunday," Mick said. "We won't leave until Monday, at the earliest. As for Sofia, I'll do my best."

"Okay," the Ambassador said, resigned to the idea. "You're right. She'll be safe with you and the boys could use some attention from their dad. I'll take them out tomorrow."

They all ate breakfast together Sunday morning then returned to their rooms. As the Ambassador and his sons were leaving for the day, they dropped Sofia off at Mick's room.

She looked the same as she had at breakfast. She looked good. Only after Mick closed the door and directed her to a chair did her posture change. She became tense and sat formally on the chair, almost rigidly.

Mick looked over to Taylor, seated nearby, and nodded slightly towards Sofia, urging him to use some of his famous bedside manner to put her at ease. Taylor shook his head negatively. It was almost imperceptible, but Mick caught it. Then Taylor jutted his chin forward slightly to say this is all on you. Taylor had been the only one of the three of them who thought it was too soon to interview Sofia. Now he was making Mick bear the full burden of his own decision.

Mick sat down in the remaining chair, directly across from Sofia. He leaned forward at the edge of his chair.

"Sofia, you don't need to be scared," Mick began. "We are just going to talk about what happened. If, at any point, you need a break, we will take a break. We are in no hurry today."

"Do you understand?" Mick concluded, seeking affirmation.

The moment Mick said do you understand, tears leaked from Sofia's eyes and rolled down her cheeks. Mick knew immediately what he had done. That was exactly what he had said to her when they had entered the office and he had first encountered her. In fact, all throughout her rescue, he had sought constant affirmation of her understanding of his actions and his directions to her. At the time, it had been necessary. He had been gauging her level of traumatization and trying to communicate clearly so as not to add to her trauma. Now, with one question, he had thrown her mentally back to the most traumatic time in her life.

Unfortunately, he could not start all over so, instead, he tried to be gentler in his tone and questioning. "Sofia, it would help me if you would tell me as much as you remember about what happened to you."

Sofia nodded her head and took a deep breath. She was silent for a long moment. Then she began to talk quietly, methodically going through the events.

She started in the morning, with her and her brothers walking in the Plaka with Nikolas. She described separating from her brothers, with the boys going to see ruins and her going to a church. Her story was the same as theirs had been. She described sending Nikolas to the car and going into the church alone. It was the same as Nikolas Pappas had described. Her description of what happened in the church was almost identical to that told by Athena Vassaly, except Sofia included what was said to her and what she was thinking during that time. She admitted that it was the threat to her brothers that was her undoing. It overwhelmed her thinking. With a split-second choice between saving herself or saving them, she had immediately chosen them.

She described the time in the van and the time on the fishing boat, being kept in a closet. She explained how she spent her time in the closet thinking about what had happened in the church or sleeping to avoid thinking about what had happened in the church. Her final conclusion was that she had made a grave mistake. They had given her no proof of a real threat to her brothers. Just saying it had been enough to make her choose to submit.

It was clear to Mick that Sofia was still deeply conflicted about her choice. She knew that she would always choose her brothers over herself. But she had started second guessing herself on the boat. She had started to question whether the boys had really been in danger. And, after the fact, seeing that the boys had not been harmed was cementing in her mind the conclusion that she was the one at fault, that she had done the wrong thing. She was the victim and, yet, she was blaming herself.

Mick resisted the urge to comfort her, to explain to her in detail that it was not her fault. He had seen it before, and he knew it was true, but he was not really qualified to deal with Sofia's emotional struggle. That was a job for the doctors. Mick knew that, if he tried to help her, he could actually do more harm than good. He knew more about her kidnapping than she knew. He had to stay in his own lane.

When Sofia described being bound with duct tape and being put into a body bag, she began sobbing.

"I thought they were going to kill me," she said over and over again.

Taylor got up and went into the bathroom. He returned and handed Sofia a box of tissues. She thanked him and wiped her eyes and blew her nose as she struggled to gain control again.

Sofia described being hit in the head and losing consciousness for a while. She described waking up in the pitch blackness, her arms and legs bound and duct tape over her mouth. She described the terror she felt when she realized that she was in the body bag. She had never been so scared in her life. She was sure they were going to kill her. But they didn't.

When they took her out of the body bag, she was in the room where she was found. They had bound her to the chair with duct tape and they kept her bound from then on, except to eat and use the bathroom. To go to the bathroom, the French speaking man cut the tape off of her legs and arms and he always went into the bathroom with her. He re-taped her legs and arms when she was back on the chair in the room. To eat, the same man would take the tape off of only her mouth and one arm. He replaced it when she was finished eating.

As Sofia spoke, she subconsciously rubbed her arms where the tape had been. On the smaller side of the average woman to begin with, she seemed to shrink even smaller in the chair as the interview wore on.

Sofia described hearing gun shots and not being scared. She just knew it had to be a rescue attempt and she was anxious for them to succeed and to get to her. She refused to consider any possibility other than a rescue attempt. After the gunfire stopped, she had gotten impatient while waiting for the door to open. She did not know what was happening then, but she heard English being spoken periodically. When the team came through the door, she knew they were there for her.

Sofia began to cry again. But she was smiling slightly, while wiping the tears away with tissues balled up in her hands.

"I'm sorry," she said, looking directly first at Mick then Taylor. "They are tears of relief. So much happened and I just knew you were there to rescue me."

They waited a moment for Sofia to regain control of herself. Now that she had related the whole story all the way through, they needed to ask questions. They asked about the French-speaking man. They were careful to call him the French-speaking man because that was what she had called him. She did not know his name, so they did not speak his name.

In answer to their questions, she said that he was in charge. He told the other men what to do. On the boat, he was the one she saw most often. She knew the other man was called Ali because she heard the French-speaking man call for him using that name. She knew others were on the boat, but she never saw them. She thought they were speaking Arabic, but she could not be sure. In the office, the French-speaking man was the only man who dealt with her. Again, she knew there were other men around because she heard them occasionally, but she only saw one man sitting by a door when she was taken across the hall to use the bathroom. She heard what she thought was Arabic and a different language she also did not know.

"Describe the French-speaking man's mood while at the office?"

"He was cross," Sofia said. "He was yelling at the others. Not really yelling, but like barking orders at them."

"Did his mood change between when you were on the boat and when you were in the office?" Mick asked her.

"Yes," Sofia replied. "On the boat he was nice. Not really nice, but not mean. And he was patient with me. He let me go up on deck at night to stretch and get fresh air. Then once they put me in the body bag, everything changed. He had no patience anymore. He was rougher and meaner."

"Did they ever hurt you?"

"Just once, really," Sofia said. "Of course, it hurt to be cramped in the closet, it hurt to be taped to the chair, it hurt when the tape was pulled off of my skin. But if you are asking if they beat me, no, they did not. The only time they intentionally hurt me was when Ali hit me in the head."

Sofia subconsciously touched the scab on her scalp under her hair. Mick paused, to gather his thoughts and to formulate the next question.

"It gave me hope," Sofia continued, unasked. "I thought it meant that they were treating me like a hostage and not a prisoner, if that makes sense."

Mick and Taylor both nodded to show her that they understood what she was trying to explain. Then Mick drilled down about the French-speaking man, trying to find out if she knew anything more about him. Other than a very accurate physical description, that he was in charge, and that he spoke French and likely Arabic, she could not provide any useful information.

Ahmed was clearly excellent at operational security. He did not speak to Sofia, except when necessary. He limited the people who saw and interacted with Sofia to himself and Ali. Mick doubted that Ahmed would have provided Sofia with any useful information, even if she had understood the language he and Ali were using to communicate between themselves. A whole week with him, and Sofia did not even have a name for Ahmed.

Mick looked at Taylor to see if he had any other questions. Taylor looked up from his notes and indicated that he did not.

"Why did they take me?" Sofia asked, pleading for an answer with her eyes.

"We don't know," Mick said. "We have to assume they took you because of who your father is and that they were going to ransom you to the government. But because they did not make any demands before you were rescued, we cannot be sure."

Sofia did not know about Sami Musa's involvement and how specifically she had been targeted and they did not tell her. At this stage in her recovery, it would set her back. If she knew, she would begin to doubt everyone, including those she needed to trust. The knowledge that she had been betrayed by a friend from school would make the whole situation worse. And she would blame herself even more.

They were done. Mick always knew an interview was done when the person being questioned became the questioner. It was lunch time, so Mick suggested they go down to the dining facility. He wanted to put Sofia in a safe but public place to get her mind off of the interview and to cut off any further questioning from her.

David met them in the hallway on their way to the dining facility. He had heard the entire interview from in his own room. They had thought that three people would be too many; that it might make Sofia feel intimidated. They had installed a listening device in Mick's room and hung out the do not disturb sign before they had gone down to breakfast so the maid would not disturb anything. They had tested the device one final time right after breakfast. David had heard it all, just like they did, when they did. Only, he had not been in the room with Sofia.

At lunch, they sat at a different table on the other side of the room, a table for four. They had arrived near the end of the lunch service hours so there were plenty of tables to pick from. Mick thought that Sofia would appreciate not being required to sit in the same corner for every meal. Sitting at different tables was something that normal people did. Normal was good.

After lunch, Taylor and David were going to go to the gym. The plan was for Mick to stay behind with Sofia. But when Taylor and David mentioned going to the gym during lunch, Sofia had asked if she could go along. They all went up to their rooms and changed clothes. Mick was not sure when her father would be back, so he asked Sofia to leave a message for him on the bed saying that she was in the gym in case he came back while they were gone. Mick wanted to avoid any possibility of the Ambassador worrying about where Sofia was. The Ambassador had already been through enough.

They went to the gym, which was even larger than the bar. There were several men in the gym working out. When the men saw Sofia, they hurriedly finished their exercise routines and left. Sofia ran on the treadmill while the team worked out with the resistance weight machines. Sofia tired first so she sat on one of the machines and waited until the team finished.

When they got back to their rooms it was in the later part of the afternoon and the Ambassador and the boys were in their rooms. They dropped Sofia off with the Ambassador and went to their own rooms to shower and change.

The team gathered in Mick's room, where David removed the listening device and the do not disturb sign from the door. They did not have a lot to say to each other about the interview of Sofia. They now had a complete picture of what had happened, from Sami Musa's first involvement through to the rescue of Sofia and her return to her family. But they were no closer to finding Ahmed. He was a ghost. He had appeared for the kidnapping and disappeared just before the rescue. There was nothing left for them to do in Germany.

Mick called Bronwyn to see if she had any new information. She did not. They had come to a dead end. They agreed it was time for the team to go home.

Bronwyn arranged their travel on a commercial flight out of Munich to Dulles International for the next day, Monday, and a ride to the airport in Munich. Because they would be flying commercial, gear could go home with them. Their kit would make it home by alternate means.

They ate dinner with the Sopko family one last time that evening. The Ambassador had insisted. He suspected they would be leaving soon and wanted one last opportunity to share a meal with them and to talk with them.

At dinner, Mick advised the Ambassador that they would be leaving in the morning. There was no visible reaction to the news from Sofia. The Ambassador thanked the three of them again. No details, just for all they had done.

"I will always be in debt to you men," the Ambassador said. "I can never repay you. But if you ever need anything, anything at all, I hope that you will contact me. I will never forget what you have done for us."

He handed each of them a card. It was a personal business card, not a government card. It had only his name and a telephone number on it.

Then Peter handed each of them the same kind of card. A plain business card with just his name and phone number on it.

"That goes for me, too," Peter said. "For the rest of my life."

It was clear that the Ambassador had no knowledge beforehand of Peter's plan. The Ambassador's eyes shown with pride at his son. The team placed both cards in their wallets and thanked them both.

"I am resigning my position as Ambassador," the Ambassador said, changing the subject. "I have already advised the administration. We are moving back to Virginia. We will leave directly from here when we are ready to go."

"No," Sofia said softly, with despair in her voice.

"It is of no consequence, Sofia," the Ambassador said to her. "I would have been replaced eventually by the new administration anyway. Now it will just be a little sooner rather than later."

Sofia said nothing. No one at the table spoke for a long moment.

"Summer is a good time to move," he continued. "We can get settled in before you all have to start back to school. I would rather do it on my own schedule than wait until the administration and the senate determine my replacement, which will probably happen in the middle of Matthew's school year."

"We, as a family, need to make this move now," he concluded. "It is what is best for us."

Back in his room later, Mick shaved and showered to save time in the morning then went about packing up his stuff. He laid out what he would wear for the flight home the next day.

Then he picked up the hotel pen and the hotel stationary. He wrote his name and his personal telephone number on the paper with a short note asking the Ambassador to let him know how Sofia was doing periodically. He tore the sheet of paper off of the pad and folded it in half. He wrote the Ambassador's name on the outside. Then he laid the note on the nightstand on top of a printout of his flight itinerary. They were being picked up very early in the morning to be taken to the airport in Munich. He would give the note to the security man outside the Ambassador's suite on the way out.

CHAPTER TWENTY-SEVEN

Mick walked along one of the rows of grape vine cuttings that he had recently finished planting. It had taken him weeks of working in the evenings and on weekends but he had two good-sized fields planted with cuttings from three different sources. He had obtained most of the cuttings from a friend of his that owned a vineyard in central Virginia. They were all in one field. He had ordered a number of cuttings from a reputable seller on the internet. They had arrived in good condition and were all planted in the second field. Last, he had received twenty cuttings in the mail, a completely unexpected gift from Kostas Panopoulos. Those cuttings he had given the honor of placement at the front of the second field. It was the cuttings from Greece that he walked among.

Mick had called Kostas Panopoulos on Saturday after he had returned home from Germany just to check in with him, to thank him again for all of his assistance, and to strengthen their bond. He had found that it was beneficial to keep in touch with people he met in various parts of the world. He never knew when having a relationship with someone would make a difference to a mission, so he built relationships with people he came in contact with in different parts of the world and made the effort to keep those contacts. Kostas was one such contact, one he did not want to lose, so he had made the call.

It was a good conversation. Kostas was pleased to have been a part of finding Sofia and very pleased that she had been found alive. Kostas did not ask for details over the phone and Mick did not volunteer any. Instead, Mick turned the conversation to Kostas and, eventually, they had gotten around to talking about growing grapes. Kostas had been a wealth of information about growing grapes and about making wine. Before the call ended, they exchanged contact information, including their personal addresses and phone numbers, and promised each other that they would keep in touch.

Mick had called Kostas again a few months later. Another good conversation. It was mostly about planting grapes as Mick had been preparing his fields in anticipation of planting in October. In the first week of October, the unexpected box of cuttings from Kostas had arrived in the mail. That generated the third call from Mick to Kostas. Mick thanked him for the cuttings and had invited Kostas to come see them after they had taken root and grown, in a year or two.

As he walked among the newly planted cuttings, he could not help but think about Sofia's kidnapping. It had been five months since his return from that mission.

The Musa families had been given new identities and moved to the United States, though not on the east coast. They were starting over in middle America. Sami had been given assistance in changing schools. The only restrictions on the Musa families were that they could never return to Lebanon, they could never go to any countries in the Middle East, or to Iran, and they could never contact anyone in Lebanon, which included Mr. Musa's oldest living son. Their identities, former and current, had been flagged in a database which would send an alert should any of them travel outside of the United States. Their foreign travel would be monitored for the rest of their lives. They would never know, unless their travel took them too close to or into a restricted area. Mick doubted that Mr. Musa and his wife would ever leave the United States. But the younger family members might. They still had long lives ahead of them.

Ambassador Sopko had called Mick twice since Germany. Once in July and once in September. He had said that Sofia was doing well. They had moved back to Virginia and his children had all started back to their various schools. He had tried to get Sofia to change schools, but she was a senior and had insisted on finishing where she had started. She still did not know about Sami Musa's involvement. Mick had assured the Ambassador that Sami was no longer attending her school. The Ambassador had very subtly asked about Ahmed during each call and Mick had told him each time that there was nothing new on that front.

Ahmed had remained a ghost. They had his picture. They had even managed to get his fingerprints from the van in Greece and the compound in Northern Cyprus. They were continuously looking for him but, so far, nothing. He had completely disappeared. It was frustrating for Mick. Ahmed was on their list and, sooner or later, he would surface. Mick hoped that it would be sooner. As the months had gone by, he began to think it would be later, a lot later.

The only new information that Mick had learned since returning from Germany concerned the State Department. Bronwyn had found out that the Lebanese Ambassador to the United States had been called into the State Department for a face-to-face meeting the day before the news of Sofia's kidnapping had hit the press. He was told about Sofia being kidnapped and he was told that Lebanon would be held responsible if she was not returned safely. The Lebanese Ambassador had protested and said that the Lebanese government could not be held responsible for acts of terrorism. According to Bronwyn, the Lebanese Ambassador was told in no uncertain terms that Hezbollah was responsible, and Hezbollah was the Lebanese government. The politically convenient fiction of separation between Hezbollah and the official Lebanese government had been stripped away.

When she had told Mick about it, Bronwyn had been seething about the State Department interference with their mission, without even consulting them. Mick was indifferent to the information. Every new administration goes through an adjustment period, some were tougher than others, but none were easy. Every department and agency jockeyed for position at the beginning of every new administration and sometimes they got out over their skis. The State Department would have considered Sofia one of their own. At times like that, shit happens. Mick had a bit of his grandfather's distrust of the government so, for him, it was not shocking. It was not even surprising. The only surprise had been that someone at the State Department had finally had the guts to speak the truth.

Later, when he had time to digest the information and put it in context, he thought that maybe the State Department had unknowingly helped them rescue Sofia. A direct threat to Lebanon by a new administration meant Hezbollah could no longer enjoy the protection offered by the convenient fictional separation between official Lebanon and Hezbollah. That threat may have been the reason Ahmed changed course and ended up in Northern Cyprus, at an inferior location and without the manpower to defend it. If so, Ahmed had been treated as nothing more than a Hezbollah pawn, who had been sacrificed for the strategic greater good, when it became necessary to maintain the safety of Hezbollah's position in Lebanon. Cut loose in the middle of an operation, just like the Cuban exiles had been cut loose at the Bay of Pigs.

It was late at night, very late, well after midnight. Technically, it was very early in the morning. Mick had spent the day at work, the evening inspecting his new vineyards, and the night reading a book about making wine. The time had gotten away from him as sometimes happened when he was engrossed in a book.

He had just finished showering and getting ready for bed. He was wearing an old pair of sweatpants as he went around checking that the doors were locked before going to bed. It was fall in Virginia and the nights had turned cold. He had been using the gas fireplace while reading so his last stop was at the fireplace. He turned it off.

Five tones sounded in rapid succession from the cell phone in the pocket of his sweatpants. He reached into his pocket and took the phone out. The display showed that he had new text messages. Five of them.

He tapped the text message icon and the messages opened. "911 411," five times, once in each of five text messages. He knew where the text messages were originating from. They were from work and they meant that urgent information had been received. Five messages to catch his attention. Some people ignore one new text message when it arrives, particularly in the dead of night. No one ignores five tones indicating five new text messages in quick succession. Everyone feels compelled to look at the messages. If he did not call in soon, they would call him. It was a polite system. First, they send the text messages. It's urgent, but finish brushing your teeth, or taking your shower, or waking up, and then call in. It is only information, after all, nobody is dying, yet. But if you did not call within ten minutes, they called you. Because it was urgent. It was a good system to use, especially at night. It worked.

Mick called in. After identifying himself, he was placed on hold. Urgent, but not so urgent they cannot put you on hold, he mused to himself while he yawned. His call was being transferred to the person who had ordered the text messages to be sent out. He was on hold for several minutes. Apparently, that person was not at their desk and Mick knew they were being hunted down. There were no cell phones allowed in the office so the call had to be transferred to a desk with a hard line. All of the hard lines were monitored. Mick waited patiently on hold.

"Bronwyn Richards," the call was finally answered.

"Mick Turek," Mick said in kind.

"Mick," Bronwyn said, sounding excited. "I've been waiting for your call. We have had two hits on your special project in the past hour."

Mick was annoyed and it came through in his voice. "Why didn't you just call me?"

"Well, Mick," Bronwyn said, drawing out both words. "I have been bouncing between two sections and you are not the only person that needed to know."

"I'm sorry, Bronwyn," Mick said, sincerely. "How significant is it?"

"You need to come in," she said, smugly.

"On my way," Mick said, as he ended the call.

His tiredness evaporated and he felt energized. Mick ran to his bedroom and dressed as fast as he could. His special project had been Bronwyn's way of telling him that it was Ahmed. Ahmed had shown up on their radar somewhere, not just once but twice.

He was dressed. Black tactical pants, black hiking boots, a forest green polo shirt, and a black jacket. Wallet, cell phone, and keys in his pockets. He felt he was missing something. He looked around his room. Then he walked over to the dresser, picked up his brass compass, and clipped it to his belt.

He turned off the lights as he went through the rooms on the way to the front door. He went out the front door and locked it behind him. He got into his Jeep Cherokee and drove to work in northern Virginia. Not the main building at Langley. The Agency had outgrown that building decades ago. His office and Bronwyn's office were not there.

On the way, he made one stop, at a coffee shop that was open all night. He bought three large coffees which they put in a cardboard cup carrier for him. One was just plain black coffee. The other two were what he thought of as fancy coffees. The type of thing that has a fancy name and comes with whipped cream on top. He did not have any idea what the names meant so he had let the barista pick the two most popular kinds of the fancy coffees. The barista had written the names of each coffee on each cup. Bronwyn liked fancy coffee.

Mick parked his car at the building, turned his cell phone off and put it in the console, then got out and locked the car. He made his way through security and headed directly to Bronwyn's office with the coffees. She was not in her office. He set out to hunt her down. He met up with her in the hallway. She was in a hurry, walking fast, on her way back to her office. Mick turned around and followed her.

In her office, Bronwyn sat at her desk and made two quick calls. When she was done, she sat back in her chair and looked at the two large cups of coffee Mick had set on her desk.

"For me?"

"Of course, for you," Mick said.

"This is why I love you, Mick," she said, with a smile, as she examined the names written on each of the cups and chose one.

Bronwyn took a drink of her coffee and tilted her head back in delight, savoring the flavor. Mick sat down with his cup of black coffee. He took a drink and waited patiently for Bronwyn to re-engage. It was pretty good coffee.

"Ahmed has a new name," Bronwyn finally declared. "And a new passport."

"Don't tease me, Bronwyn," Mick chided her. "What do you have?"

"Facial recognition," Bronwyn said, as she picked up a thin file from her desk and handed it to Mick. "Ahmed Bari is now Saleh Hallal, with an Algerian passport. He flew from Algiers to Paris today."

Mick flipped through the few photographs in the file. It was Ahmed.

"Go get your team ready," Bronwyn said. "After I spoke to you on the phone, I called them all in. You need to be in Europe and able to react as soon as possible. The arrangements are being made now."

Mick stood up and walk out of Bronwyn's office and went to the team's equipment room. On the way, he thought, five months is either too short or too long. If Ahmed was worried about being identified after Northern Cyprus, he should be laying low for a year or more. And, if he was not worried about being identified, he should have been on their radar months ago.

CHAPTER TWENTY-EIGHT

Mick walked into the team's equipment room. The equipment room was shared by two teams. It was on the door, Det. 3 and Det. 4. His team was Det. 3, short for Detachment 3. A meaningless name, other than the number three, which separated his team from the other teams. Detachment 3 was an intentionally meaningless name.

Taylor, David, and Jason were all already in the equipment room. Mick quickly brought them up to speed on Ahmed's new identity and current whereabouts.

"Saleh Hallal," David said. "It means righteous resolver, I think. What is he going to resolve?"

No one had any response to that statement.

Mick moved on. He told them to pack up and be ready to leave as soon as arrangements could be made. They each began by unpacking their kit bags which were always packed and ready. There were four large tall tables in the room, one for each of them. They each took a table and spread the contents of their kit bag on it. They checked each of the firearms and made sure that they were clean and serviceable. Then they examined the other equipment and repacked the bags.

The AR-15s that had been used in Cyprus had been replaced with new ones. The AR-15s used in Cyprus could no longer be used by the team. It was sometimes possible for ballistics analysis to match a fired round with the barrel that it had been fired from. To avoid that possibility, in the event an AR-15 was left behind on a future mission, the AR-15s used in Cyprus had been sent to a training facility for continued use in training.

Next, they unpacked their gear bags. Mick went into the large closet marked Det. 3 and pulled two shirts, two pairs of pants, two pairs of underwear, and two pairs of socks off of his shelf. His gear bag was generally packed with four of every clothing item and one light jacket, which could comfortably last him for a week. He wanted more this time because he felt they might be out longer. Ahmed had a good head start on them and they still had to get across the ocean.

The others saw Mick come out of the closet with additional clothing and they each went into the closet to get more clothing for themselves. There was often no time for laundry when they were on a mission. The clothing was provided by the Agency and everything was considered disposable. Any items that did not come back to the equipment room, or that came back torn or otherwise deemed to be in need of disposal, were replaced in short order. When their bags were packed, they were almost ready to go.

"Personal items," Mick said, holding up a box of gallon-size resealable thick plastic bags.

They each placed their wallets, jewelry, and other personal items in a plastic bag. They checked all of their pockets, putting loose change and other pocket litter in the bags. The sealed plastic bags were place on the table near Mick. Then Mick put the four plastic bags in the Det. 3 safe.

When they were done, they sat around waiting for Bronwyn. Mick had gotten no sleep and he needed more coffee. He had finished his large cup of coffee while packing. He looked over at the coffee pot and noticed that someone had made a pot of coffee so he went over to the small kitchen counter and refilled his disposable coffee cup with fresh coffee. One drink and he knew who had made the coffee.

"David, when are you going to learn how to make coffee?" Mick asked. "Two scoops of coffee per pot. Two scoops."

"Hey, you should just be happy I made it at all," David replied. "You didn't think to make it, Mr. Coffee."

They all laughed. Taylor and Jason also poured themselves cups of coffee. Then they sat around drinking David's weak coffee. David was not much of a coffee drinker, which probably explained why he could not make decent coffee. David was drinking a can of Coke he had taken from the small refrigerator.

Bronwyn came into the room in a flurry, with two men in tow. "You are leaving from Dulles as soon as you get there," she announced.

Then she nodded to one of the men with her and he handed out manila envelopes to each of them. "Two sets of identities, one real, one not," Bronwyn said. "Matching credit cards and cash."

She nodded to the second of the men with her. He handed Mick another large manila envelope, this one bulging at the sides.

"Untraceable international cell phones," Bronwyn said. "Use them as needed. Dispose of them, if necessary. Updates will be sent to the plane. Your initial destination is Paris, but it could change while you are in the air. Any questions?"

There were no questions. "Your ride is downstairs," Bronwyn said. "Good luck, gentlemen."

With that she turned and left as hurriedly as she had entered. The team quickly checked the contents of their document envelopes. Identity papers were crucial so they each checked to make sure they had passports and credit cards in their own name and in one of their alias names. When satisfied, they put the envelopes in their gear bags. Then they each picked up two bags, one kit and one gear, and went down to their ride.

Their plane had been diverted to Tirana, Albania, while in flight. They would arrive about an hour before midnight, local time. Ahmed had spent most of the day in Paris. Then he had caught a flight to Tirana in the early evening.

The team had slept for most of the flight. The steward had just served them meals. They were eating and mulling over Ahmed's actions.

Taylor asked, "Why Tirana?"

Jason asked, "Why did he go to Paris?"

"Why two flights in one day?" David chimed in.

"He is in Albania so let's deal with Albania first," Mick said. "Albania is a predominately Muslim country. But it is no hot bed of terrorism. Nothing ever happens in Albania. It would be unlikely that he would have an extensive support network in Albania."

"Albania shares a land border with Montenegro, Kosovo, North Macedonia, and Greece," David said. "By sea, it is a short distance from Italy."

"If he were going to Albania, why not fly there directly from Algeria?" Jason added to the conversation. "Why go to France first?"

"You are right, Jason, it makes no sense," Taylor said. "France is an EU country. If he wanted to enter the EU and go through immigration control in a country that was not his final destination in the EU, France would make sense. He did that in Cyprus when his final destination was Greece. But Albania is not in the EU. Unless he had something important to do in Paris, he didn't need to go through EU immigration control, and I would think that he would have wanted to avoid EU immigration control.

He is not stupid. He knows we have good working relationships with the EU countries."

"For that matter, he could have gone from Algeria to Albania by sea," Mick said. "He didn't have to fly at all."

"I think we should give more thought to his name," David said. "After all, he probably picked it."

"What are you thinking?" Mick asked.

"I think righteous resolver means he is on his way to resolve something," David explained. "The only thing we know of that, for him, is unresolved would be the kidnapping. We all agree that Ahmed is good at what he does, very good. The rescue of Sofia had to sting a guy like that. He knows he escaped only by sheer luck. It's a failed operation for him. He needs to redeem himself. He needs to do something that shows how good he is again."

"What?" Mick asked.

"I don't know," David said. "But I have the feeling that he entered the EU on purpose. Maybe he was testing his new identity. Maybe he wants us to know he is active again. I don't know. It just doesn't feel right."

They were all quiet as they each thought it through. Mick thought again, Ahmed's period of inactivity was either too long or too short. Mick broke the silence.

"Do you think he could be using himself as bait to lure us into something?"

"Yes and no," David replied. "That's what is bothering me. We think we are hunting him. But I think he might be hunting us. I wonder, how would he prove that he was better than the Americans? What would he want to do? My answer is, he would want to take us out. Just like we want to take him out. We both want to finish the job. To resolve it. And if he has people watching the airport in Tirana, our arrival will be obvious to them. He would know that he has lured us out, that we are on his trail. That could be why he chose Tirana. Because of its small size, relatively speaking, he wouldn't need a network to confirm that he was being hunted. But I don't think he would try to take us out there. Once he knows that we are after him, he could lead us to where he is prepared to make his stand."

"Okay," Mick said, as he looked around at each of them.

They all gave some credence to David's thinking. They knew Ahmed was intelligent, too smart for his current actions to be mistakes on his part.

"We can't afford to make a mistake," Mick concluded.

Mick rose from his seat, meal tray in hand, and walked toward the cockpit. On the way, he handed his tray to the steward. Then he went into the cockpit and spoke to the captain.

Their plane landed at Fiumicino Airport in Italy shortly before midnight. They were met by someone from the Agency and they were escorted through immigration control. Because they were using diplomatic passports, their bags were not subject to search.

They were driven to the U.S. Embassy in Rome, where Mick was able to have secure communications with Bronwyn. Ahmed was still in Tirana, as far as Bronwyn knew. She agreed that Rome was a good positioning location for the team.

Their bags were left at the Embassy. They each took a small duffel bag out of their gear bags and put a change of clothes inside of it. Then they were driven to a hotel, where they got rooms, and settled in for the rest of the night. It had turned into a waiting game. They were waiting for Ahmed's next move.

CHAPTER TWENTY-NINE

The team had been waiting for three days in Rome. They spent their days in the U.S. Embassy and their nights at the hotel.

They were sitting around a small table in the conference room they had been assigned in the Embassy. They were bored with the waiting. The small trash can near the door to the conference room was full of coffee cups and drink cans and bottles.

"It's been almost three full days," Mick said. "With no movement by Ahmed."

"None that we know of," Jason added, qualifying Mick's statement.

Mick had ordered no surveillance of Ahmed in Tirana. If Ahmed was waiting for them, there was a chance that he would make any surveillance operatives, which would confirm for Ahmed that he was being hunted or, at the very least, that his new identity was blown.

"If he is testing his new identity, he has to be pretty happy with the results," Taylor said.

"Yes, if he is testing his identity, he is happy we didn't arrive, that no one did," David added. "But if he was waiting for us to arrive, he has to be disappointed. Either way, he should move on soon as he has nothing more to gain, assuming he has nothing planned for Tirana."

"I don't like assuming he has nothing planned for Tirana," Mick said. "But I don't see that we have any other choice. We are taking a gamble here. But I don't want to walk into a trap, if that is what Ahmed is setting."

"Gamble or not, we already made our choice," Jason said, ending the conversation. "I'm ready to go back to the hotel and get some dinner."

The team had arrived back at the Embassy the next morning to begin another day of waiting. They were all seated around the conference table in their assigned room drinking coffee or orange juice.

Mick was summoned to the secure communication facility. Bronwyn advised him that Ahmed had made reservations for a morning flight from Tirana to Algiers. Bronwyn had arranged for one surveillance operative to be at the airport, near the assigned gate, to confirm whether or not Ahmed got on the plane as scheduled. Mick went back to the conference room and told the others.

"He could be going home," David said. "Algeria is a Sunni Muslim country and was a French colony so Arabic and French are both widely spoken there. Or it could be just another stop on his journey."

"He started in Algeria with the new identity," Taylor said. "But he is too smart for that to be his home base. He would not lead us to his home base that easily. His home base is probably in a contiguous country. One with loose borders."

"Algeria shares land borders with Morocco, Mauritania, Mali, Niger, Libya, and Tunisia," David said. "Take your pick of loose borders."

"Okay," Mick said. "Which countries have major population centers relatively close to Algiers?"

"There is Rabat in Morocco, Tunis in Tunisia, and Tripoli in Libya," David responded.

"In which of those is French widely spoken?

"Morocco and Tunisia were both former French colonies, like Algeria, and Arabic and French are widely spoken in both countries," David said. "Libya was a former Italian colony. Italian, not French, is the primary secondary language in Libya, followed by English."

"Morocco or Tunisia then," Jason said.

Mick asked, "Which is easier to get to from Algiers?"

"By air, they are both short hops," David said. "Rabat, Algiers, and Tunis are all on the coast. By water, Tunis is closer than Rabat. And by road, the same, Tunis is closer than Rabat."

"Which of the two has the loosest borders?"

"I would think that they are both the same when it comes to border security, especially if you are traveling with an Algerian passport," David said. "Algerians should be able to pass easily between all three countries, Morocco, Algeria, and Tunisia."

"Where do you think he would feel more comfortable?"

"In Tunis," David said. "Morocco and Tunisia are both Sunni Muslim countries, but the city of Tunis has slightly more religious diversity, including a small number of Shia Muslims."

"Okay," Mick said. "If it is confirmed that Ahmed got on the flight to Algiers, we will move to Tunis. I'll put the plane on stand-by."

Within the hour, they received confirmation. The surveillance operative had seen Ahmed get on the plane to Algiers.

The flight to Tunis was short, less than an hour and a half. It had taken longer to get to the Fiumicino Airport, to get onto the plane with their bags, and to get take-off clearance.

It was mid-afternoon when they landed at the Tunis-Carthage International Airport. They were met by two Agency men from the Embassy with transportation in the form of a large passenger van bearing diplomatic plates. They were escorted through immigration with no luggage search.

They were not taken to the Embassy. Instead, they were taken to a three-bedroom house located on the outskirts of the main downtown area. Tunis was an ancient city. It's defining feature was white paint. The buildings were practically all painted white to reflect the sun and to help keep the interiors cooler than the outside air temperature. Those that were not painted white were either the light gray color of unpainted cement or a yellowish beige. The primary accent color was bright blue.

The house they had been taken to had been painted white, with a bright blue door and matching bright blue window shutters. It was a typical Tunisian exterior.

The inside of the house, however, was not typically Tunisian. The furniture was all clearly American. Big American furniture contained within the architecture of a typical Tunisian house. The two larger of three bedrooms each contained two sets of bunk beds, for a total of eight beds. The smallest bedroom had a full-sized bed which took up most of the available space in the small bedroom. The dining room had a large wooden table and six wooden chairs. On two of the dining room walls, there were large white boards screwed into the walls. On the third dining room wall, there was a large mounted cork board. Maps of Tunis, Tunisia, and north Africa had been thumb tacked into the corkboard. In the living room, there was a small wooden desk with a router and modem. Several laptop computers were laying on the desk. There was only one bathroom, which was small by American standards. The kitchen, too, was small by American standards and sparse, just the bare necessities. The cupboards and the refrigerator were full of recently purchased food and drink.

The house had two final features that were not typical in Tunisian homes, an elaborate security system and a safe room. They were shown how to access the safe room by one of the Agency men. The smallest bedroom was so small because the safe room had been built behind the closet. To get into the safe room, they had to go into the closet, open a concealed door in the back of the closet, and enter a numeric combination code into a keypad which opened a steel door and allowed access to the safe room.

They each took a couple days' worth of clothes and toiletries out of their gear bags and then deposited their gear bags and kit bags in the safe room. Then they all met in the dining room with the two men who had picked them up at the airport.

It was decided that they would go out in pairs, one pair at a time, to purchase business casual clothing. David and Jason went first. One of the Agency men drove them to a shopping district to buy clothes. It was a modern shopping district with modern stores selling modern American and European clothing. It was not a tourist area. They each purchased two pairs of khaki pants, several button-down shirts, a sport coat, a brown leather belt, and a pair of lace-up leather dress shoes.

As soon as David and Jason returned to the house, Mick and Taylor were taken to the same shopping district where they bought similar clothing. The items were intended to give them the appearance of businessmen, after work hours, enjoying the sites of Tunis as one of the perks of their business trip. Including the polo-shirts they already had, they could create a number of different looks to change their appearance from day to day, as necessary.

When everyone was back at the house, Mick and Jason and the two Agency men left. Mick was dropped at the Embassy to use the secure communication facilities and Jason was taken to pick up a previously rented car for their use.

Mick contacted Bronwyn. She told him that Ahmed had landed in Algiers and had taken a taxi to a hotel where he had checked in. Discreet surveillance was being maintained. Mick told Bronwyn which of the team members was using which phone number.

Jason picked Mick up outside the Embassy and they returned to the house in the rental car. The team gathered in the dining room, again, where David was studying the map of Tunis on the corkboard. David had an affinity for geography and a very good inherent sense of direction. He was able to study maps and move around on the ground like a native, or as close to a native as a foreigner would ever get. He might not know the quickest way to get somewhere during peak rush hour, like a native would, but he always knew how to get where he was going, even when he had never been there before.

"It looks like we were right about Algiers," Mick said to the group. "It's most likely not his home base. Ahmed has checked into a hotel in Algiers. Not what I would expect, if he lived there."

"So now we wait again," said Taylor.

"Now we wait again," Mick confirmed.

"Then let's get dinner, while we wait," Jason said.

They dressed in their business casual clothing and went out to dinner. Jason drove the rental car with David as his navigator. They found a restaurant downtown and had dinner.

Mick was awakened a few minutes before seven o'clock the next morning by the ringing of his cell phone. He answered the call.

"He's moving by car," a male voice said, then disconnected the call.

Mick got out of bed, went into the bathroom, brushed his teeth, shaved, showered, and returned to his room. He got dressed in business casual clothing. Khaki pants, a white button-down shirt, brown leather belt, and leather dress shoes, with his compass on his belt. Then he went into the kitchen.

There was only one long counter in the kitchen. On the counter was an automatic drip coffee maker. Mick looked in the cupboards and found the coffee and the coffee filters. He placed the filter in the coffee maker basket and added two heaping scoops of ground coffee. He turned the coffee maker on and waited impatiently for the coffee to brew and drip down into the glass carafe. While the coffee was brewing, he found the coffee cups and placed four cups on the counter. When the carafe was full, he filled one of cups with coffee and took a sip.

As expected, the smell of freshly brewed coffee brought Taylor into the kitchen. Taylor took one of the cups from the counter and poured himself a cup of coffee. Then he headed back to his bedroom to get ready for the day, without having said a word.

As Mick was leaving the kitchen for the dining room, David came into the kitchen.

"Morning," David said, as he took a cup from the counter and poured a cup of coffee for himself.

"Morning," Mick said. "Two scoops."

"Got it," David said.

Then Mick went into the dining room where he studied the map of Tunis, while drinking his coffee. He did not know how David could study a city map and learn the area so quickly. Mick was good with large geographic areas, like countries, he could remember where cities and towns were in relationship to each other and to the country overall. He was also good with small towns or rural areas with a few main roads and geographic features. But cities teeming with streets were not so easy. The mishmash of streets on the map of Tunis was definitely a challenge.

Mick heard someone rooting around in the kitchen and went to see who it was. Jason had poured himself a cup of coffee and was hauling food out of the refrigerator. Mick saw that Jason had already placed butter and eggs on the counter.

"Who puts tomatoes in the refrigerator?" Jason asked no one in particular.

Mick ignored the question and, instead, asked one of his own.

"Any bacon?"

"Of course, there is no bacon, Mick," Jason replied. "And no sausage. And no ham."

"Just checking," Mick said.

Jason laughed.

"How do want your eggs?" Jason asked Mick. "I'm cooking this morning."

"Whatever you want to make works for me," Mick replied, thankful that Jason was cooking breakfast.

Mick refilled his coffee cup and made a new pot of coffee. By the time Jason was finished cooking, there were four cheese omelets on four plates on the table in the dining room, each with two slices of buttered toast and several slices of tomato. Mick had found the silverware and set it out on the table.

Of the four of them, Jason was the best cook by far. He could make a palatable meal out of about anything. With decent ingredients, he could make an excellent meal. His cooking skills had no bearing on his becoming a member of the team but they all appreciated his skill in the kitchen. It was a pleasant bonus for the team.

"Breakfast," Mick called down the hall to the others.

They all refilled their coffee cups and went into the dining room to eat.

"Ahmed is on the move," Mick said, as they ate. "He is traveling by car. Obviously, we don't know yet if he is leaving Algiers or just moving around in Algiers."

"If he drives from Algiers to Tunis, it will take him between seven to nine hours, depending on how fast he drives and if he stops for more than just gas," David said.

"So, if he is headed here, it will take him all day to get here," Mick said.

"If it looks like he is leaving Algiers and heading for Tunis, we should use the morning to get acquainted with the city," Taylor suggested.

They all agreed.

Taylor and Mick washed the morning dishes. There was no automatic dishwasher. Jason had cooked then had gone to get showered and dressed. David was studying the map again. As Mick dried that last of the dishes, his cell phone rang. He answered it.

"He is headed your way," the male voice said, before disconnecting the call.

They spent the day driving and walking around in Tunis. Jason drove them all downtown then Mick and Taylor walked the city center on foot while Jason and David covered a larger area by car. In the afternoon, they moved out to the suburbs, at the outskirts of the city proper, and worked their way back into the city center.

Tunis is not a centrally planned city. Like Athens and Rome, it had grown up over the course of thousands of years. It sits on the southern coast of the Mediterranean Sea by a sheltered bay. It also has two major lakes within the city limits. Tunis had been colonized by the Phoenicians, the Carthaginians, the Vandals, the Byzantines, Arab and Berber tribes, the Ottomans, and the French. And they all left their mark on Tunis. The streets in Tunis tend to follow the natural terrain and to meet at all kinds of different angles. The *medina*, the old town in the center of the city, is full of narrow twisting cobblestone streets, many no wider than alleyways, between white painted buildings with brightly painted blue or green doors. The *ville nouvelle*, new town, was built by the French and has some straight streets and even an extremely wide and perfectly straight avenue that starts at the old town and goes toward the harbor, Avenue Habib Bourguiba. French colonial and post-colonial buildings line the avenue. The old co-exists with the new throughout the city. In short, Tunis is a central planner's nightmare.

In the evening, the team stood around the dining room table at the house. Large aerial photographs were arrayed on the table. Ahmed had taken a northerly road that generally followed the coastline from Algiers to Tunis, which had allowed for non-invasive aerial surveillance. Non-invasive of Algerian or Tunisian land, but not non-invasive of territorial air space. Both Algeria and Tunisia claim territorial waters out to twelve nautical miles, including the air space above the territorial waters.

The aerial photographs were clear and detailed. They followed the travel of a Toyota SUV, with Algerian license plates. The car had been determined to be a rental, rented in the name of Saleh Hallal the day before he flew from Algiers to Paris, and had been left at the hotel until his return to Algiers.

The driver, Ahmed, had stopped in Sidi Bou Said, a coastal town in Tunisia, and had then gone on foot to a house. Sidi Bou Said is a resort town on the coast, east by northeast of the Tunis-Carthage International Airport. Within an hour of Ahmed getting out of the rental car, a different man, unidentified, got into the rental car and it was headed back toward Algiers.

"He could be staying the night, or a week for all we know," Mick said. "Let's check out the town and see if we can get a place nearby where we can observe."

Jason and David went out to the car and drove to Sidi Bou Said. It was an eighteen-kilometer drive, eleven kilometers beyond the airport. They located the house that Ahmed had gone into and drove through the surrounding area. There were a number of hotels and vacation rental properties. David wrote down the addresses of the most promising vacation rentals, those nearby the house that Ahmed had gone into. When they returned to the house in Tunis, it was late at night.

"There are a number of good possibilities," David said, when they were all gathered in the dining room. David stood by the map of Tunis on the corkboard.

"We are here," he said, as he pointed out the location of the house that they were using on the map.

"This is the airport," he said, as he pointed out the Tunis-Carthage airport, which was clearly depicted on the map.

"Ahmed is here," he said, as he pointed to the location of the house where Ahmed was in Sidi Bou Said.

"Eighteen kilometers from us," David said. "And eleven kilometers from the airport."

"It is not far from here," Jason added. "But it is too far for surveillance. We need a good location close by Ahmed."

Mick asked, "What did you think of the town?"

"It was getting dark when we got there," Jason said. "But it was well lit. My impression of the town is that it is a high-end tourist area, which is why it is well lit. It is small. A village more than a town. It is built on the side of hill. The hill slopes down to the sea. And every building is painted white with blue trim. The only other color you see in any abundance is the green of trees, bushes, and plants.

"Because it is a tourist area, and this is the off-season, it shouldn't be hard to secure a decent observation post," David added. "I wrote down some addresses."

Jason pulled a laptop computer over to himself and started it up. It connected automatically to the house network. He began searching for vacation rentals in Sidi Bou Said.

"This is when we should have a woman on the team," Taylor said. "A man and a woman would be a natural for a vacation town. Inconspicuous."

"Well, we don't have a woman on the team," Mick replied. "We will have to limit our number in Sidi Bou Said to no more than two at a time, until we get a feel for the place. Two will observe for a couple of days then we will reconsider."

"I got something," Jason interrupted. He turned the computer monitor outward so that the others could see it. It showed a small two-bedroom apartment on the second floor of a white building. It was on the same street as the house that Ahmed had gone into.

David picked up another laptop computer and started it up. It also connected automatically to the house network. He asked for the address of the apartment and Jason supplied it. David brought up a detailed aerial map of the area showing both locations.

"The apartment is three houses or buildings from the target house," David said. "And it is on the opposite side of the street and up the hill. It should be a good location."

"See if it's available, Jason," Mick said. "If so, book it starting tomorrow."

Jason made an inquiry regarding the availability of the apartment and, within seconds, received notification that it was available for rent.

"One week or two?" Jason asked Mick.

"Two," Mick said. "Better to have two and not need it than the other way around."

Jason reached into his back pocket and took out his wallet. He then took out one of his credit cards and made a two-week reservation using his alias identity, requesting early access at ten o'clock in the morning. Within minutes, the reservation, including early access for a small additional fee, was confirmed and an address to pick up the keys was provided.

"Jason has to go first in case anyone asks for proof of identity when he picks up the keys," Mick said. "David, you go with him to get a lay of the land."

They all agreed that Jason and David would leave in the morning for Sidi Bou Said. They would get the keys to the apartment and begin the surveillance. At least one of the others would stop by in the early afternoon with groceries for the apartment. They would stock up for a week to avoid unnecessary trips out of the apartment.

Mick placed a phone call and ordered a second rental car to be delivered to the house in the morning.

CHAPTER THIRTY

After breakfast in the morning, Jason and David left in the rental car for Sidi Bou Said. Jason drove and David navigated. They were dressed casually in khaki pants and polo shirts.

They arrived at the address provided to pick up the keys for the rented apartment at precisely ten o'clock. It was a small house, white with bright blue trim, being used as a commercial property, a vacation rental management company. Jason went inside while David stayed in the car. Within five minutes, Jason returned to the rental car.

"Any problems?" David asked Jason as he shut the driver's door.

"None," Jason replied. "The woman was expecting me. She didn't ask for any identification."

"The magic of credit card charge authorization," David said. "She was probably thrilled to have the off-season rental."

Jason handed David a map of the town and several brochures the rental woman had given him. Then Jason drove them to the apartment building. It was two stories tall and was painted white with bright blue trim. It had assigned parking spaces behind the building. There were several empty spaces.

B. René Shekmer

They parked the car in the spot with their apartment number on it, took a bag each, and walked into the building through a rear door. Once inside, there were no elevators, just a stairwell. Looking toward the front of the building, there was a small lobby, with a glass door. They walked up the stairs to the second floor. As they stepped out of the stairwell and into a hallway, they saw four wooden doors, two for apartments at the front of the building and two for apartments at the rear of the building, none of which were painted blue. The number of their apartment was on the door for one of the two apartments at the front of the building.

The apartment was nicely, but sparsely, furnished. It had everything someone on vacation would need with no extra pieces of furniture to clutter the space. The interior was painted white. Furniture in neutral colors gave the place a rental feel; it had no local character. There were two bedrooms, each with a double bed. One small kitchen and one large bathroom. It was a typical vacation rental unit that could be found almost anywhere in the world.

David and Jason went into each of the rooms at the front of the building. In the front bedroom, there were two windows, one on the front wall and one on the side wall. The target house across the street was visible looking downward from both windows. In the living room, there was a door with large windows which led to a small balcony, containing two white plastic chairs. The front of the target house was clearly visible from the balcony.

David and Jason went back into the front bedroom. They agreed that the window on the side wall had the best view. They rearranged the furniture in the room to accommodate surveillance through the side window. David went out to the kitchen and brought one of the stools into the bedroom and placed it next to the left side of the window. Then he sat on the stool and looked out the window, at an angle and downward, directly at the target house. He could see the front of the house and part of the near side of the house. Perfect for night surveillance. With the bedroom door closed and the lights off in the bedroom, no one would be able to see them watching.

David and Jason went back out to the balcony and settled into the two plastic chairs. David took the seat to the left. He opened the town map and began studying it. Jason took the seat on the right and watched the street below, regularly scanning the front of the target house. Just two men relaxing on a balcony in the late morning sun.

As morning turned to afternoon, Jason went inside to his gear bag and got a pair of sunglasses. Then he returned to the balcony. It was warm with a pleasant sea breeze on the balcony. The sun was shining brightly. They were on the top floor so there was no shade from a balcony above them. The street was quiet, with only the occasional car or pedestrian passing by below them.

A little before one o'clock in the afternoon, there was a knock on the door to the apartment. David went and opened the door. Mick and Taylor stood in the hallway with bags of groceries. It took the two of them three trips to bring all the groceries up the stairs to the apartment.

"Nice rear entrance," Mick said, when he had completed his final trip up from the second rental car.

"And good surveillance positions," David said. "In the bedroom and on the balcony."

David took Mick and Taylor into the front bedroom to show them the view from the side window. They did not go out onto the balcony. Too visible from the target house.

"We haven't seen anything yet," David said.

"Do you want to go out to eat or make something from what we brought?" Mick asked within hearing of both David and Jason.

"I'll make something here," Jason said. "David, trade places with me."

David went out on to the balcony and Jason went into the kitchen, where he started unpacking the groceries.

"We will leave then," Mick said. "We are going to drive the area then head back to the house."

David and Jason were drinking iced tea that Jason had made on the balcony in the late afternoon.

"Movement," Jason said, quietly.

David did not turn to look.

"A woman coming out of the house," Jason said. "Mid-thirties, average height, white, with shoulder length brown hair, and a child, looks like a boy, three or four years old, short brown hair."

David still did not turn to look.

"Ahmed, coming out of the house now," Jason said.

David got up from his chair and went into the apartment. He opened the front door and went out into the hallway. He went down the flight of stairs and stood in the bottom of the stairwell with his phone in hand. His phone vibrated. It was Jason calling.

"They just passed by our building," Jason said. "They are heading up the street on foot. Ahmed, the woman, and the child."

David disconnected the call and went to the front door of the building. He stepped out of the doorway, into the sunlight on the street, and saw Ahmed, the woman, and the child walking up the street to his right. He followed them. They continued to walk up the street, out of the residential area and into a more commercial area, with shops and restaurants. David continued to follow at a distance.

Ahmed, the woman, and the child went into a pharmacy. David walked past the pharmacy and stopped a short way farther on. He browsed the shop windows for a while. Then he took his cell phone out of his pocket, and began taking photographs of the commercial area. He stood near an outdoor display of birdcages, painted white and blue, like the whole village. After ten minutes, they came back out of the pharmacy and continued walking up the street. The woman was now carrying a plastic shopping bag.

David had continued to take pictures, like a tourist. He made sure to get a photograph of Ahmed, the woman, and the child in the background of the birdcage display when they came out of the pharmacy. He was able to capture the faces of the woman and the child who had turned toward him, but only the side of Ahmed's face was captured in the photograph as he came out of the pharmacy last.

David put his cell phone in his pocket before Ahmed turned his way. He began looking at items in the window of a store again. David followed their progress by watching their reflections in the store window. They passed behind him and continued to walk up the street.

As David followed, he saw the child, who was holding the woman's hand, take Ahmed's hand and begin swinging between them as they went up the street. It looked natural to David. The child was used to swinging between the two adults as they walked together. David quickly took a picture of the child swinging. A few minutes later, Ahmed bent down and spoke to the child. The child stopped lifting his feet and swinging. But he kept hold of both of their hands as they walked.

They came to a shop that sold breads and pastries. Ahmed held the door open for the woman and child. They all went inside the shop. Again, David walked past the shop and stopped further up the street. He looked into the window of another shop.

Within ten minutes, Ahmed, the woman, and the child came back out of the shop. Now the woman was carrying two plastic shopping bags. The newest bag was quite full, but obviously not heavy. David could see two baguettes sticking out of the top of the plastic bag. They did not come toward David. Instead, they headed down the street, back the way they had come. David followed again but from further back.

David followed them all the way back to his apartment building, where he went around to the back, and went in through the rear door. As he had approached, he had seen that Jason was not on the balcony. David ran up the flight of stairs and into the apartment. Jason was in the front bedroom by the window, taking photographs as they went back into the target house.

"They went to a pharmacy and to a bakery shop and then came right back," David said.

"I saw the baguettes," Jason said. "Did you get any for us?"

"I thought you only got fresh baguettes in the morning," David said, seriously.

"Beggars can't be choosers," Jason replied, as he went back out onto the balcony.

David sent the photographs from his cell phone to Mick's cell phone. Then he called Mick.

"Is that a family?" Mick asked David, referring to the photographs.

"I'm not sure but they are not strangers," David said. "The child is comfortable with Ahmed."

"We will be over for lunch tomorrow," Mick said, and ended the call.

There was no further movement out of the target house during the evening. At eight o'clock, David suggested that Jason go to bed because, if there was movement tomorrow, it would be Jason that conducted the foot surveillance. Jason went to the back bedroom and David kept vigil on the target house throughout the night, using a night-vision monocle. The target house went completely dark at eleven o'clock at night. David paid close attention for several hours after the lights went out. If Ahmed was going to slip out of the house in the middle of the night, he would do it within a few hours of the lights going out.

Jason came into the front bedroom at four-thirty in the morning, after he had shaved, showered, and dressed.

"No movement overnight," David said, as he handed Jason the night-vision monocle. Then he walked out of the front bedroom and to the back bedroom. A few minutes later, Jason could hear the shower running. David was showering before going to sleep because there was a greater probability of movement from the target house during the daylight hours.

Mick and Taylor arrived at the apartment at noon. They had parked in back and come in through the rear door and up the stairs. David was standing watch on the balcony while Jason was cooking in the kitchen. Taylor walked over to the kitchen and laid two fresh baguettes on the counter. Jason smiled his thanks and turned his attention back to the pot he was stirring on the stove.

Mick stood inside the apartment near the balcony and spoke to David. "Any movement?" He asked.

"No," David replied. "Nothing since the pharmacy and the bakery yesterday."

"Do you think it is his family?"

"No way of knowing." David replied. "But whoever they are, they are close to him. They might as well be his family."

"It complicates things," Mick said.

"You think?" David responded, turning for the first time to look at Mick briefly.

"Food's ready," Jason called out to the others.

Mick and Taylor moved the small table over by the balcony, followed by three of the four chairs. Then Taylor put silverware on the table and Jason went out onto the balcony.

"Go eat," he said to David. "I'll watch."

Mick and Taylor followed David into the kitchen, where Jason had spaghetti pasta in a bowl with serving tongs, spaghetti sauce in a pot with a ladle on the stove, and six-inch pieces of baguette cut in half, spread with butter and garlic, and toasted in a shallow baking pan. A bowl of shredded Romano cheese was on the counter with a spoon.

They each helped themselves to a plate of spaghetti and a piece of garlic bread and went out and sat down at the table by the balcony. They were silent as they ate. The only sound was of utensils on plates. When David was finished, he took his plate to the kitchen sink, grabbed another piece of garlic bread from the pan, and went out onto the balcony. Jason went inside the apartment, got his own plate of spaghetti and garlic bread and sat down at the table to eat.

"Thanks for making lunch," Mick said to Jason. "It was excellent."

"No problem," Jason said.

Then Mick turned the conversation to work.

"The woman and child are a problem," he said.

They all nodded in agreement.

"He is not acting like he is hiding," Mick continued. "Thoughts?"

"He doesn't know we are here," Taylor said. "He didn't see us in Cyprus and maybe he believes that we didn't see him."

"He could believe that we know there was another man involved," David said, while keeping his eyes on the target house. "And still believe we don't know that other man was him."

"His trip from Algiers to Paris to Tirana and back to Algiers could have reinforced the belief that we don't know it was him," Jason added. "If the purpose of that trip was to watch his back to see if he picked up any followers, he might be convinced now that we don't know he was involved."

"So, either he was never hiding," Mick said. "Or he was hiding but now he is not."

"I think that all we can safely say is that for now he feels safe," David said.

"What about your theory that he is hunting us?" Mick asked David.

I could have been wrong," David replied, again keeping his eyes on the target house. "I don't think so, but I admit it's possible. And if he was hunting us, he didn't get anywhere with it because we didn't show up during his travels. There is nothing he can do about it right now. He will have to devise a new plan."

"That he feels safe is a major plus for us," Mick said. "But the woman and child are a real problem."

No one responded to Mick's statements for a long moment. "The woman and child are out of bounds," Taylor said, breaking the silence. They all murmured their agreement.

"Getting him out of the house could get messy," Mick said. "A bigger risk for us."

"We don't need to get him out of the house," Taylor said. "We need to get the woman and the child out of the house."

"And we don't have forever," Jason added. "This is a resort town in the off-season. We can stay for a week, maybe two at the most. But after that, our continued presence will draw attention to ourselves."

"We need more information about the woman," Mick said. "The house looks like a permanent residence but looks can be deceiving and maybe it is a rental. Is it her house and he is visiting her? Is it their house? Or are they just renting the house for a week or two?"

"Nothing yet from Bronwyn?" David asked Mick, from the balcony.

"No, nothing yet," Mick replied. "I sent her your pictures."

"Then all we can do now is wait and watch," David said, ending the conversation.

Mick and Taylor got up from the table, picked up the plates and silverware, and went into the kitchen to do the dishes. By hand, again, no automatic dishwasher. After the dishes were done, Mick and Taylor left the apartment.

David and Jason took turns watching the target house. There was no movement from the house all day or all night.

Jason was watching the target house from the window in the front bedroom. At eight-thirty in the morning, a car passed below their apartment, pulled up in front of the target house, stopped, and sounded the horn. Two quick honks. Within a couple of minutes, the woman and the child came out of the target house.

"Movement," Jason said, just loud enough for David to hear.

The woman helped the child into the back seat of the car then she got into the front passenger seat. Jason took photographs of the car, of the woman, and of the child. Jason had the impression that the driver of the car was also a woman but the driver was not clearly visible so it was just an impression, not a fact. The car drove off, headed away from the apartment building, down toward the sea.

David came into the front bedroom. "They are up," Jason said. "A car came and picked up the woman and child."

"I'll take the balcony," David said. "You be ready to leave, if Ahmed leaves."

David walked out onto the balcony and took a seat. He pretended to be reading a book. Jason checked the photographs on the digital camera. The license plate on the back the car was visible in one of the photographs. Jason transferred the photographs from the digital camera to his cell phone. Then he sent the photographs to Mick's cell phone.

They waited all morning. The woman and child did not come back to the target house and Ahmed did not leave the target house. Shortly after noon, Ahmed came out of the front door of the house.

"Movement," David said, from the balcony.

Jason left the apartment and went downstairs to the first floor. His cell phone vibrated, and he answered the call.

"He is on foot, headed the same way he went before," David said. "Give him a minute to get up the street."

Jason walked out the back door of the building and around to the front. Ahmed had already passed the apartment building. Jason waited until Ahmed was a reasonable distance away then turned the corner and began following him. They walked through the residential area and up to the same commercial area. Ahmed went into a restaurant. As Jason walked by the restaurant, he could see that Ahmed was being seated.

Jason continued on and went into a small shop. It offered a bit of everything for sale. Sunglasses, tourist trinkets, snacks, and drinks. Jason walked around the shop and picked up several items. He paid for the items at the front of the shop; a tourist guidebook for Tunis and the surrounding area, a pack of gum, and several postcards. The shopkeeper put the items in a plastic shopping bag and handed it to Jason.

Jason left the shop and walked to the restaurant where Ahmed was already seated. The restaurant was only about half full. There were plenty of open tables. Ahmed was seated by himself at a small table near the front of the restaurant. Jason spoke in French and asked for a table in the back. He was seated at a table for two. Jason took the seat that gave him a clear view of Ahmed's back.

A waiter came up to Jason, handed him a menu, and asked for his drink order. Still using French, Jason ordered an orange Fanta to drink, with no ice. The waiter nodded knowingly to confirm the no ice part of the order then left the table. Jason had learned that lesson the hard way once before. Ice is just frozen local water. Local water is not always fit to drink. Ice in a drink is the same as drinking a glass of the local water. Risky.

The menu was printed in Arabic, French, and English. Prices were both in dinar and euros. Jason scanned the menu for something quick to prepare. Jason had to assume that Ahmed's order was already being prepared.

The waiter returned with Jason's Fanta. He placed a large empty glass, no ice, on the table in front of Jason. Then the waiter took a bottle opener from his pocket and opened the cold bottle of Fanta in front of Jason. He then poured the Fanta into the glass and placed the empty bottle on the table. The waiter clearly knew the drill.

No ice also means open the bottle at the table so the customer can see the bottle was unopened. Generally, the bottle ceremony, as Jason thought of it, the formal opening of the bottle at the table was used for bottled water, even in the finest restaurants throughout Africa. Empty bottled water containers can be refilled with tap water and recapped. The bottle ceremony, with the cracking of the plastic cap seal at the table, assured the customer that the water in the bottle was not tap water.

Jason had been gifted the bottle ceremony for a bottle of Fanta. Not really necessary for a bottle of soda. No ice alone was sufficient. He thanked the waiter, to properly acknowledge the gift, then ordered a fricassé. Fricassé is the go-to sandwich of Tunisia, a fried roll, split open, and filled with tuna, hard-boiled egg, boiled potato, black olives, and harissa, the local condiment, a spicy chili pepper and garlic paste.

When the waiter left to put the order in, he took the empty Fanta bottle from the table. While Jason waited for his food, he took the tourist guidebook out of his shopping bag and began browsing through it. Although almost all of the tables were filled by then, he did not have to keep an eagle eye on Ahmed. He would know when Ahmed was getting ready to leave. Casual occasional glances around the dining area were sufficient.

Ahmed's food was delivered to his table after Jason had ordered. It appeared that Ahmed had ordered a full meal, not just a light lunch. Jason sent a text message to David, "Eating." David would know that he had time to get something to eat himself while Ahmed was eating lunch in town.

Jason's fricassé was delivered to his table by the waiter a short while later. Jason paced himself. Ahmed had a full meal to consume, while Jason had only a sandwich. He ate slowly while appearing to be engrossed in the guidebook. The fricassé was very good, and spicy hot. Very hot. Jason caught the waiter's attention and ordered a second Fanta.

After the second Fanta was delivered and the bottle ceremony was again completed, Jason asked the waiter for the bill. He wanted to be able to pay the bill without delay when Ahmed left the restaurant. Ahmed took his time with his meal, eating at a leisurely pace. He appeared to be in no hurry to leave the restaurant.

Jason had finished his meal and was nursing his second Fanta. Thankfully, the restaurant was still not completely full, and the wait staff was not trying to move finished customers along so that they could seat waiting customers. There were no waiting customers.

Jason was finding that the guidebook was actually interesting. Ancient Carthage had been near modern day Tunis. The history of the area was fascinating. Jason made a mental note to give the guidebook to David.

Ahmed was finally done and was paying his bill. Jason reached into his pocket, retrieved his wallet, and left euros on the table with the bill, including a substantial tip for the waiter. The bottle ceremony, twice, while unnecessary, was worth a reward.

Jason waited for Ahmed to leave the restaurant before standing up from the table himself. He returned the guidebook to his shopping bag while he watched through the front windows. Ahmed turned right, heading back down the street in the direction of the target house. Then Jason left the restaurant and followed behind Ahmed, at a distance.

Ahmed went directly back to the target house. Jason went back to the apartment. David was watching out the window in the front bedroom.

"I got you something," Jason said, as he reached into the shopping bag and handed the tourist guidebook to David.

"Thanks," David said. "What did Ahmed do? Where did he go?"

"He went to a restaurant and ate lunch by himself," Jason replied.

"That's it?"

"That's it."

"The woman and the child are still not back," David said, as he went out onto the balcony and sat down to read the tourist guidebook, while watching the target house.

The woman and child returned to the house, in the same car, at six-thirty that evening. Mick and Taylor came to the apartment at seven o'clock that evening. They had all already eaten dinner. Mick was carrying a cardboard box of bambalouni, Tunisian doughnuts, round dough with a whole in the center, fried in oil, and sprinkled with sugar. The bambalouni were still warm in the box.

Jason was on the balcony and David was reading a guidebook at the dining table. Mick set the box of bambalouni down on the dining table near the balcony. They had not moved the table back to its original position.

David checked the box, saw the doughnuts, and picked one out of the box. He stood up, moved around the table, and over to the door to the balcony, where he handed the doughnut out to Jason. Then David returned to his seat at the table and took a doughnut out of the box for himself. Mick and Taylor also sat at the table and they each took a doughnut from the box. After the four bambalouni had been consumed, Mick started the discussion.

"Taylor and I are moving over here," Mick said. "We have our bags in the car and will bring them up after dark."

"Makes sense," David said. "This was not just an overnight for Ahmed. He seems pretty settled in."

"We missed an opportunity today," Mick said. "We can't let that happen again. We need to be ready."

"We had no way of knowing that the woman and child would be gone all day," David countered.

"Granted," Mick responded. "But we have to be ready the next time."

"We have received new information from Bronwyn," Mick continued. "The woman's name is Gabriel Duval. She is a French national and she owns the house. It is in her name. She bought it four years ago, with no financing."

"This is an expensive area," David said. "Where did the money for the house come from?"

"No idea," Mick said.

"Is she his wife?" David asked.

"We still don't know," Mick responded. "If she is, she hasn't taken his name. She is using her own name. We do know that there are no marriage records for her in France."

"Better for him if she keeps her own name," Jason said, from out on the balcony. "That way he can have assets, like that house, which are not in his name."

"Does she live here full time?" David asked.

"That's the way it looks," Mick said. "Flight records show that she travels to Paris once a year and stays four or five days. Other than that, no recorded travel."

"What about the boy?" David asked.

"No information at all on the boy," Mick said. "He doesn't fly to Paris with her when she goes."

Taylor had not been actively participating in the conversation. He had already known the information from Bronwyn that Mick relayed to David and Jason. He began participating by changing the topic.

"This is the woman and the child's permanent residence," Taylor said. "It may also be Ahmed's permanent residence. At the very least, he is comfortable here and we can expect him to stay or, if he leaves, to return. But this can't be our permanent residence. We need to start gaming this out, so we are ready at the next opportunity."

"With the four of us all here, we can do more than just watch," Mick said. "We can follow them if they all leave the house as a group or separately and, at the same time, we can check out the inside of the house."

The discussion turned to assignments. David and Jason would continue to be the only visible residents of the apartment, the only ones to go out on the balcony. They would also do most of the foot surveillance. It was a small town. People would expect to see their temporary neighbors around town. Mick and Taylor could help with the foot surveillance if they were prepositioned in the commercial area of the town. Mick and Taylor would assist with surveillance of the house from the front bedroom, particularly at night, so everyone would be well rested. And Mick and Taylor would be responsible for getting inside the house.

When it was dark outside, Mick and Taylor went down to their rental car and brought the bags upstairs to the apartment. Mick told David and Jason to sort through their bags and to put everything they thought they would need into one bag. One kit/gear bag would stay with them, one kit/gear bag would go back to the safe room in the house in Tunis.

David emptied his gear bag on the floor in a corner of the living area. He sorted through the clothing. They were no longer businessmen. They were now tourists on vacation. Polo shirts, khaki pants, and hiking boots went into one pile, with a pair of black tactical pants and a black jacket. Dress shoes and sport coat in another pile.

The plan was to get inside the house. Items like handguns and night-vision monocles went into the bag staying with them. Items like the rifles and night-vision goggles went into the bag going back to the safe room.

It was almost midnight before all four of the team had completed sorting through their bags. Mick and Taylor carried the bags headed for the safe room down to their rental car. Then Taylor got into the rental car and drove the bags back to the safe room in the house in Tunis.

Mick changed into all dark colored clothing. Black tactical pants, a dark blue polo shirt, and a black jacket. He put on his hiking boots last. Then Mick put a night-vision monocle in his thigh pocket and left the apartment. He went down the stairs and out the door in the rear of the building. His compass was used to oriented himself. Then he walked up the hill, searching for a high point where he could look down on the town. He was in no hurry as he had all night.

Mick ended his upward journey when the town was laid out below him. He could see the lighted main streets and lights shining out from windows. He could see out over the town to the sea, where the lights of ships stood out against the blackness of the water of the Mediterranean Sea. Mick waited for the light to lessen as businesses closed and people went to bed.

A little after three o'clock in the morning, the ambient light from the town was as low as Mick thought it would get. He pulled the night-vision monocle out from his thigh pocket and began to look around. He could see the dark residential areas well, there was still too much light in parts of the commercial areas for clear definition. He patiently scanned the entire town and focused on the area where the target house was located.

Mick began his walk back down the hill and into town at about three-thirty. There were no cars or people moving in the streets. Mick had the town all to himself. He walked slowly, veering off onto side streets to see where they went then crossing over, or backtracking, if necessary, to his main route. Cross streets were not in abundance, the blocks of houses along his route tended to be long.

He approached the target house from the street behind. The street behind the target house was very dark. It was filled with private homes, all of which were dark, except for the occasional exterior light. Mick quietly walked down the driveway to one of the houses and moved to the back of the house. He stood in the dark and used the night-vision monocle to scan the back of the target house. Then he walked back out to the street and continued walking down the hill.

Mick walked all the way down to the end of the houses. He had to negotiate the sand dune buffer area between the last house and the shore road. The beach was across the shore road. It was mostly a thin strip of sand between the road and the sea. He walked north along the shore until he got up toward the marina, where the beach area became large and wide.

Mick walked on to the marina. It was man-made and sheltered. The boats in the marina were very nice and very expensive. Leisure boats, not commercial working boats. Obviously, the boats belonged to the wealthy people who owned homes there. It was possible that some were used as commercial boats that catered to fishing excursions for tourists.

Mick came to the far north end of the marina and turned east. He could just see the twilight occurring on the horizon. He turned to the west and headed for the road, where he turned north again. Avenue John Kennedy continued north for a little way then turned west in a gentle curve following the track of the coast. At the curve,

Mick could see the lights of La Villa Bleue, a hotel, beyond the barrier dunes. He negotiated his way through the dunes and up to the commercial area, with hotels, restaurants, and other businesses.

As Mick walked on through the commercial area, he started to see people, working people. The pre-dawn deliveries were being made to the hotels and restaurants. Mick walked through the commercial area and headed downhill again, back to the apartment. He arrived at the apartment just as dawn was breaking in the town. He slipped in through the rear door of the apartment building, climbed the stairs, and went inside the apartment.

Taylor was manning the front bedroom surveillance position. David and Jason were asleep.

"I saw you behind the house," Taylor said.

"Only because you have night-vision," Mick responded.

"Did you have a good walk?" Taylor asked.

"Very good," Mick said. "Want coffee?"

"Of course," Taylor replied.

Mick went out to the kitchen and made a pot of coffee. He was quiet about it but the smell of coffee brought Jason to the kitchen. Mick poured three cups of coffee. He left one on the counter for Jason and took two into the front bedroom. He handed Taylor one of the cups.

"You take a break," Mick said to Taylor. "I'll watch until David gets up."

"Don't you want to get some sleep?" Taylor asked.

"I can wait until David gets up," Mick said. "And if I wait long enough, Jason will make us breakfast."

Taylor laughed as Mick took Taylor's place by the window and looked out at the target house.

After lunch, in the afternoon, the team was sitting around in the apartment. Jason had the watch on the balcony, having relieved David after lunch. Mick, Taylor, and David were sitting at the dining table waiting for something to happen. There had been no movement from the house during the morning. It was almost two o'clock when something happened.

"Movement," Jason said, from the balcony.

"They are all out of the house," Jason said next.

"They are walking up the street, like before."

Mick, Taylor, and David all hurried out of the apartment, down the stairs, and out the rear door. They walked up to the corner and David turned right, following Ahmed's group from a distance. Mick and Taylor waited until they could no longer see David then they walked in the opposite direction, toward Ahmed's house. As they crossed the street, they looked for others out and about. They saw no one.

They came to stop near the front of Ahmed's house. They looked up at Jason. He had the better observation position on the balcony. He gave them a go-ahead signal.

Mick and Taylor moved down the near side of Ahmed's house and to the back door. They paused at the rear, pulled gloves from their pockets, and put them on. Then they went to the rear door. It was at the back of the house but on the side wall, not the rear wall. It was a sturdy wooden door, painted bright blue like the front door. Mick studied the lock. It was an old key lock, not hard to pick. He removed two lock picking tools from a small set in his thigh pocket and set about picking the lock. It only took a minute and the door was unlocked.

Mick and Taylor went inside with handguns drawn. They quickly cleared the small house. As expected, no one was in the house. They walked around memorizing the layout and taking photographs of the interior rooms with their cell phones. They did not search, except for weapons in the obvious places. There was a loaded semi-automatic pistol in the bedside table, to the left of the bed, in what they determined was the master bedroom. There was another loaded semi-automatic pistol in an upper kitchen cupboard by the refrigerator. The third loaded semi-automatic pistol was in the only drawer of a small decorative table, an accent piece, near the front door. When they were done, they left the way they had come, through the rear door. They removed their gloves as soon as they got outside.

Instead of going back out onto the street at the front of the house, they climbed over a short masonry wall at the rear of the property and went into the back-neighbor's yard. They skirted around the house and went down the driveway to the street. Then they walked leisurely down the road, downhill, until they could cross over. They turned left at the cross street and continued walking. They crossed the street the apartment building was on and kept going straight to the next street. They turned left again at the corner and walked up the hill until they were at the next cross street. They turned left again and walked to the parking area of the apartment building and entered the building from the rear. Then they climbed the stairs and went up to the apartment.

"Eight minutes," Jason said, when they walked over toward the balcony. "You were inside for eight minutes. I can just see the top of the door on this side of the rear of the house."

"It's not a large house," Mick responded. "Any word from David?"

"David says they are shopping for groceries in the souk," Jason continued.

Mick and Taylor sat at the dining table and sketched out the layout of the house, checking the photographs on their cell phones to refresh their memory. They plotted out the position of the furniture on their sketch. When they were done, they set the sketch aside and waited for David to return. They waited for more than an hour.

"They are coming down the street," Jason said, as he walked into the apartment from the balcony and went to the window in the front bedroom. "They are carrying shopping bags."

A short time later, Jason called out, "In the house."

A little while later, David came back into the apartment. He moved the fourth dining chair over to the door by the balcony and set it where he could sit inside and still see the street in front of the house. Taylor asked David to move over to the dining table where he could see the sketch better and Taylor sat in the chair David had vacated and watched the street below.

Mick called Jason into the living area. Jason took the remaining seat at the dining table. Mick set the sketch in the center of the table, facing David and Jason.

"Small house, basic layout," Mick began. "If you enter through the front door, you walk directly into the main living room. Off of the living room, at the back of the house, there is an eat-in kitchen, with a table and chairs. Only two bedrooms. The bedroom at the front of the house is the boy's room. The bedroom at the back of the house is the master bedroom. The house appears to have had some extensive remodeling work done."

"It looks like what might have been three bedrooms was turned into two bedrooms," Taylor explained. "There is a large walk-in closet in the master bedroom. That is not typical for an older house. There is also a fairly large and newer bathroom with doors leading into the master bedroom and out to the living area. Again, not typical of an older house. All of that is between the two bedrooms, probably in the space that was once the third bedroom and a small bathroom."

"I wonder why they didn't open up the kitchen and the living area, to make it all one open space," Jason said.

"Probably a roof support issue," Taylor said. "Some walls can't be removed without weakening the entire structure. They wouldn't have had that problem with the new closet or the bathroom because they were actually adding to the number of walls."

"At the rear of the house, through a door off the kitchen, there is a bump-out that contains a laundry room, with a washer, a dryer, and a large sink," Mick continued. "It was probably an addition. It is behind the master bedroom. It looks like they chose to give up the rear wall window in the master bedroom to keep the window in the kitchen. Now, instead of a back door that goes out the back of the house, the back door comes out of the laundry room onto the side of the house, right behind the master bedroom."

"It also looks like the old back door was moved and is now the new laundry room back door," Taylor added. "Probably something to do with requirements for the town aesthetics. Otherwise, I think anyone doing extensive remodeling would have replaced that door with a newer door."

The sketch had not been drawn to scale, so David and Jason asked questions about the distances between certain points to get a feel for the size of the rooms. Mick and Taylor gave approximations for the distances.

"Only two ways in," David said. "The front door fully visible from the street. Or the back door, somewhat visible from the street, if a person is in the right position to look down the side of the house."

"We need to start watching the house behind this house, too," Mick said. "It looked unoccupied when I was out last night. It still looked unoccupied when we went out that way today. It is two stories tall and a newer building. All of the blue window shutters were closed both times. It's a good access and egress route, as long as it remains unoccupied. There is only a short masonry wall between the properties, more of a boundary marker than a security wall."

"If it is occupied, we should see lights on in the house later in the evening, even with the window shutters closed," Jason said.

"I have seen no lights on in that house at night," David said. "It is close enough to the target house that I would have noticed if there were lights on through the night-vision monocle, even if the shutters were closed."

"Good," Mick said. "Let's hope it stays that way. Let's take a break and think about our options. Then we can go over our thoughts together after dinner."

Jason and Taylor decided to go out for dinner. Since Ahmed had not left the house in the evening since they had been watching, there was a good chance he would not leave this evening either. Mick and David stayed at the apartment, just in case. Jason and Taylor had agreed to bring dinner back to the apartment for them. They trusted Jason to bring back something they would eat. He was a food guy and he knew their food preferences were not as adventurous as his own.

While Jason and Taylor were out, Mick and David stayed in the front bedroom. David kept watch by the window and Mick laid on the bed. They talked about Ahmed.

Ahmed seemed to have no job. The woman also seemed to have no job. Yet, the woman owned the house, a small house but a very nice house in a very affluent resort town. It was an expensive place to live. Neither left the house regularly, just short trips by foot up to the stores and restaurants in town during the day, except for the one day-long trip away from the house that the woman and child had taken. They did not go out in the evening, so they were eating at the house. In short, they were homebodies, preferring to stay at home than to go out.

"This is it," David said, while looking out the window. "This is Ahmed's home."

"I agree," Mick said. "I have been in the house. He is not visiting, he lives there. I would never have guessed that he would live here. It is so public, with the tourists that regularly come to town. And the town is so small. I would have thought that he would live anonymously in a big city, easily lost in the crowd."

"His wife or girlfriend is French," David said. "It's a compromise. It is somewhere she feels comfortable because it is a safe upscale tourist town where French is widely spoken and, at the same time, it is somewhere he feels comfortable because it is in north Africa, not Europe."

"She has to know about all the loaded handguns he has around the house," Mick said. "Two of the three we saw are in locations where the boy could get to them."

"Love is blind, as the saying goes," David replied. "She wouldn't be the first person to do something stupid for love. She either knows what he is or she suspects and doesn't want to know. Either way, the handguns cannot be an issue."

Taylor and Jason came back to the apartment after dinner late in the evening. Jason took over the watch at the front bedroom window. Mick and David went to the dining table and sat with Taylor. Jason had brought them shawarmas and fries. Mick and David each opened a foil wrapped shawarma. They were still very warm inside the foil. Mick took a bite. Warm fresh pita bread wrapped around slow roasted lamb, with spices, was just what he needed. He could taste the tahini, garlic, and onions complementing the lamb in the shawarma. After eating one, he slowed his pace and ate some fries. They were some of the best shawarmas he had tasted. He lingered over the second one, enjoying it, instead of simply inhaling it. David was similarly enjoying his meal. When Mick and David were done eating, they cleaned up and threw away their trash. Then they all gathered in the front bedroom, where Jason was still on watch.

"Thanks for the shawarmas," Mick said to Jason. "They were great."

"I thought you would like them," Jason replied.

As they all got comfortable in the front bedroom, Mick got back to business.

"We have to take the next opportunity we get," Mick began. "When the woman and child are out of the house."

"What are you thinking when the times comes?" Taylor asked.

"Obviously, I would prefer to go in at night," Mick said. "But that is not going to happen because the woman and child are there at night."

"It has to be during the day," Taylor acknowledged.

"If the woman and child go out, we have to assume that Ahmed will be awake and in the master bedroom, the bathroom, the kitchen, or the living room," Mick said. "He wouldn't be in the boy's bedroom. And it is unlikely he would be in the laundry room."

"Entry through the front creates too much exposure for us," he continued. "We would be visible from the street and we would have no cover inside the house. He would have a clear shot from the bedroom doorway, the bathroom doorway, the kitchen doorway, or anywhere in the living room. So, we have to enter through the rear door."

"The laundry room will bunch us up, but it also narrows his field of fire and gives us some cover," Taylor agreed. "He would have no immediate shot from the bedroom, the bathroom, or the living room. Our only initial concern would be if he were in the kitchen."

"We can check the kitchen through the rear window before we enter," David said.

"It is a small house," Mick said. "My thought is that only two of us go in. One of us conducts overwatch from our balcony, in case he tries to run out the front door."

"He won't run," David interjected.

"And one of us conducts overwatch on a rear balcony of the house behind, covering our rear," Mick concluded.

They discussed the plan for the better part of an hour and debated who would have what roles. All of them wanted to be in the house but they all agreed to assign roles based on each of their particular strengths.

The lights in the target house went out shortly after eleven o'clock. At midnight, Mick and Taylor left the apartment. They left the building through the rear doorway and retraced Mick's steps from the night before, in reverse. They came to the house behind the target house. There had been no light from the house before they left the apartment.

They walked around the house, checking the windows on every side. The window shutters were all still closed. There was still no light coming from the house. They examined the two doors into the house. The locks were newer but would not be a problem. They decided to enter from the rear door. There was no rear window in the master bedroom of Ahmed's house. and they would not be exposed to the street at the rear of the house.

They put gloves on and Mick used his tools to open the lock. He pushed the door open and waited for a security alarm to sound. There was no audible alarm. Mick went inside the house. It was completely dark inside. He examined the walls through a night-vision monocle, looking for a security system keypad, in case there was a silent alarm. There was no keypad. Mick signaled for Taylor to enter the house. They went to the front door and looked again for a security system keypad. There was no keypad near the front door. They went up the stairs to the second floor in the dark.

They examined the windowed doors out to small balconies in the two back bedrooms. In each room, they opened the door and one side of the exterior shutters to get the view from the balconies. The balcony in the bedroom to the left had a view of the back of Ahmed's laundry room, but not of the back side door. It also had a view into Ahmed's kitchen through the window, but the angle was not good because it gave a view of the side wall of the kitchen. The balcony in the bedroom on the right had a good view into Ahmed's kitchen through which they could see the doorway from the living area into the kitchen.

They closed the shutters in both bedrooms, they left the windowed doors to the balconies unlocked but closed, and went back downstairs to the rear door. They left the rear door closed but unlocked as they left the house. Then they walked out to the street and took a long route back to the apartment building, where they entered through the rear door. David was at the front bedroom window. Jason was asleep in the back bedroom. Mick went into the front bedroom.

"Starting in the morning, we keep everything in our bags, and we keep our bags in one of the cars, ready to go," Mick said to David.

"Got it," David replied.

CHAPTER THIRTY-ONE

Taylor was at the front bedroom window when Mick woke up in the morning. David and Jason were still asleep. The sun had yet to come up. Mick started the coffee maker then went into the bathroom and shaved and showered. When he was dressed, he put all of his things in his bag and placed the bag by the door. He got two cups of coffee in the kitchen and went into the front bedroom and handed one to Taylor. Mick took over Taylor's position at the window and sipped his coffee. As dawn broke, he could see that the sky was overcast. The air was cooler than it had been recently. Maybe it would rain and they would not look totally out of place wearing light jackets during the day.

Taylor went to the bathroom to shave and shower. Then he dressed and put his bag beside Mick's bag at the door. A short while later, David and Jason woke up. Jason went into the kitchen for a cup of coffee and David went into the bathroom. Jason walked into the front bedroom with his coffee.

"What's with the bags?" Jason asked Mick.

"When you are dressed, pack your bag, and put it by the door," Mick answered. "We will leave the bags in the car from now on. We will be ready to leave at a moment's notice."

"Okay," Jason said, as he walked out of the front bedroom. "You are on your own for breakfast today. Just FYI."

David finished shaving, showering, and dressing. He walked out into the living room and placed his bag beside the others. Then he got a cup of coffee in the kitchen and walked past Taylor at the dining table and out onto the balcony.

"I'm on," David called back into the apartment.

Mick left the front bedroom and took a seat at the dining table.

"Jason is not cooking this morning," he said. "You want me to scrounge what I can?"

"Sure," Taylor replied.

Mick went into the kitchen, made a fresh pot of coffee, and started bringing items out to the dining table. Four bananas came first. Then a while later, a plate full of buttered toast. Finally, three containers of yogurt.

David had already eaten one of the bananas. Mick handed him a couple of slices of toast through the doorway. He knew David would not eat the yogurt.

When Jason was finished shaving, showering, packing, and putting his bag by the door, Mick and Taylor took all four bags down to one of the rental cars and put them in the trunk. Then they went back up to the apartment.

"The bags are in your car, Jason," Mick said.

Jason nodded his understanding.

"Movement." David called quietly into the apartment.

Woman and boy," David said next.

A car passed underneath David on the street below and stopped in front of the woman and boy standing outside of the target house. The woman helped the boy into the back seat and got into the front passenger seat. Then the car drove away. It was eight-thirty in the morning.

David came into the apartment and Jason went out onto the balcony. Taylor went into the front bedroom, picked up the stool, and put it back into position at the kitchen counter. David went into the front bedroom and pushed the furniture back where it had been when they arrived. Mick turned off the automatic coffee maker in the kitchen and emptied the glass carafe.

Mick, Taylor, and David checked their clothing to make sure they had everything. They double checked their weapons. Then they went out of the apartment, down the stairs, and out to the parking area at the rear of the building. They got into the second rental car, and Taylor drove them around to the house behind the target house. From the street it still looked unoccupied. Taylor backed the car into the driveway by the side of the house, off the road.

They got out of the car and went to the rear corner of the house. They put on their gloves. Mick looked across the short wall and into the kitchen window of the target house and did not see anyone. He slipped around the corner and went into the house through the unlocked rear door. Taylor and David followed.

They all went upstairs to the back bedroom on the right. Taylor opened the windowed door to the balcony and looked through the louvers. He could see down into the kitchen through the kitchen window. He saw no one in the kitchen.

Mick and David left Taylor and went back downstairs and out the rear door. They slipped over to the left and approached the short masonry wall behind the laundry room. Mick went over the wall first and stopped on the other side with his back to the laundry room wall. Then he took out his lock picking set while he waited for David to come over the wall. David joined Mick behind the laundry room wall.

They both watched the second-floor balcony on the house behind for a signal that they were clear to go. Within a minute, Taylor slowly opened one of the blue wooden shutters then closed it again. There was no one in the kitchen. It was clear.

B. René Shekmer

Mick and David slipped around the corner of the Ahmed's house. Mick went to the rear laundry room door and began to pick the lock. David stood at the corner of the house and watched for any sign from Taylor on the balcony.

The lock opened. Mick reached out and tapped David on the shoulder. David gave one last look at the balcony, saw no warning sign from Taylor, and turned to follow Mick. Mick stood to one side of the door and David stood to the other side. Mick reached out and opened the door, slowly. When there was just enough room, David went inside. Mick followed.

The blue wooden shutters on the balcony slowly opened and closed again. But they were already in and did not see it.

David passed the dryer and the washer. The door into the kitchen was open. David started to turn left into the kitchen. Ahmed was coming from the living area into the kitchen, with a pistol in his hand. David fired from his hip, at the ready position. Ahmed fired a second later. Two loud gunshots rang out in the quiet house. The smell of burnt gunpowder filled the air.

Ahmed had been hit. So had David.

Mick rushed around David and advanced on Ahmed. Ahmed was bleeding profusely from his right shoulder. The bullet had torn through an artery, possibly two. His right arm was useless, just hanging limp by his side. He had dropped his pistol. He was leaning into the wall for support and holding his right shoulder with his left hand. Blood was smearing on the white wall. The smell of gunpowder lingered in the air.

Mick's hearing was greatly diminished. He knew that Ahmed's was too. Mick looked at Ahmed and Ahmed looked back at him, defiant, despite the pain he was in.

"Sofia." Mick yelled loudly and clearly. He saw the recognition flash in Ahmed's eyes. Then Mick shot Ahmed in the chest. Ahmed slowly sank to the floor, leaving a smear of blood on the white wall all the way down. Mick did not need to check him as Ahmed was clearly dead.

"How bad?" Mick called back to David, while removing his cell phone from his pocket and taking two pictures of Ahmed, one full body as he lay and one of his face.

"In the calf muscle," David answered.

"Hold tight," Mick said, as he went around Ahmed and into the bathroom. He grabbed a towel then went into the bedroom. He found extra bed sheets on a shelf in the walk-in closet. He grabbed them and went back out to the kitchen.

Mick knelt down and checked David's wound. The bullet had gone into his calf on the outside of his left leg. There was no exit wound. The wound was bleeding but not excessively. Mick saw a hole in the wall between the kitchen and the laundry room. The bullet had gone through the wall and ended its flight in David's calf as David had been turning left out of the laundry room and into the kitchen. Mick was surprised that the wall had offered only concealment and not cover. Mick folded a pillowcase horizontally and tied it tightly around David's calf. Then Mick went to the sink, wet the towel, and wiped up the small amount of David's blood that had reached the floor.

Mick located David's spent cartridge on the kitchen floor, picked it up, and put it in his pocket. Then he went and located his own spent cartridge on the living area floor and put it in his pocket. He returned to the kitchen.

"We have to leave," Mick said.

David did an ungainly hopping turn, so he faced back into the laundry room. Then he wrapped his left arm over Mick's shoulders, and they went through the laundry room and out the rear door. Taylor was at the short masonry wall separating the two properties. He had heard the shots, and seen Mick at the sink in the kitchen, and he had known that it was over. He had closed the shutters and the windowed door in the second-floor bedroom and come down the stairs and out the rear door, prepared to leave. When he had seen Mick assisting David, he altered his course and had come to the wall to help.

Mick helped David up and over the wall and Taylor helped him down on the other side. Sirens began to sound as David was crossing the wall. They did not wait for Mick. David wrapped his left arm around Taylor's shoulders and they headed for the car. Mick climbed over the wall and followed behind.

Taylor helped David into the back seat then went to the driver's seat. Mick got into the back with David. Taylor checked for traffic on the road in front of the vacant house and pulled out of the driveway, turning right, headed uphill, at a normal speed. The immediate concern was just to get out of the neighborhood. From the car, Mick called Jason's cell phone.

"Go," he said, when Jason answered.

Jason went into the apartment and closed the glass door to the balcony. He went out the door into the hallway, down the stairs, and out the rear door to the rental car. He got into the driver's seat, pulled out of the parking area, and drove away. Local police cars, with sirens blaring, were headed into the neighborhood as Jason was headed out.

Jason was the first to arrive at the house in Tunis. He unloaded two bags from the trunk of the car and carried them inside. Then he returned to the car for the remaining two bags. Once the four bags were inside, he opened the safe room and put all of the bags inside. Then he went to the kitchen where he got a plastic trash bag.

In the dining room, he began removing all of the items pinned to the cork board and placing them in the trash bag. He erased all of the notes they had written on the white boards, first with a dry eraser then with a wet towel he got from the kitchen. Last, he opened each of the laptop computers to ensure that the browsing histories had been deleted. Then he sat at the dining table and waited. The three gunshots weighed on him but, if anyone had been injured seriously, they would have notified him.

An hour later, Mick and Taylor helped David into the house in Tunis.

"How bad?" Jason asked.

"Not bad," David said, through clenched teeth.

"The bullet went through a wall first," Mick added. "It is lodged in his calf muscle."

"Put him on the table in the dining room," Jason said, as he headed for the safe room.

Jason was the team medic. They all carried some medical supplies, but Jason was trained to work in the field. He came into the dining room carrying his medical kit. He put the kit on the table and went into the kitchen.

Mick and Taylor had removed Mick's pillowcase field dressing and had placed David face up on the table with towels under his left leg. They had cut his left pant leg off at the thigh and removed his shoe and sock.

Jason washed his hands and arms thoroughly in the kitchen, grabbed a large bowl and returned to the dining room. He took surgical gloves from his kit and put them on. Then he looked the wound over, pushing and prodding at the muscle. He cleaned the wound with Betadine.

"It's not deep," Jason said. "I can get it out."

"Do it," David said.

"Morphine?"

"No, just do it."

Mick looked around for something for David to bite down on. Seeing nothing useful in the dining room, he went into the kitchen. He returned with a large wooden spoon which he handed to David.

Jason put his forceps and other instruments into the large bowl. Then he poured half a bottle of alcohol over the instruments. He opened a sterile pad and placed it on the table beside David's leg. Then he removed the instruments from the alcohol and laid them on the sterile pad. He dipped his gloved fingers in the bowl of alcohol and shook them dry. Then he put sterile gauze pads on the pad.

When Jason picked up a scalpel, David put the wooden spoon in his mouth, between his teeth. David bit down on the wooden spoon as Jason cut down from the wound, to make it a little bigger so that he could maneuver the forceps so the bullet would come out easier. Then he cleaned away the blood with sterile gauze pads and inserted the forceps into the wound. After a minute of maneuvering to get a good grip, he pulled the bullet out of the wound, dropped it into the bowl of alcohol, and looked at it intensely. Satisfied, he flushed the wound out with saline solution and sutured it closed. Finally, Jason covered the sutured wound with a square of quick clotting gauze and used an ace bandage to wrap the leg in the area of the wound.

"You'll live," Jason said, as he began cleaning up his equipment and supplies. David swung his legs over the side of the table, and sat up.

"Thanks," David said. "But will I walk?"

"Not today," Jason said. "At least not well."

"When?" David asked.

"Whenever you can stand the pain," Jason said. "The muscle is damaged but the bullet didn't go in very deep so it should heal well. In another day or so, you will need to start moving the leg, flexing it. But right now, the more pressure you put on it, the longer it will take to heal."

"You should use crutches," Jason concluded, "but I don't have any."

"Lucky shot," David said, changing the subject.

"That's for sure," Mick agreed. "I would not have thought a bullet would go through those old walls. That wall was once the exterior wall of the house."

"Bullets do strange things," Taylor said, also surprised that the bullet had gone through the wall.

"You hit him in the shoulder, it threw his aim off, and probably saved your life." Mick said.

"I guess there is that," David said. "I was aiming for his chest."

"You hit him right in an artery," Mick said. "Lots of blood. He knew he was dead while he was still standing there bleeding. If I hadn't shot him, he would have bled out. No question about it."

"Thanks for getting me out of there," David said, seriously.

"Anytime," Mick responded, equally seriously.

"Let's get you onto the couch in the living room," Jason said.

Mick and Taylor each got on one of David's sides. David put his arms around their shoulders and stood up on his good leg. They moved him into the living room and he laid on the couch and put his injured leg up on the back of the couch. Then Taylor went to get David a new pair of pants and a new pair of socks.

"I have a call to make," Mick said, as he walked back into the dining room.

When Mick was done with the phone call, David was changed. Jason put David's discarded clothes in the trash bag with the papers from the dining room. Then they gathered their bags at the front door and prepared to leave.

They were driven in a van to a marina where they boarded a yacht. The yacht took them from Tunis to Valletta, in Malta. The yacht was met in Valletta by a doctor who came aboard and talked to Jason then looked at David's wound. After David's leg was re-wrapped, he was given an antibiotic and pain killers. Then they transferred to the Agency jet and flew back to Dulles International Airport, in northern Virginia.

They were met at a private aviation hangar at the airport and taken, with their bags, to a black van with deeply tinted windows. They were driven to the office. They dropped their bags in their equipment room, emptied the contents of their pockets into plastic bags to be sorted through later, and retrieved their personal items from the safe. Then they left the office to go home and rest before the next day's debriefing. Taylor left first. Jason and David left together, with Jason helping David. Mick was the last to leave.

When Mick got into his Jeep Cherokee, he took his cell phone out of the console and powered it up. Then he began driving home. At a stoplight on the way, he made one call.

"It's finished," Mick said, when the call was answered.

"Thank you for letting me know," Ambassador Sopko responded.

ABOUT THE AUTHOR

B. René Shekmer is an attorney living in Western Michigan, with a passion for reading and travelling. She has lived in seven countries throughout the world and visited many more.

BOOKS IN THIS SERIES

Detachment 3 Novels

RESTORING ORDER

A young college student is kidnapped while on summer vacation. Her father, a U.S. diplomat, has the connections to involve the CIA and he does not hesitate to use them. Detachment 3 is given the assignment to find and retrieve the young woman. From Northern Virginia to the Mediterranean, the team follows the available clues in the search for Sofia and her kidnappers, who turn out to be more than mere criminals.

NOC OUT

A CIA NOC has gone missing while on an operation in South America. Detachment 3 is sent to find and retrieve him. They follow a trail of lies, deceit, and revenge as they unravel his various identities in their search for the missing NOC.